Bella's Point

By

Elizabeth Seckman

WCP

World Castle Publishing, LLC
Pensacola, Florida

Copyright © Elizabeth Seckman 2014
Print ISBN: 9781629891224
eBook ISBN: 9781629891231
First Edition World Castle Publishing, LLC, July 13, 2014
http://www.worldcastlepublishing.com

Licensing Notes

Cover: Sprinkles on Top Graphics
Editor: Eric Johnston

For Rose
For teaching me simplicity.

Acknowledgements:

Thanks to my readers and critique partners who never let me chuck this story, no matter how frustrated I was becoming—Annalisa, Celeste, Chad, Kari, Sonya, and Tammy. You guys rock and I'd have been lost without you!

Thanks to Karen for putting up with my obsessiveness.

And thanks to my readers for coming back for more. I love you. God bless.

Chapter 1

As Nero passed through the tiny town of Macon, North Carolina, Bella's heart skipped a beat. If Sam was right, the prison should be over the next roll in the road. She squinted to see through the fog enveloping them as the wagon bumped and lurched its way through the stretch of land the locals called Purgatory. In this stretch of ground, rolling green hills bathed in sunshine gave way to slanted climbs and hidden shadows.

Seated beside Bella on the unpadded bench, Tessie crossed herself and mumbled a prayer. Bella's nerves were brittle. The reminder that a holy intervention was appropriate made her flash Tessie a look. Raised not to cross her mammy, she kept her tongue in check, no matter how much ire she felt.

She gave Nero a snap of the reigns and urged him to move faster. The horse slapped its lips in response. Nero didn't seem to be worried about the half mile ride through the ominous gulley. A ride that had her shivering and sweating at the same time.

"This is foolishness, Bell," Tessie finally said, her lips tight. "Driving half a night, with a little boy. And for what?"

"For everything," Bella's words were tight, but not so clipped to be called rude.

"Hah. We'll probably be robbed by bandits or killed by ghosts."

Bella would never admit being plagued by the same thoughts. Instead, she forced assurances from a dry throat, "That's nonsense. We're almost there, and we haven't passed a soul. Dead or alive." Bella looked back over her shoulder at Manteo. He was still wrapped in blankets and sleeping peacefully.

Nero labored as he pulled them up the last few feet of rutted road. Bella worried the poor old horse would tucker out and drop dead in the mud, but he made it. She breathed a sigh of relief. The fog thinned as they crested the hill, and just as she was told, the pine palisades of the makeshift prison appeared.

Constructed at the end of the Civil War, it was a hasty replacement for the original brick structure, which was little more than a pile of rubble now on the corner of Main and McKinsy. A new jail was a must, because it's a simple fact of life: where there is carnage, the vultures flock. This new jail was an ugly, crooked structure that didn't fit into the rolling green of the landscape, but it was a sight for her sore eyes.

She pulled Nero under a grove of trees next to the prison. The structure was bigger than she imagined. The ten-foot-high wall of roughhewn logs spread out in a circle hundreds of feet in diameter. Large gates like double barn doors seemed to be the only way inside. Bella hopped down from the wagon.

Tessie looked the place over and shook her head. "This is all wrong. Shouldn't there be guards? Ain't a soul outside." Tessie tapped Bella on the shoulder. "I'm telling you, child, this place is full of evil spirits. And it's the thirteenth."

"Oh pooh. You and your superstitions." Bella rubbed the goose bumps on her arms.

Manny stirred. His little head popped up from the side of the wagon. "We here already?"

"Sure are," Bella whispered, still staring at the wall before her.

"You change your mind, Miss Bell?"

His words shook her from her worries. She turned and ruffled his hair. "Not at all. You stay here and keep Miss Tessie calm, okay?"

He nodded his dark head and smiled.

"Keep me calm," Tessie muttered. "You want to keep me calm? Let's turn around and go on home. Buying a prisoner from jail? Who ever heard of such a thing?" Her dark head shook with her words.

"Sam said people do it all the time."

"Well, it can't be legal. Fellas willing to bend the law this way can't be trusted for much of anything else. You have no idea what you are walking into." Tessie crossed her arms over her chest and spoke to her charge as if she was still a wayward girl. "I declare, child. You have done some dim-witted things, but this is, by far, the craziest thing yet!"

Bella laughed, "Now who's crazy? I honestly can't believe you said that with a straight face. I have certainly done more foolish things than this!"

Tessie patted her heart. "Jesus, have mercy. The child doesn't listen to reason."

Bella snorted. "I'm extremely reasonable. As a matter of fact, this is probably the most sensible thing I've ever done."

"I suppose that's what's worrying me most... you calling this craziness sensible. Crazy people don't know they're crazy. They think they're making perfect sense."

"Oh pooh. You'll see." Bella brushed off the comment, though she partly agreed. It was crazy. What kind of men sold other men's freedom? She could be getting in over her head, but she had a duty to her family and quite honestly, she was fresh out of options. She kissed Tessie's cheek, then Manny's, and assured them, "Sam told me to talk to Tom Clark. Sam wouldn't send me somewhere unsafe."

"Sam shoulda come here for you."

"You know he has his own business to look after."

"Business," Tessie said. "Getting lost in a bottle of booze is his business."

Bella sighed. "Forget Sam. This is my life. I have to take care of it." Bella pulled the hem of her dress up to her ankles and walked, head bowed, carefully choosing each footstep as she made her way across soggy earth.

Engrossed in her foot falls, she nearly jumped out of her shoes when someone overhead barked, "Halt!"

Bella looked up to find a guard stationed in the tower, a gun aiming at her head. Her knees shook and her belly flip-flopped.

"State your business."

"I, uh, I was told I should speak with Sergeant Clark. My, uh, fiancé is incarcerated here. I was told I could post bail?"

"Wait right there."

Bella's heart pounded and the early morning air was suddenly too thin to breathe. It seemed like forever passed before the door swung open, and a man motioned her forward. Inside the gate, not a blade of grass survived, just puddles and sticky mud all around. Wide boards, laid down as walkways, bowed, and bent with every step, squishing sloppy earth up around the edges. Her nose wrinkled at the stale smell. A large building made of more of the rough cut pine covered the largest part of the interior. High wire fencing surrounded that building. Inside the fence, men stomped through the mud and gazed through the wire mesh.

A union soldier met her at the gate. "Come with me, ma'am. I'll take you to Sergeant Clark." Armed soldiers eyed her as she passed. She rolled her shoulders forward, wishing she still owned a corset or anything to keep her supple body in check. Even after a hungry winter, she still had her loathsome bosom. A prisoner inside the fence yelled something at her, but she couldn't make out his words. A guard gave him a swift punch in the head with the butt of his rifle. The man dropped in the mud and the rest of the inmates scattered like scared birds. Bella gasped, but said nothing. Hadn't Tessie warned her that prison was no place for a well-bred lady?

And Isabella Francine Troy Stanley was well bred, though whether or not she was a lady was still being determined in public debate.

"Sergeant Clark? A lady here to see you. Told the guard she wants to spring her fiancé."

Tom Clark stepped from behind his desk and waved Bella inside. Another man lounged in the corner.

"Can I help you, ma'am?"

"Yes, sir, you can. I have a friend, Mr. Sam Cleary? He says he knows you and…"

"Sam?" Tom Clark wrinkled his brow in thought.

"Undertaker," said the man in the corner. Bella looked at the man as he stood and stepped into the light. He looked familiar, but she wasn't quite sure how she knew him. He sounded like a Yankee and she didn't know too many Yankees.

"Oh, yeah, Sam buries our dead." Tom nodded his head. "Of course, how could I forget?"

Bella smiled. It took a lot of effort, but she managed it. "Sir, Sam, uh, Mr. Cleary, said that you could help me."

"Well, I suppose that depends. What exactly do you need?"

Bella brushed back a wayward hair with trembling hands. Her honey blond tresses were a riot of curls and they proved unruly no matter how she styled them. "I was told I could pay a man's bail and get him out of here."

Tom's eyebrow shot up. "How you looking to pay?"

The man from the corner snickered.

Bella bent over and grabbed the hem of her skirt. She tugged, ripped a seam, and then pulled out three gold coins. She stood back up and held out her hand to Sergeant Clark. He took it from her and rolled the coins around in his palm.

"Who's the lucky man?"

"Jack Byron," Bella answered.

"Byron..." Clark said as if the name rang no bells.

"Byron," the other man offered, "the English? Quiet guy, exceptin' when he's stirred...you know him, Tom, dark-haired guy? He's the one who tends the horses."

"Of course, Jack. Hate to lose Jack. Sure I couldn't interest you in a couple of others? For this much gold, I could let you have two."

Bella's palms started to sweat. "No. I came for Jack."

"She said she was collecting her fiancé." The other man reminded Clark with a chuckle. "A girl only needs one of those."

"Seems Jack had a different fiancé when he came in here. Didn't he, Joe?"

Joe's eyes squinted. "That I don't recall. He has the hefty sister who visits. Her and her husband."

"No, I'm pretty sure there was a red-haired girl."

"Hell, Tom, your memory is about as good as my grandmother's, and she's pushing ninety."

"I suppose." Tom scratched his head. "Let me have a look." He went to a file cabinet and flipped through the files.

Joe stepped closer, looking Bella over more closely. "I swear, you look familiar. What'd you say your name was again?"

"Isabella Stanley, though Jack would know me as Bella Troy."

"Well, I'll be damned." Joe spit a line of tobacco on the floor. "You're the one who married Charlie. I used to play cards at your house."

Bella blushed. "Yes, I was. I thought you looked familiar. I apologize for my memory lapse, but Charles didn't like me to come around while he was entertaining."

"A damned jealous beast if I remember correctly. So, how the hell is Charlie? And how the hell you married to Charlie and engaged to Byron?"

Bella's hands went cold. She gripped them together as she tried to explain. "I suppose to say Jack is my fiancé is a bit of a lie, but he is the oldest and dearest friend I have. He used to work for my father at Bella's Point."

"You don't say." Joe perched himself on the edge of the desk. "Son of a bitch, but it's a small world. Why didn't Charlie come with you?"

"I, uh, I divorced him."

Joe's mouth dropped open, and Tom turned from his search at the cabinet to stare wide eyed like she suddenly grew a second head on her shoulders.

Joe shook his head. "No way in hell he let you get away with that. He felt pretty damned full of himself that he married a Troy."

"Well, evidently the charm for the arrangement only lasted as long as Daddy's money held out." Bella dropped her gaze and stared at her clasped hands. "Truth be told, Charles grew quite bored of marriage rather quickly. Setting it aside was his idea. He didn't want to be bothered with a wife who was suddenly poor and homeless." Bella wiped at a tear that rolled from her eye.

"My apologies, ma'am. Didn't mean to stir up bad memories for you."

"So, given, my situation…no money, no family…" She stifled a little sob. "You see, Jack is my only option."

"Are you sure about that, miss?" Tom asked as he pulled a file from the drawer. He read over it. "Jack can have a pretty mean temper when provoked."

"That may come in handy should Charlie come back. You do realize just because you divorced him doesn't mean he won't be back?"

Bella nodded. "Another reason to get Jack."

"Wouldn't you be better off with a respectable man? Surely there are plenty of…"

Bella shook her head. "Sadly, there isn't plenty of anything anymore. All the good, decent men are either married or dead. And besides, what respectable man would have proper intentions for a divorcee? Oh no, I'll take my chances with the devil I already know. Jack owes my family, and I'm using the last of my gold to have him set free. Surely he has enough honor in him to not allow a couple of women and a child starve to death this winter? And if he doesn't? Well, I suppose that'd be my problem to contend with." Bella dropped her face into her hands and cried. Tom looked at Joe, and they shared a look of fear that one of them might have to comfort an emotional woman.

Tom patted her shoulder gingerly, his head bobbing. "It'll be all right." He cleared his throat and turned to Joe and said, "Why don't you take her on outside? I'll bring Jack out."

"Now he really will be free, right?" Bella asked as she made a quick, but very proper recovery.

"Yes, ma'am, records will show he was paroled."

"Why thank you." Real tears sprung to her eyes, and she couldn't contain the bounce in her step. She did it! She freed Jack.

Tom scribbled a note in the file and said, "Now scoot, girl, get on out of here."

Bella didn't argue. She followed Joe out of the room, past the inmates, and out the gate. She took a grateful gulp of fresh air. Tessie's dark eyes were glued to the door. When Bella emerged, Tessie called, "Thank you, Jesus," to the heavens as her skinny fingers eased back the hammer on the pistol she held on her lap.

Manny's dark head popped up from the back of the wagon. "You all right, Miss Bella?"

Bella strode to the wagon and gave the boy a lingering kiss on the top of his head. "Everything's fine. Did you keep Miss Tessie calm?"

"I tried, but she was still nervous. She had the gun cocked the whole time."

"Well, seems she didn't charge the door and shoot anyone," Bella grinned. "So you must have done a good job."

Manny smiled, his eight-year-old face glowed with success.

"I never should've allowed this. Behavin' like a stupid, willful child." Tessie's face was stern, but even her irritation couldn't hide the perfect structure of her face. Her rich dark skin was unlined, though she guessed her age somewhere around fifty.

Bella grinned. "It worked. They said they'll bring Jack out."

"And that's supposed to solve our problems? Now we're out of gold and gonna have a criminal under roof." She looked to the sky. "Lord have mercy. We should've moved. Gone somewhere and got work. Someplace where men don't know you or me and they treat us with some decency."

"And what about Noah? What do we do about him?" Bella asked.

Tessie turned away hiding the sudden tears.

Bella touched the woman's arm. "He'll be back. I know him. If we leave, who can we trust to tell him where to find us?"

Tessie sniffed and dried her eyes with a piece of towel she carried as a hanky. "But this? Buying a man out of jail? We don't even know why he was locked up. Could've been for murder...or rape. Child, you have no idea."

"I know Jack. He didn't commit murder or rape."

"Oh, phooey. You know him as well as a girl in petticoats can know anything. Having a crush on him doesn't mean you knew a thing."

"I did not have a crush!" Bella blushed and her mouth dropped open.

"Course you did. Everybody at the Point knew it. You followed that boy everywhere."

"I liked horses. He took care of the horses."

"Mmm, hmm. Funny how that interest was lost when Jack moved on."

"I..." Bella's cheeks turned cherry red. "I had my studies to consider."

"You minded your studies! That's a hoot. Child, you were forced to study every word...you paid attention to your studies." Tessie snorted.

"Why I..." Bella's argument was interrupted when the door opened again. The three of them turned in silence. Tom led a scruffy man out by the irons that bound his hands and feet.

Tessie gasped and turned her head, covering her mouth with her towel. Bella stepped forward and grabbed Tom's arm. "Oh, Mr. Clark, please set him loose. This breaks my heart."

Tom shook his head. "Guess I shoulda considered a lady's sensibilities. Hold out your hands, Byron." He spoke to Jack as he freed him, "Now listen, I'm warning you, you better not give these ladies any trouble. None! Or you're right back here, understand?"

Jack Byron nodded as he let the chains drop into the mud and rubbed his freed flesh.

Tom turned his attention to Manny. He reached into his pocket and pulled out a marble and offered it to the boy. Manny's eyes flashed to Tessie for approval, she smiled and nodded. The boy snatched the marble from Tom's hand. His face glowed and he breathed, "Thanks, Mister. It's mighty fine."

Tom rubbed the child's silky black hair. "So, where the hell'd you two pick yourself up an Injun?"

Tessie's eyes sparked, but Bella smiled sweetly. "We helpless females needed a strong brave to see us through the winter."

"So, you're the man of the house, eh, boy?"

Manny nodded, eyes still focused on his new marble.

"Thank you, Mr. Clark. You've been more than helpful." She squeezed his hand. "And thank you for the gift for Manny. You're such a kind man."

Tom mumbled and helped Jack into the back of the wagon. Jack was thin and barely recognizable through the shaggy hair and beard. He slid in next to Manny, who immediately scooted tight to the front of the wagon and clutched Tessie's hand. Bella looked Jack over and frowned before climbing into the wagon and taking the reins. She gave the skinny thoroughbred the command and he sauntered off. She turned and waved again at Tom until he disappeared from sight.

They traveled less than a mile when Jack finally spoke, "What the hell are you up to, Isabella?"

Bella kept the horse on track and moving forward as she answered, "I needed a husband, so I bought me one."

Chapter 2

Bella yanked on the reins and halted the horse outside a brick farmhouse. Jack expected she was making a stop on the way to The Point, but she jumped to the ground and announced, "Home sweet home."

Jack looked the place over. It was humble. Two stories, simple rectangular design. Jack opened his mouth to ask about the whitewashed brick antebellum mansion with its east and west wings and sprawling roll of tobacco fields. That's where Bella belonged. Not here. The place was smaller than the stables of her childhood home.

Bella must have read the look on his face. "It's not quite as impressive as The Point, but it seems to be solid."

Jack hopped down. The roof looked sound, the white trim on the place was chipped and peeling, but it looked structurally fit. Judged independently, it stood out among its post war counter parts; judged against his memory of Bella's Point, it looked sad and neglected.

Bella pulled off her riding gloves. "Manny, rub down Nero and put him in the stable. Then you better have a bite to eat and get on to bed. It's getting late. Tessie? Would you please make Jack something to eat? Jack, you come with me. I'll show you where you can clean up."

Tessie nodded but failed to move a step. Bella raised an impatient eyebrow and shook her head. "Go on. Sun's dropping."

Tessie's frown deepened, but her feet moved hesitantly toward the house.

"We don't have a bath house, but Tessie and I created our own version of one." Bella was proud of their ingenuity. Her father had built a room for bathing with a large stone fireplace and an oversized tub. It was one part of The Point that she did miss, but as with everything else, she learned to make do.

Jack ignored the obvious pride on her face and her chatter about her makeshift bath. He grabbed her by the arm and pulled her to a stop. "Have you lost your mind, Isabella?"

Bella looked confused. He seemed angry with her; probably because she spoke of bathing in mixed company. She flushed red. Her mother had taught her better manners. She supposed those manners were as tarnished as her reputation. But that etiquette belonged to a different time, a time when she knew nothing of hunger, loss, or pain.

"I apologize for my crudeness, Jack, but there are no man servants to show you to your, um, bath."

Jack's mouth hung open and he shook his head. It took him a full minute to speak, "It's not that." The tension in him made his shoulders stiff and his cheeks red. "Blast it, Bell. It's this whole crazy notion of bringing a man here. You're a beautiful woman and damn it! Men get ideas."

Bella smiled. She couldn't help but be flattered. She spent many a day in her youth wondering if Jack Byron even noticed she was a female. "Why, thank you, Jack."

"Jesus, Bella! That wasn't a compliment. I was stating a fact."

Bella grinned. It still counted as a compliment by her estimation.

"You ARE crazy. You've gone plum insane."

"Oh pooh." Bella pulled her arm free and resumed walking. "My *sanity* is the one thing I haven't lost. And you can move on, Tess. I see you round that corner. I swear, you all are the crazy ones. Jack's mad that I sprung him from jail and Tess acts like she never met you before."

Jack tugged at his bushy beard. "I'm not mad at you. I just worry about your motives."

"I offered to marry you."

"That's my point! What makes you think you can simply buy a man from jail with the intention of marrying him? You don't know what kind of trouble you could get..."

"Oh, for cripe's sake. I didn't buy *a man* from jail. I bought Jack Owen Byron. A man I believe is trustworthy and true of heart."

"People change."

"Have you changed?" Bella asked.

Jack rolled his eyes and shook his head.

"Have you become untrustworthy? Or are you the same person who opened my eyes to the injustice in my world? The guy who risked his neck to save me from a berserk horse?"

"Anyone would've done that."

"The barn was filled with hands, but when that snake spooked Caesar, you were the one who jumped in to save me."

Jack sighed and looked to the trees in the horizon as if they might offer the words he needed to speak sense to a child, or a simple debutante. "But marriage? Seriously? You don't just marry anyone. What's Master Troy think of this? He'll have my hide if he hears I even consider..."

"Father's dead."

"I'm..."

"Don't apologize. Thankfully, father died before he saw everything he loved come to ruin. Well, almost everything." Bella crossed her arms over her chest. "This is my decision, my choice. I've had enough of people making choices for me. I'm offering to marry you. I don't have money, land, or anything of value. I realize that's a sad bargain, but it's all I have. And as much as I hate to admit it, I'm finding this world to be a harsh place without a man. So, if I have to have one, I prefer one who knows how to work the land and is willing to bend his back."

"So, you're buying yourself a worker? Some strange twist on indentured servitude? On slavery?"

"No, not at all. I'd rather call it an arrangement. A mutually beneficial arrangement."

"How am I benefited?"

Bella's face fell. She never considered this would offend him. But how could it not? She still acted like a princess. What made her think he would ever want her? Her shoulders sagged and her eyes watered. "I...oh...I'm sorry. I guess I offer no benefit. Forgive me, Jack. I only thought of myself. Well, I thought about Tessie and Manny. But I never thought about you. I guess I assumed you'd be so happy to be out of jail." She swallowed the tears and sighed. "I suppose that was mighty arrogant of me."

He reached out for her hand, but she spun away.

"Bella, I didn't mean..." He tried to explain.

"Let's not speak of it." Bella walked on toward the barn, ignoring his calls, filling the awkward moment with chatter about the outdoor tub hidden by hanging blankets on clotheslines. She and Tessie had filled the tub that morning to warm it in the North Carolina sun. She dipped her fingers in the water. "It's near perfect. You can clean up. I, uh, well,

Tessie and I fixed you up some new clothes to wear. We kind of figured you'd need them." She pointed to trousers and a shirt hanging with the blankets. "When you're done, come in and have a bite to eat."

"Bella, what you did was foolish but…"

"I really am sorry. You have to forgive my arrogance. And the fact that I never once considered how you would feel about this. I suppose I'm still…"

"Be quiet a minute and listen to me." He reached for her, but she circled the tub to avoid the contact.

"Jack, please, don't. I don't want to make you feel bad. Let's get you cleaned up, have a bite to eat and then we'll…well, we'll figure something out."

"Bella…"

"I don't want to speak of this anymore. Do you understand? I realize what a stuck up, foolish little ninny you must think I am. So, please just stop talking." She readjusted the blankets on the line. "Besides you smell and you need a bath."

Jack looked her over, jaw clenched, hands on hips. He unbuttoned the sleeves on his rough wool shirt and mumbled, "Don't know why I'm surprised. You always were stubborn and spoiled. Shoulda known you'd grow up to be a crazy willful woman."

"Excuse me?"

"I asked if you had a razor."

"Hmmph." Bella's lips pursed and her foot tapped. Then she nodded. "I'll be right back."

By the time Bella returned he was scrubbed clean and had a blanket from the line tucked around his waist. She handed him a mirror and the razor and watched as he cut away the fur which hid the once familiar man. Finishing, he splashed his face with water then dried it on the towel. He handed the razor to Bella and sat on a stump. "Shave it off. Bound to have lice in it, so be careful."

"Tessie's lye soap and kerosene rinse didn't kill it?"

"Do you want to take the chance?"

Bella shook her head and sawed away at the wiry mess of hair. Jack was much skinnier than she had ever seen him. She could count his ribs, front and back. His hands, once so big and strong looked long and bony.

"Tom said you were there two years?"

"Going on."

Bella's heart broke for him. "If only I had known, but I only heard last week. I would have gotten you out immediately...I swear I would've come. Even a lashing from Charles wouldn't have stopped me from getting you out of there."

"Who's Charles?"

"My husband."

Jack jerked his head around. Bella gasped. "Be careful. I nearly took a chunk out of your scalp."

"If you've got a husband, what the hell am I here for?"

"Well because, I also got myself a divorce."

Bella anticipated his shock, lifting the razor above his head as he turned to gape at her again. She placed her hands on his shoulders and ordered, "Stop moving."

"You did what?"

"I think you heard me the first time."

"How? Why? A divorce. You got to be kidding me."

"We weren't a good match. It's better this way. But, it's also why I can't just let you live here. The rumors would be devastating."

"So, what's your husband going to think of you marrying another man?"

"Trust me. He'll never know."

"How can you be so sure of that?"

"I just am."

"What the hell's going on? Why aren't you living at the Point? What about your mother?

Your brothers?"

"Gone. All gone."

His thin body slumped. "I'm sorry Bell. What happened? The war?"

"The boys died of fever a few years after you left the Point. Father died of a heart attack right as the war began. The day after the firing on Ft. Sumter to be exact. Mother died a few years after Father."

"And the Point? It's gone, too, I assume?"

Bella sighed. "It's still where it was. It's just owned by someone else."

"I don't know what to say."

"I don't want you to say anything. I'd rather not think about what was."

"But you…"

"Shush. I didn't exactly find *you* in a gilded cage. I, at least, have Tessie and a roof over my head."

Jack nodded, then looked over the house. "So, your husband let you stay on in his house?"

"Oh no. This place doesn't belong to Charles," Bella gasped. "It's in my name alone."

"Seems like a nice place. House looks solid, foundation looks square. Fields look lush, should be good for planting. You got several outbuildings and a couple of barns." Jack looked over the land with a farmer's eye. "The land lays good. Looks like it gets plenty of water; got a nice stream there with some nice woods beyond. It seems to have everything a man would need to make a living, if he's willing to work."

"I was thinking the same thing and you called me a crazy willful woman, or was it a willful crazy woman? Hmm…guess you're not going to repeat yourself while I have a razor." Bella held the razor in limbo as she gazed over the place. She knew the place could offer a comfortable living, but she didn't know where to begin. She sighed and resumed cutting away clumps of hair, "I'd do it myself, but don't know anything about farms, except harvest time is a busy time."

"So did you buy this place? You picked a good one."

"No. It actually belongs to Noah. You remember Noah?"

"Tessie's boy?"

"Mmm, hmm. He went north right before the war and ended up joining the union army. Well, he was posted as a guard at an army prison in the new Virginia. Well, you know Noah, he's as curious about people as he is about books, so he got to know all the men he guarded. And it seems one of them was from right here in the county. Jimmy Trent. Do you remember him?" Isabella paused. She leaned over his shoulder to see his face as he answered.

Jack coughed and squirmed in his chair, nodding his head. "Didn't he have crush on you, Bell?"

"Who Jimmy? No." Isabella laughed at the thought.

"He was always hanging around the Point."

"Because he loved horses and Daddy always raised the best."

Bella resumed her work. Jack crossed his arms over his chest and closed his eyes while she worked.

"Well, seems Noah got him special treatment in the prison and nursed him through gangrene that set in from a bullet wound to his leg. Then when the war was over, Jimmy was released. His leg was darn near crippled and he couldn't walk all those miles home, so, Noah practically carried him back to his family. Why James, Jimmy's dad? He was so grateful, and he always was a fair man, so when he and his family decided to move west…too many bad memories here…he traded Noah this place for the union money Noah earned in the army. But the deed is in my name, of course, being as Noah's black. But it belongs to Noah."

"Where's Noah?"

"He left almost a year ago. He's looking for Manny's mom, Wendy. He loves her so much. I told him he should have married her as soon as he came back from the war, but he could barely admit he had feelings for her, much less ask for her hand." Bella laughed. Noah Solomon's moon eyed love for the beautiful half breed Cherokee was obvious to everyone but Noah. Bella's smile disappeared as she thought of the current situation. "Now she's gone and none of us know where she went."

"She left her kid?"

"She left everything. She brought me Manny in the middle of the night. Seems some men got drunk and she lived alone." Bella cleared her throat and cleaned the razor on a towel with a little too much vigor. "It was an awful night. One best forgotten." She took a deep breath, then smiled. "Anyhow, I know Noah will find her. He was right on her trail. I pray he can talk some sense into her."

"Did someone hurt her?" Jack whispered.

"I'd rather not talk about it."

Jack's voice was near gruff. "What about you, Bell? You had that problem?"

"I won't lie to you. Men are bold, especially when your reputation is as sullied as mine. But we hold our own, Tessie and me. Everyone in this town knows we can shoot straight at a hundred yards. I only had to put lead in one man's leg to let all of them know I prefer to be left alone."

Bella brushed the loose hairs from his shoulders and then announced, "There, you're all done." She stepped in front of him to examine her work. His hair was black as night and even completely sheared, he retained a shadowy crown. He looked younger without the hair. And though his face was gaunt, she could still see the handsome man she once tried to trick into kissing her when she was thirteen.

"Making this place a producing farm will take a lot of work," he cautioned.

"I'm not afraid of work. And if you don't want to marry me...I suppose that's all right. I guess you can still stay. Anyway, what more can they say about me? Unless you're worried about your reputation." She looked at the ground. "Even being friends with me will ruin you in this town."

"Bella..." He reached out and touched her cheek stroking it with the back of his fingers. She tried to read his face. His mouth was set in a grimace, his eyes troubled. Please, please she begged silently hoping her face didn't betray her desperation. This morning she thought she wouldn't be above getting her way by any means, but now that he was here, in the flesh, she couldn't accept anything but him wanting her of his own decision.

"How did it all come to this?"

"Happenstance," she said with a sigh. She wasn't sure if he meant the entire world's fate or just her own, but she knew she didn't want to waste time thinking about how she got here. She only wanted to know the way out. Besides, she was boggled by human meanness, and as a habit, she didn't bother with things that bewildered her. "But," she said, taking a deep breath, "it'll all be all right. Why, if you'll give me one year, then I know..."

"You make it sound so simple. Life is never simple." He pulled her close and kissed the top of her head. "Have you grown up at all from the giddy girl I used to know?"

Bella tried to pull away, but he held her close. "You don't have a clue what I've been through, Jack Byron."

"That's my point." He let go allowing her a few steps so he could look her in the eye. "I won't leave you in need, so of course I'll stay. But as for marriage…"

Her muscles tightened. He was going to tell her no, but she wouldn't cry. He would stay at least. He just said so, and for Jack, that was good as a solemn oath.

"I don't know if you've completely thought it through. There are parts of being married you may not be considering."

Bella felt her heart lift a little. He wasn't ruling it out. He was talking about…her mouth went dry… sex. Of course. What man didn't? Bella understood the obligations of a woman. She bit her lip. "Jack, I've been married before, remember? You'll see, I can be a good wife. I'll try to keep my mouth shut and not be sassy and opinionated. And as for what I think you're talking about…I can endure it. I understand a man does have certain needs."

Jack studied her, a muscle twitched in his cheek, his eyes narrowed.

"What's wrong, Jack?"

"Nothing. I think sometimes questions are better left unasked and definitely better left unanswered."

"Did I say something wrong?"

Jack threw an arm over her shoulder and tucked her tight as they walked to the house. "No, Bella. I guess I realized a whole lot has transpired since that day you threw yourself on me in the barn."

"I tripped."

"Did you, now?"

Bella blushed and admitted, "I wanted you to kiss me."

"I figured as much."

Bella stopped and looked up at him. "So why didn't you kiss me?"

Jack frowned. "You really don't get it, do you, Bell?"

"Was it because I was so young?"

"No. It's because you never thought far enough ahead. Never weighed the consequences of your actions. You never did, and evidently you still don't."

"That's not true. I think more than *you'd* ever believe. *You* may still see me as a little twit who worries more for her dresses and bonnets than anything else in the world, but I do have plans for us. I've thought about nothing else the last two days. My only problem is getting you to see it my way."

Chapter 3

Jack rolled up his blankets and set them in the corner of the pantry. He heard Tessie humming as she stoked the fire in the kitchen. Then he heard the lock slide on his door. He grinned as he stretched. At least Tessie was wise enough not to trust him, locking his door before she went on to bed. Bella, on the other hand, suggested he sleep upstairs. No way was Tessie allowing that. She stomped her foot and laid down the law. As always, Bella crumbled to her mammy's authority.

He shook his head and sighed. The girl didn't have the sense God gave a goose. He supposed he had Tessie to thank for her survival, evidently Noah, too. Though the Noah he remembered was a sickly, thin fellow. He was surprised he survived the war at all. Would have figured him as one who'd die of dysentery before he ever saw a fight. But then people could surprise you.

He lumbered into the kitchen.

"Mornin', Mr. Jack."

"Mornin', Tessie. Did you sleep all right with one eye open?"

Tessie might have blushed. He couldn't tell with her dark skin. She poured a cup of tea and said, "I slept well enough knowing I had you locked in your room. I won't lie about it. I don't trust men, not even men who I used to like as a boy. Never know what kind o' man a boy'll grow into. One of us has to use some sense round here. The missy sure won't."

Jack took the cup of yaupon tea Tessie offered him. "I agree. She's a damn fool for even going to that hellhole they call a prison. How'd she survive this long without ending up like Wendy?"

Tessie frowned. "She told you 'bout Wendy?"

"No. She said she had a run-in with some men then ran away. I filled in the blanks myself."

"Injun women are 'bout as respected as a darkie, though Wendy is Lumbee and could pass for white. But she married a Cherokee and has beautiful, long black hair. My how it shimmers. That hair and having a Cherokee child marked her in this town." Tessie's face looked pinched. "Noah took after her over a year ago. Surely, he found her by now. He couldn't have been more than half a day behind her."

"She didn't tell anyone where she was going? Just left? Abandoned her kid and all?"

"I don't think she planned to ever return. Or to go very far away."

"You really think she would have...?"

Tessie nodded.

He closed his eyes. "You guys were here all alone? Doesn't Bella have an uncle or a cousin? Someone to take care of you?"

"The ones who aren't dead don't want anything to do with her. They're ashamed of her."

"Just because she divorced her husband?"

"Mmm, that's as good a reason as any."

Jack opened his mouth, but Tessie switched the subject. "So, how do you like your eggs, Mr. Jack?"

"However you want to cook 'em." He considered asking more questions, but the Tessie he remembered wouldn't answer them. She'd probably run him out of her kitchen and call him a flapper jaw. He decided to go in a safe direction. "So, I take it there's a chicken coop?"

"No, just a few scraggly birds and one randy rooster running around in a shed. Isn't much, but they've kept us in food. Them and a bit of flour is about all we have left. Had a mess of potatoes, but we're about out. Going to use what's left for seed."

"Been hard?" Jack pulled a chair from under the table and turned it so he could look out over the yard. The dew was still wet on the grass and the sun was rising over the fields.

"Been hard for everybody. I thank the Lord we've done as well as we have. We're all still living and breathing." Tessie put the eggs on a plate and brought it to Jack. "We get by." She sighed heavily. "Well, I best be getting to my chores. Hope you enjoy your meal."

"Tessie." Jack turned in his chair and laid his plate on the table. "Did you know Bella was going to ask me to marry her?"

Tessie snorted, but nodded.

"What do you think?"

"I think the child's a bit daft. She's too kind for her own good. Too trusting. Loyal beyond good sense. When she told me 'bout her harebrained idea, I told her the gold would be better spent on a mule." Her head dipped slightly. "No offense, Mr. Jack."

"None taken." He laughed. "And for God's sake, Tessie, call me Jack. I ain't meant to be a mister."

Tessie shrugged and refolded the dish towel she'd laid on the counter. "So, you gonna marry her?"

Jack closed his eyes and grimaced. "It's insanity. Doesn't she want to marry some young gent who loves her?"

"Sometimes a girl does well to find a man who'll respect her."

Jack rubbed his chin in thought.

Tessie sighed and added, "And truth be told, you're not just any man to her, Mr. Jack."

"Jack," he reminded.

"Sorry. Jack. You know she had a powerful crush on you."

"She was only a girl."

"She was a young lady of thirteen. Plenty of girls are married by fifteen or sixteen."

"I look at Bella and I still see the girl."

"Well, you're the only man in this county and the next who hasn't realized Isabella is a woman."

Jack rubbed the back of his neck. "Oh, I see how she's changed. Trust me. I see it. I hate to even look at her. I feel like a dirty old man."

"You're what six, seven years older?"

"Five. But I keep thinking, she's Bella. She's not meant for the likes of me."

"That sounds like Master Troy talk."

"It still feels wrong."

"Then tell her no. Soon as I can get her out of this county, you'll see, she'll find herself a man who'll love her."

Jack looked at Tessie and scowled.

"That thought bug you? Another man having her?"

"No, it reminds me how well she evidently picked her last man. I can only imagine what happened to lead *her* to divorce."

"Oh, Master Charles wasn't her picking. Her daddy married her off and he didn't care one lick about whether or not it was to a good man."

"Seriously? Isabella was always Master Troy's princess."

"Well, things changed."

"What happened?"

Tessie seemed ready to talk, then closed her mouth and turned her back to him. "You know these are Bella's stories to tell. I sure wouldn't want someone telling all my secrets. But I'm sure if Master Troy had known exactly what Master Charles was, he'd not have forced his baby girl to marry him." Tessie's words were quiet.

"Was her husband rough with her?"

She shook her head. "That's the missy's business; you'll have to ask her. And that's sound advice for ya. Want to know? Ask her; she'll tell you. And I suppose you should before you hear it from the people of Troy. What they think they know is half rumor, other half lie. None of them know a thing." Tessie's jaw clamped shut and her nostrils flared.

Jack scratched his chin. His whiskers scraped against his hands. "I wish I knew what to do. I've always had a liking for Bell, but..."

Tessie turned to face him. "You don't love her."

"I loved the girl. I never thought of her as anything more."

"Then explain that to her. And whether you stay or go, well that is your choice, but don't make it out of pity for us. We're doing good. We got food and shelter and Noah'll be back any day now. She couldn't rest knowing you were in that jail."

"It's not that I don't appreciate what she's done, or think I wouldn't be the luckiest man in the world to have her...I don't know if I can marry her knowing neither one of us loves each other." Jack ran a hand over his stubbly hair. "But I feel I owe her. She did save me."

"Can't go marrying her 'cause of that."

"But then I think, hell, love sure didn't work out for me."

"Woman break your heart?"

"Yeah. I was engaged to the prettiest little redhead. Then I got in trouble. Got sentenced to five years and after the first, she sent me a letter letting me know she couldn't wait four more years. Even if she could, she didn't see me as the kind of guy a gal could build a future with. Me being a convict and all."

"Now that girl had some sense." Tessie snorted. Then she sighed. "Definitely more sense than Miss Bella, 'cause I can guarantee without the slightest bit of hesitation, she'd have waited till hell froze over for you if she loved you. Maybe even if she didn't."

Jack closed his eyes and was quiet a moment. "Maybe I should use my head, not my heart. Any man would be happy to have a woman like Bella."

The back door closed with a bang. Tessie grabbed her towel and started wiping clean counters. Jack jumped in his seat, his cheeks flushed.

"Mmm, smells good, Tess. I'm starved after that walk. Young Manteo is so sick of school, but bless his heart he went. I know the kids tease him, but I think Noah was right, he'll have to learn to live in the world as it is. Can't let him hide, right?"

Tessie sputtered and stammered. Bella poured herself a cup of tea and grabbed a cold biscuit from the tin. "After this summer, we'll have jam. It'll be divine."

"I better get to my sewing. I'm taking in some of Master Charles's pants. Kind of gives me a thrill to know I'm shrinking the bastard's stuff for another man."

"Well, enjoy yourself." Bella laughed and finished off her biscuit. "And I guess I should run into town to see about buying some seed. I think it's safe to put the garden in. What do you think, Jack?"

"You could have done it at the end of April. All you have to worry about is frost being done."

"Good, then, I'm off."

"I'll go with you." Jack stood, swallowing his food whole and setting his plate in the dish pan.

"You don't have to. It's a simple trip."

"Nonsense. I'll help pick the seeds."

"I'm perfectly capable of choosing seeds."

"I'll keep you company."

"I prefer to ride alone. It clears my thoughts."

"Thought you wouldn't be saucy?"

"You don't want to marry me."

"I never said no. I said let me think about it."

"Well, I'm rescinding my offer. So, there, now you don't have to worry. Now… I have to go."

Bella grabbed her bonnet and bolted, tying the stained ribbon under her chin as she sprinted to the horse barn. She tried to drag the beast out of his stall, cursing his slow-moving hide as he made his way, easy as he pleased, to the harness. "Dammit, Nero, pick up the pace. We've got to go."

"Why the hurry?" Jack asked as he took the harness from her and began working the straps around the horse's neck.

"I've got a lot to get done."

"Really? Or are you avoiding me?"

"Nonsense." She tripped over her own feet trying to get into the wagon. He caught her by the hips and held her till she steadied herself. He set her aside and climbed into the wagon and took the reins. He looked down at her with a smug smile. "You can come with me if you'd like."

Bella stomped her foot. "Get off *my* wagon."

"You said I could stay here and I plan to earn my room and board. Now get on or I'll leave you here."

"Fine." Bella circled the wagon and climbed in. "Why do men have to be so bossy? Did the good Lord make you that way or do mommas spoil little boys and make them brats?"

"My mother passed on the first month I was in jail."

"Oh." Bella bit her lip. "I'm sorry, Jack. I didn't mean to..."

"It's all right."

"That was a mean thing for me to say."

"You didn't know. And you have every right to be mad at me. You offered me a gift as rare as gold, and I acted like you gave me coal. You're a special girl, and I do appreciate your offer. But, the thing is, you deserve a gentleman, not a dirt farmer. I want what's best for you."

"I know what's best for me. I *am* a grown woman." She lifted her chin and looked straight ahead. "But you're right. My talk of marriage was pure silliness. I don't know what I was thinking."

"You were scared. But I assure you, I won't leave you and Tessie before Noah comes back. I owe you that much."

Bella's spine stiffened. "You don't..."

Jack gave her hand a squeeze as he interrupted, "I said that wrong. I *need* a place to stay.

I *want* to stay and help you and Tessie. We can get through this together."

"Like partners?"

Jack's cheeks reddened, but he nodded. "Yeah, partners."

The birds chirped and the spring breeze blew cool and fresh. He smiled and asked, "So, boss, what are we out to buy?"

Bella pinched his arm and giggled then told him all her ideas for the garden. She chattered on the entire ride. Jack said barely ten words. He listened and nodded periodically. Bella knew he had to be tired of her voice, so she breathed a sigh of relief when they arrived at the general store. Jack offered to tie up the horse while she hastened inside.

Eager to leave fear and hunger in the past, she was raring to rebuild, but her spirits sagged as she realized Bert was working the counter. Bert Potter owned the place, but usually his wife ran it. Sue was rarely a friendly woman, but at least Bella was safe from getting her hind end pinched as she shopped.

Bella stretched a smile from one ear to the other. "Morning, Mr. Potter. I came to buy some seeds. I'm going to put in my garden."

"Really?" His grin was greasy. "You probably need help plowing your ground. If you need a horse, I could help you."

Two men loitering at the counter did a poor job of stifling laughter. Bella didn't quite understand the innuendo, but she knew it was an insult. She didn't know what to say, so she ignored the comment and headed for the seed bins. "No, I only need seed."

The three men laughed. Each offered to provide her with seed. Bella's cheeks flamed. Her hands shook as she lifted the wooden lid.

"Well, how are you on money?" Bert asked as he came from around the counter and moved in close, his body pinning her against the bins. She squirmed as he stroked her shoulders, "My offer of credit is still good. Or we could make some better arrangement. Sure we could think of something mutually satisfying." His hands slid down her arms. "I could help you in lots of ways, seeing as how you're without a man and all."

"She's got a man, you filthy son of a bitch!" boomed a voice from the doorway. Jack pounced, quick as lightning, grabbing Bert by the collar and shoving him against barrels of grain. One bin toppled over splashing oats across the floor. Bella clutched Jack's arm. "Stop it! Jack! Stop or you'll kill him!"

Jack loosened his grip and looked down at Bella. Her eyes were watery and showed all the fear she normally hid. Jack released his collar only to get his hand around his neck. He lifted Bert off his feet; the man gurgled, his breaths coming in raspy wheezes. Bella glanced at the patrons near the counter; the men stared but made no move to get involved. She turned to Jack, tears in her eyes, "Please, Jack. They'll send you back to prison for sure."

Her soft words penetrated his anger. Jack let the man's feet return to the floor, and he slowly released his grip. Bert coughed and massaged his throat as Jack said, "I don't much appreciate you talkin' to Miss Bella that way. She's a lady, and you should address her as such."

"I was just offering to help..." Bert's words hung in the air as Jack grabbed him by the collar. Jack's face turned crimson. "She doesn't need your kind of help! Ignorant pig. I should bloody your face for the hell of it."

"Stop it, Jack." Bella's voice was much more firm and confident than she felt. She positioned herself between the two of them. "You didn't mean any disrespect, did you, Mr. Potter?"

"No, ma'am." Bert's voice trembled.

"Now, I came here to get supplies for my garden, not to witness men behaving like white trash in a bar room." Bella lifted her chin and straightened her crooked bonnet.

Bert stared at the floor. "My apologies, Miss Bella. I didn't realize you and Jack were..."

Bella covered her mouth and gasped. Her skin drained of color. "Oh no, Mr. Potter. You don't understand. I hired Mr. Bryon. He's going to be working on the farm." She gave Jack a scathing look. "Me and Jack? Why that's just silly. Why, he was Daddy's stable boy. Oh my, I could laugh about *that* all day…but I can't with so much to get done. So back to business. Mr. Potter, would you be so kind as to wrap me up some carrot and lettuce seeds? Oh and some pepper." She took a deep breath, then added, "And onion, and hmm, some cabbage. Oh, and tomato, can't forget tomato. What else." She looked around the store. "And certainly beans and cucumbers. My, this will be so much to plant. But won't it be wonderful come fall to have so much to eat?"

No one answered her directly, but the men mumbled. Jack looked furious, so she ignored his gaze.

She sidestepped Bert and went to the counter. She held out the last of her coins. "I suppose you *could* put the rest on credit. It *was* so kind of you to offer. I'll be sure to mention to Sue what a fine gentleman her husband is."

Bert followed behind her, assuming his place at the register. "No need to mention anything to the missus." He scooped up the coins and dropped them in the till without counting them. "I'm sure this is payment enough. Seeds aren't as expensive this year."

"Oh, good then, maybe I'll grab a bag of flour, too. Jack," Bella commanded pointing to a 50 pound sack of flour, "make yourself useful and grab that."

Jack grabbed the flour, and Bella took her paper wrapped parcel and offered a sickeningly sweet smile at the men as she passed. For Jack, who held the door for her, she cast an icy glare.

He followed right on her steps. "Bella, I…"

"Get in the wagon."

"Bella..."

Her head whipped, and the muscles in her jaw twitched. Jack shook his head and threw the flour and a sack of beans he grabbed into the bed. Bella climbed into the driver's seat and snapped the reins. Jack stood, mouth hanging open in the dust as he watched her drive away. Once he realized she wasn't slowing down or turning back, he ran after her, hurling himself into the bed. He maneuvered to the front, trying to get in the seat as she aimed for every bump and hole in the road.

Bella never looked his way. She rode out of town with her head high, evidently not noticing that Jack teetered on the back of the seat or that everyone she waved to as she passed ignored her. Jack settled in beside her. He said nothing until they were safely out of town.

"I was only trying to help you."

Bella urged the horse to move faster.

"Slow down before you kill yourself."

"Don't tell me what to do!"

Jack grabbed the reins and pulled Nero to a stop. "Thought you said you would be obedient?"

"I suppose that's why I'm not the marrying type."

He grabbed her by the shoulders and uttered a curse. Before she could be shocked by his language, his hands locked behind her head and he pulled her to him. His kiss, a near brutal assault, left her breathless. She told herself she should feel ashamed, instead she felt thrilled. He did want her. He didn't want to, but he did. She placed a hand on his chest and gently pushed him away. She touched her lips, reveling in the feel of them.

She cleared her throat and shook her head to clear her thoughts, "Kindly remember, Mr. Bryon, contrary to popular opinion, I am *not* a whore."

Jack's cheek blazed. Then he muttered more curses. "I'm sorry, I didn't mean…"

"Speak of it no more. And be mindful of what you tell people in public. By marking me as your territory in there, you simply added fuel to their fires. I know you meant well, but you have to think about what you say. When you leave? I'll have sunk so low as to being my father's servant's trollop. Doesn't exactly elevate my status."

More curses.

"And watch your language. Goodness. You sound like a field hand."

"I am a field hand," he said quietly, then said nothing more till they arrived home.

As Bella unhooked the reins, Jack grabbed her hands and turned her toward him. "I'm sorry, for everything."

"No need for sorry. I just think if we are to live side by side for a time, we set a few boundaries."

"No. We *will* get married. You're right. I never should have said that in town. And I can't seem to remember, my, uh, manners. It's the only rational thing to do."

Bella shrugged, "Don't be a ninny, Jack. Who wants to be rational when we can hope for love?"

Elizabeth Seckman

Chapter 4

Bella raced from the barn, bypassed Tessie's curiosity, and bolted to her room.

She pressed her ear to the door to see if Tessie followed her, or Jack. Though she doubted he'd approach her again. Not for a while, anyway.

She touched her chest. Her heart thumped against her hand. What just happened didn't seem real. His hands, his lips? She wanted him to touch her like that forever. She closed her eyes against the thought. Thinking like that made everything people said about her true, and she was raised better than that.

But still…his kiss…it was so beyond lips, slobber, and pressure. It was heat. It was being completely lost in a moment. She hadn't wanted it to end and now she wondered, if she hadn't broken away, would she have burst into flames?

She dropped onto her bed and covered her burning face with her hands. She was twenty-four years old. Far too old to believe such nonsense. She needed to clear her head and be as rational as she said she could be. Problem was… rational thought was never her best quality.

She stood and straightened her skirts. Lying around in the middle of the day certainly was not *rational*. She paced the length of her room. Forcing herself to look at the whole situation. Jack was a good man. He protected her from Bert. But he'd have done that for any woman.

As for that kiss, she didn't understand why he did it. She heard him with her own two ears say he didn't love her, that he loved someone else. She gasped and covered her mouth as her stomach twisted. Surely he didn't think she was a fallen woman and it was acceptable to prey upon her?

She couldn't bear Jack thinking of her like that. She always cared for him. Not because he was handsome, which he was, but because he was gentle and sweet. He never treated her like the master's daughter either. He talked to her like she had some sense.

No, no, she thought as she paced. Even if Jack thought she was a Jezebel, he wouldn't kiss her for sport. And he certainly wouldn't have said he'd marry her.

So why the sudden change of heart?

Tears stung Bella's eyes as the answer became obvious. He pitied her. Jack knew she was vulnerable; knew she was an abhorrence in the town which bore her name.

Pity wasn't a good enough reason to marry someone, or was it? Rational thought said, *certainly; without him, you'll likely not survive another winter.*

But her heart couldn't agree with her belly. Pity and fear of starvation wasn't a fair reason to marry him. If only she had something to offer him in return.

She thought of all she had… another man's farm…an absolute ineptitude in running a house without servants?

She had nothing…no assets, no skills. Why, if it weren't for Tessie, she wouldn't have survived the winter. She didn't even know how to cook for herself. She had nothing to offer any man, especially one as fine as Jack. Unless she counted what was up her skirts.

Bella groaned and shook the memories from her mind. Men were fools to be so weak over something so...so...she couldn't even describe the feelings of revolt that washed over her. But that's how men were, and she realized, with a pain in her heart, Jack was no better.

"So, I have his pity and his lust...is that enough?" Her rational mind chimed in fast with, *use whatever you have, just get him to marry you,* but her heart, that damned infernal beast without any sense, said to her, *Jack deserves to have love.* A fat tear slid down her cheek. Jack didn't love her, so she must let him go.

She comforted herself with the fact that Jack would stay till Noah came back. He would never leave her stranded. When Noah returned, well, then he could move on. She'd even give him her blessing, so that he could find his true love.

Even if it was with the trollop who abandoned him. Bella's cheeks stained red with irritation. The room felt hot, so she went to her window for a breath of fresh air. The spring breeze whipped the lacy curtains and felt cool against her hot cheeks. She looked out over the lush green hills before her. The trees were filling out their winter skeletons with leaves of green. She heard a whinny and looked down in the barn lot. Nero pranced, lifting a hoof gingerly. Bella held her breath, hoping beyond hopes that her childish tantrum riding out of town hadn't crippled the poor beast. Jack bent over Nero's hoof. He dug at it with a knife, then set the hoof back on the ground. Nero put his weight on it and was fine. Bella exhaled. Jack really was the finest of men. If only he loved her.

Bella imagined the other woman, the lucky woman who would have him in the end and her Troy pride was pricked. Troys never accepted loss, at least not without a fight. She'd win his heart, one way or another.

She was so sure of her ability to make him fall in love with her that she had half a mind to go ahead and accept his proposal! Why, she'd be doing him a favor; saving him from a disloyal woman who cast him aside when he needed her most.

But she'd already said no and how would she ever go down and say yes. It would be awkward. She would have to get him to ask her again! It was that simple.

She went to her vanity and poured some water. Too bad she had no scented oils. She washed her face to get rid of the road grime and pinched her cheeks for added color. She loosened her hair, brushing it till it shined, then twisted it back into its knot. The humidity made her curls go wild, so she dabbed them with a bit of water to tuck them behind her ear.

She wished she had one nice dress to wear. Maybe a pink gown to set off her complexion. She felt as giddy and hopeful as the girl who dressed "just so" to run down to the stable.

But then, all those years ago, after all her efforts, Jack never did notice her. By the age of thirteen she could charm most men into doing anything she wanted, but never Jack. So, why would he now? She tossed the brush on the dresser realizing she was the same foolish little twit she was ten years ago. Only now she was poor, without so much as a full pantry as a dowry.

Thoughts of wooing Jack evaporated like a dream.

Stripping off her brown muslin skirt and the once white, now tea-stained cream top, she donned her trousers. She had no corset or proper undergarments, so Tessie had made her some tight fitting camisoles. She pulled one of those over her head before slipping into one of Charles's long-sleeved shirts, which she tied heart her waist. Charles had been a big man. His clothes were easily reduced to make double the clothes for her and Manny. But this shirt she left large. Its looseness let in the cool air while she worked.

She looked at herself in the mirror and frowned. She'd sneak out the back door and get to work. If Jack saw her like this, any hopes she might have of seducing him would be dead.

The garden plot was already plowed from the previous owner, but the soil had hardened and was difficult to dig. Bella put on work gloves and began to hack at the clumps with her shovel. They broke into smaller clumps, but nothing smooth enough to dig up and plant a seed. She worked till her back ached, but there was absolutely no visible difference to be seen. She plopped herself down at the edge of the garden and cried. She didn't try to stop. She let the tears fall. How hard was a garden to plant? Evidently pretty damned hard, or she was pretty damned useless. Fresh tears welled up as she fell onto her back, laying prone on the hard earth. "I am a useless failure." She covered her face with her gloved hands and sobbed.

She felt him before she saw him. She didn't know if she subconsciously heard his footsteps or if she knew he was there, seated beside her in the grass. He stroked the top of her head. "It'll be all right. Please don't cry."

She kept her hands over her face and shook her head, not caring that her bun was loosened by the motion. He pulled her hands away from her face. She squeezed her eyes closed as the sun bore down red and angry against her face. "Ah, Bella," was all he said as he scooped her off the ground and onto his lap like she was a child. He cradled her against him. Kissed her cheek and loosened stray hairs that stuck to her tear-stained cheeks. His eyes were soft and sad as if he'd come upon a box of dead puppies. "Bella," he said again, then said nothing more. He tucked her head under his chin and held her tight. Bella thought of a time when she dreamed of Jack holding her like this, back in a time when she was certain of everything. Now she didn't *know* anything. Her body shook with sobs. Jack's arms tightened around her, his breath tickled her ear as he whispered, "It's gonna be all right. I promise."

Bella nodded her head.

He kissed her forehead and tipped her chin until she looked up at him. "I swear."

She nodded, tried to smile.

The pressure of his hands tightened and he frowned. "I have no right, but hell with it." His lips descended. The urgency of before was gone. His kiss was gentle and slow as if they had forever. The idea of stopping it never crossed Bella's mind. She allowed her body to melt against his. She didn't care if it *was* wrong. The feeling he awakened might very well sustain her through any bad that may come. She felt safe and loved…and treasured. He pulled away, rubbed a thumb across her lower lip. "What are you doing to me?"

"I didn't…I'm sorry."

Jack kissed her cheek. "It's not your fault, Bell. Don't be sorry."

Bella blushed. "Well…no. I think I do owe you an apology." She swallowed. "I planned this. The thought crossed my mind that I might, um, use your desires against you."

"And you chose this outfit?" He grinned as he tugged at the sleeve of her shirt.

Bella looked down at her clothes and her cheeks burned red. She covered her mouth and nearly cried again from embarrassment. "Oh!"

He took her hand and kissed it like a gentleman. "I've never seen you more lovely."

Bella searched his face and was shocked to realize he seemed to be telling her the truth. Men were such odd creatures.

"So, sweet little Bell, why are you crying by the garden?"

"Because," she said as she flailed her arms at the untilled earth, "I can't do it! I can't even plant a seed. I'm totally useless. I have been digging in this God-forsaken dirt for over an hour and nothing good has come of it. So, if I can't even grow food, what good am I? I keep hoping Noah will come up the road and we could leave. Maybe go north where I could get a job in a factory or something. Because," –fresh tears erupted though she bit her lip and tried to make them stop– "I'm completely useless. Useless! Do you realize unless I'm willing to hike my skirt for the swine in town, I have nothing? Nothing at all. Do you understand me? Nothing." She plopped her head back into her hands and sobbed. Jack rubbed her back, tucking her closer into him.

"Don't cry, Bella. I can't stand to see you cry."

"Then go away and let me wallow in misery all by myself."

"I can never do that. It's all right. You know I won't let you starve. Why you could have used that piece of gold to buy a whole 'nother year of food and supplies."

She shook her head. "No, I wouldn't have been able to. Bert usually cheats me because he evidently thinks people with breasts can't count. He always charges me double. Him and his wife. Everyone in this damned town hates me. Why do I stay?"

"For Noah?"

Her tears slowed. "Yes. For Noah. But for all I know he's never coming back."

"He'll be back."

"Even if he came back, I'm probably still too much of a coward to leave. I don't even know what a factory is."

"I'll take you away. As soon as Noah comes back, I'll take you somewhere where you can be free of all this. A place where people wave back at you and men treat you with the respect you deserve. Until then, I'm here and I'll see to it you're taken care of."

"You don't have to do that. I'm just pouting like the spoiled brat that I am."

"You're scared. And you have every right to be scared. This whole world is upside down, but soon it will come to rights. Just be strong and let me help you. You're not alone." He brushed away a tear with his thumb. "You know I would never leave you, right?"

Bella nodded. "That's a truth I have been counting on." She needed Jack to stay with her and she didn't care what his reasons were. She sniffled. "I suppose you were a good investment."

"You know, I've never even thanked you." He tipped her chin till she was looking at him. "You saved my sanity, if not my life. That place was becoming more and more like hell every day. I won't let you starve. We'll start with this garden and tomorrow, we'll check out the fields to see what we've got to work with. All right?"

Bella nodded, relaxing in the knowledge he was there, his hands holding her firm. He gave her a gentle squeeze nuzzling his lips to her ear. His voice was sharp as he warned her, "But don't ever, ever think of selling yourself to any man. You're much too precious for that. It's rare to find a woman who's beautiful inside and out."

So why don't you want me? she thought, but asked instead, "Tell me, honestly." She picked at one of his buttons. "Could you be interested in me if you weren't in love?"

"Who said I was in love?"

"I heard you talking to Tessie."

"Ahh. I wondered."

"So…"

"Well…" He wiped dirt smudges from her face. "Yes, I thought I loved her, but Tessie had a good point. True love would have lasted no matter what. I don't know if what she and I had was ever real."

Bella mulled over his words a moment then offered, "After this summer, you can leave. Without feeling any obligation. Maybe you can find this girl and see if she is what you need."

Jack opened his mouth, but Bella closed it by gently pinching his lips together. "I don't want you to feel sorry for me. Teach me what I need to know to survive. Like how to plant and how to harvest, and then you can go."

"All that in one summer?"

"Oh, I'm a quick learner."

"Bella Troy, honor student?" He laughed.

"Oh, I can be. It's just before I never had any need to know. Now I do."

"I see." His grinned remained. "So, at the end of summer…what if I don't want to leave?"

Bella shrugged. "I don't know how long I can keep you here before I ruin *your* reputation, too." She stood and adjusted her loosened hair. "I'm going to go remind Tessie to get Manny from school, and then I'll be back to help."

"Bring a bucket of water and Nero."

"Nero?"

"You might try to work up a garden this size with a shovel and hoe, but me, I'm going to plow it."

"A plow." How, she wondered, could she grow up on the biggest plantation in Macon County and know nothing about agriculture? She shook her head and sighed. "That's a good idea."

She made arrangements with Tessie and returned with Nero and the water bucket. Jack got to work plowing. She followed behind him, as instructed, and planted the seeds. She paid careful attention so she could do it alone next year. She even watched intently as he harnessed the horse to the plow. I can do that, she thought. She was feeling more confident as the day wore on. Manny came home, and he and Tessie joined in the planting and watering. By the time the sun set, they were done. They had a garden ready to grow. Bella looked it over with satisfaction. And hunger. All the work left her famished. And sore. Her back ached, tightening as she stood idle. Tessie had a half bag of potatoes left over. "Looks like I may as well cook these up for dinner."

Manny smiled and rubbed his stomach.

Bella massaged the small of her back to ease the stiffness. Jack came over and squeezed her shoulders, his strong hands kneading out the kinks, leaving her warm and relaxed. "Mmm…" The low moan escaped her lips involuntarily.

Jack leaned down and placed a gentle kiss on the side of her neck. "You're a remarkable woman, Bella."

Bella grinned and stepped away. "Glad to hear I'm a woman now."

"You are definitely a woman. I don't know how I didn't notice. Maybe I was blind."

He placed his hands on her waist, but she pulled herself free, making a nervous check over her shoulder. "Tessie will kill us both."

Jack's cheeks reddened. "I forgot myself." He took Nero by his strap and walked away.

She watched him till he disappeared over the horizon, then she went to the barn to wash up. She filled the bucket with water from the well and dumped it in the barrel behind the blankets. She repeated the filling and dumping until the barrel was full of icy cold water. She stripped out of her clothes and stepped in, holding her breath until her body adjusted, then grabbed the soap and began to scrub. The cold water was refreshing. It was only the first of May, but the temperature had climbed to a muggy eighty degrees or more. It made her skin feel tight to be free of the grime and sweat. She decided to submerge and wash her hair, too. The water sloshed over the sides as she scrubbed and rinsed. Her eyes were closed, so she didn't notice the blanket lifting until she heard Jack's gasp and profuse apology.

She ducked her body below the edge of the tub and covered her breasts with her arms. Jack continued to stare and apologize, but he failed to leave or turn away.

Bella cleared her throat, an eyebrow raised in a high arch. "Jack." She finally spoke breaking his stare.

"Oh, I'm sorry, Bella. I wanted to speak with you but now is probably not the time."

"Darn right it's not. Scoot!" Bella commanded trying to sink even farther, but it was no use.

"Can I get you a blanket?"

"No. Just leave." Bella figured her red hot embarrassment was enough to make the water boil.

Jack came to his senses and walked away, though much slower than good behavior allowed. Once alone, she climbed out and wrapped herself in a towel and hurried to the house where she changed into a clean undershirt, blouse, and skirt. She brushed out her hair and wrapped it in a loose bun. When she reached the kitchen, dinner was done. Jack came in moments later, also washed and changed into the clothes Tessie fitted for him. They took their plates out on the porch to eat and watch the sun set. Bella wondered if the reds and pinks that lit up the sky were this beautiful when she was a girl, or was she learning appreciation? She turned to ask Jack, blushing again when she realized his eyes weren't on the melting sun, but fixed on her. Bella smiled shyly, hoping he hadn't seen too much of her in her bath.

Chapter 5

Bella was half asleep when her door cracked open and a shadowy figure slipped into her room. She assumed it was Manny running from a nightmare. Then the lock turned. Its click made her jump.

"Bella. It's me."

"Jack?"

He sat on the edge of her bed.

"What are you doing here?"

"I waited until everyone was asleep."

"Why?"

"We need to talk."

"Now?" She pulled her quilt up to her chin. Her shift was threadbare. If he hadn't seen her in the tub, the moonlight would definitely reveal all.

"I changed my mind. I want you to marry me."

"Why?" Bella's voice was accusing, distrustful.

Jack was quiet a moment. Then he whispered, "I thought that was what you wanted? Isn't that why you got me out of jail?"

Bella's mind buzzed. It was what she wanted, but now that he was here in the flesh? She no longer wanted him to marry her because it was the sensible thing to do. Or because he wanted to bed her. She chewed on the inside of her cheek. What did she want? *Oh, please don't say you want him to love you,* she warned herself. She had to remain practical. Marrying Jack solved her problems. He was a man of honor. Marrying him would mean protection and survival. That meant more than love.

But what was best for Jack? She didn't want him to have regrets. She sighed and forced herself to ask, "Are you certain this is what you want? I have nothing to offer you. I have no money, no land, no…" She looked away from his shadowed face, her cheeks burning hot in the darkness. "I don't even have any honor left. You'd be chastised for marrying me."

Jack was quiet a moment. Bella's heart ached with each passing second as he rationally chose his future. He wasn't smitten enough to toss logic out the window. A tear dropped from her eyelash splattering cool and damp on her hand. She took a deep breath and willed the tears to stop.

"Well," Jack answered, "seeing as how I've never had money, or owned any land… I don't expect those things. And I guess me being an ex-convict, I can't throw stones at another person's honor."

So, if you had a good reputation, you'd never want me? Bella closed her eyes with the thought. She reminded him, "One day people will forget. Your honor will be restored and you could marry any woman you want." She took a deep breath. "Besides, you're feeling guilty over what happened in town. Forget about that. I'm used to their behavior. It never goes beyond words…and once Noah comes home, I'll leave this place and never have to deal with it again."

"So you're saying you don't want to marry me?"

"Oh Jack. When I told you that, I was being rash. Why, you know how flighty I can be. Like you said, I rarely think things through properly."

"But…" Jack sputtered, "I've found the idea has its merits."

Not exactly declarations of undying love, but a smidge better than pity. Bella smiled and patted his hand. "Something this important can't be decided hastily. Let's forget about this for tonight. Go to bed, Jack. You'll think more clearly in the daylight." She drew the blanket tightly around her shoulders and rolled over, turning her back to him.

He retreated to the door. The lock was freed and the knob turned, but before he left, he added, "I know my mind, Bella. I'll feel the same way in the morning."

"We shall see. Good night, Jack." Bella bit a trembling lip.

He stood in the doorway as if hesitant to leave, but finally sighed and was gone. Bella hugged her pillow. Part of her wished she had told him yes and married him. She knew she could make him happy. Tears fell on her pillow as she admitted to herself that she loved Jack too much to rob him of his choice. She couldn't let him make a decision based on pity and loyalty.

She swore she'd never sleep, but she must have drifted off at some point in the night, because it was the birds chirping outside her window that wrestled her from her slumber. She dressed quickly in her work skirt and brushed out her hair. She drove thoughts of last night's conversation from her mind as she concentrated on what work needed to be done today.

Bella checked her hair, tucking the wayward curls behind her ears, took a deep breath, and opened her door. She smoothed her skirt nervously as she entered the kitchen in time to hear Manny complain about having to go to school and hear Tessie admonish him for his disrespect for learning. "An ignorant man is easier to control, Mr. Manteo. Stay ignorant and be a slave to all. Learn and at least be master of your own mind."

"Who ever heard of an injun going to school?"

"Who ever heard of a darkie reading Shakespeare?"

"Well, Miss Tessie. You bein' able to read books ain't made yer life none better."

Tessie sighed and hit him over the head with her dish towel. "*Ain't it?* Why, I do believe I woke up this morning a free woman. Don't have to answer to no one but the good Lord Himself and a sassy young man who dallies about making himself late for school."

"Don't even try to argue with her, Manny. Tessie once whipped me with a switch for throwing my school books in the fire pit. I once cut up my mother's best silk gown to make doll dresses and only lost dessert. You won't win this argument with her."

"But it don't matter whether or not injuns can read."

"*Doesn't* matter. And yes, it does. The world is changing, Manny. From all this ruin, we'll make something better." Bella stroked his hair and kissed his cheek. "So, stop letting other people tell you who you are. You're not *an injun*. You're Cherokee—a proud and fearless people. And Lumbee, who if you had a proper education, you would know are one of the tribes who helped the white settlers and rescued run-away slaves. You're a brilliant young man who can look to brave warriors and noble people as the root of his character."

"I'd rather hunt bears than go to school. One day, I'm gonna find the bear that killed my dad and I'll wear his hide."

"I have no doubt you will, little man. But not today." Bella smiled.

"Then when? I'm tired of waiting."

Tessie shook her head and frowned, though her eyes sparkled with pleasure. "One day, Manteo Smith. One day, you'll be your own master. Until then you're stuck with bossy women who say it's time for school."

He grumbled, but cleaned his plate and grabbed his books. Bella headed for the door when Tessie spoke up, "I'll take him today." Bella looked confused. Tessie grinned. "Mr. Jack headed out right before breakfast. He told Manny and me you two were getting married today."

Bella's heart pounded. She dared not speak. The oxygen needed to talk would be more than she had available and she might well pass out on the floor.

"He didn't ask you?" Tessie asked.

Bella gripped the back of the chair and nodded. "Yes, but I assumed he'd change his mind."

Tessie grabbed her hand and cradled it to her chest. "This is what you want, isn't it, child? I don't want to see you with the wrong man again. I haven't said much about this because I always knew you had a powerful crush on Mr. Jack."

"I never…"

Tessie laughed. "You most certainly did. I knew about you sneaking up in the hayloft so you could watch him do his chores. Child, you never escaped your mammy's eye."

Bella blushed. "Remember? It was the horses."

Tessie pushed Manny gently toward the door. "Mmm, hmm. Don't try to lie to me, child. I know you better than you know yourself."

"Am I making a mistake, Tessie? If I say yes?"

Tessie smiled. "No. I think it'd be the right thing."

"But he doesn't love me."

"He will. If the man has any sense about him, which I believe he does, he'll know he got himself a real treasure."

Bella felt her eyes fill with tears. Tessie was the only person on this earth who would say she had any redeeming qualities. "Thank you, Tess."

Tessie took a moment to give her child a hug. "I love you, Isabella Francine. Couldn't love you any more if I gave birth to you myself. You go on and marry this man and make him happy. He'll not regret it. I promise."

Bella squeezed her back and gave Manny one for good measure. She had tears in her eyes and Manny looked up at her, his face full of concern. "Why you cryin', Miss Bella?"

"Because I'm happy."

Manny looked at her as if she were insane. She kissed the tip of his nose, "Now scoot, you'll be late." He nodded quietly and left with Tessie, looking back over his shoulder to see if Bella really was all right. As he passed the barn, Jack came out and waved at them. "Have a good day at school, Manny."

Manny answered him with finger shake and an order, "You better not be making Miss Bella cry. I come from warriors and I could hunt and kill bears with my bare hands. So, you better be afraid of me."

Jack took two steps back throwing his hands up in surrender. "I don't want any fight with you, young warrior."

Manny stood a little straighter and added, "And if you're marrying her, you better get her some flowers. Girls like flowers, don't they, Miss Tessie?"

"Oh, yes," she agreed winking at Jack. "Now, come along, little brave. Come along."

Bella hurried upstairs and changed into her better attire. She was back downstairs, washing up the breakfast dishes when Jack came in. He carried a bouquet of wild flowers. He dropped to one knee and handed them to her asking, "Bella, I don't have a ring...or anything of value for that matter...but I can assure you, I'll never mistreat you and I'll work hard to give you all you deserve." He let out a sigh and said with a bit less formality, "I've thought it over. Been up most of the night, and I know there's nothing I'd like better than to have

64

you as my wife." His cheeks turned pink. Then he took a deep breath and asked, "Will you marry me?"

Bella took the flowers and fought back an unladylike squeal. She nodded her head and whispered a barely audible yes. Jack smiled and stood. He kissed her cheek and said, "Let's find the minister. I don't see any reason to wait."

Bella relished in the feel of his hand as it gripped hers. It was warm and strong; a hand she could trust. He might not love her, but he'd never hurt her. She knew Jack would never raise a hand to strike a woman or a child. If she never had more than that, that alone was enough.

They rode into town making nervous conversation about the weather and Manny's dislike of school. They arrived at the church and Jack hopped off the wagon and went to the small, but meticulously neat parsonage, and knocked on the front door. Bella couldn't hear the conversation, but she felt the minister's eyes on her, and saw the fury in Jack's movements. The minister handed him something and Jack tucked it into his pocket. The minster closed his door, which Jack appeared to spit on. Bella gasped and covered her mouth with her hand. She couldn't ask the questions quickly enough when he returned. "What happened? What did he say? What did he give you?"

Jack looked her over, and the fury in his face melted. "He doesn't have time to marry us. He gave me a certificate and told me to fill it out. Said I could give it to Judge Fox when he comes back next month. It'd be a legal marriage, just no ceremony."

"It looked like you were awfully angry."

"Well, who ever heard of a man of God not having time to do God's work?"

"That made you that mad?"

"Well, I guess I had my hopes set on giving you a nice wedding."

Bella smiled. She reached over and took Jack's hand. "You wanting to make it nice makes it the best it could be."

"Bull. This is the worst wedding day a woman could have."

"No. I can think of worse." Bella's laugh was nervous.

Jack was quiet a moment. Then he cast her a quick glance and asked quietly, "Was your first wedding beautiful?"

Bella looked down at her wilting flowers and thought they were the loveliest she'd ever seen. "It was...quite an affair. Father spared no expense." Bella looked to the horizon and sighed.

Jack's words were bitter. "I knew I didn't deserve you."

Bella touched his arm gently. "At the fork in the road up here, take a right." Jack nodded and followed the directions she quietly gave him. He pulled the horse to a stop at a cemetery. It was situated on a knob and looked down over lush green tobacco fields that rolled into to the waters of the Oconaluftee River. Jack recognized this peninsula as the namesake of Bella's Point. Below, past the river bend, rolled the acres and acres that made up the massive plantation of Henry Troy, Bella's father.

Bella didn't even look toward the place that was her home. Instead she moved between the white marble markers to a roughhewn rock. It had no markings and any who stumbled upon it would think God had settled it there. But here Bella stopped and knelt. She plucked the growing blades of grass from around the stone and pruned the wild rose that grew in front of it.

Jack knelt beside her, wrapping an arm over her shoulders.

"This is what I have left of that wedding, Jack." Her eyes filled with tears that overflowed and dropped, staining her cheeks and reddening her eyes. "Charles Stanley was a horrible man. He only wanted money. When Daddy was gone and all his money wasted, he made no pretenses of kindness. He was a cruel man who..." Bella stopped and covered her face with her hands. Jack held her tighter.

"Is he buried here?"

Bella shook her head, then buried it against his neck. "No. It's my baby. He was born early and had Daddy's French coloring. You remember Daddy's dark eyes and dark skin? Well, baby Henry looked just like him. Daddy would have been so pleased, but not Charles. He immediately accused me of cheating. Accused me of the most horrible things. Baby Henry was only a month old when Charles came home drunk, furious, saying Henry wasn't his. He'd been playing cards and the men kept taking jabs at him about his wife being a whore...and a nigger lover... and that his child didn't even resemble him. He grabbed Henry from his bed and shook him... and he shook him. I tried to stop him, but he was a big man."

She had to take a few minutes to calm herself before she could continue. "I never thought I could tell this. I can hardly think of it." She pressed her face to Jack's chest.

He stroked her hair. "You don't have to tell me. Not if it hurts you like this."

Bella shook her head. "I have to make you understand." She took a breath. "Understand why none of that," she said and pointed over the hill, "means anything anymore."

"All right then, you tried to stop him. Did he hurt you?"

"He slapped me and I fell." Jack's jaw clenched. Fury made his blue eyes as cloudy as water after a storm. Bella took a deep breath. "Tessie heard the commotion. She came running in. She had the fireplace poker... and she held it up above her head, and oh my, she looked possessed by the devil himself. She told him, 'Master Charles, touch that child again and I swear I will split your skull. I'd gladly hang from a tree to rid the world of you.' I think Charles knew she would, too. He dropped Henry back into the cradle and stormed out of the house."

"Did he kill him?" Jack whispered.

Bella shook her head. "No, but after that, his eyes looked vacant. He didn't learn like other children. He was three years old before he could say 'Momma.'"

"Did Charles ever hit him again?"

"Oh no. Charles told everyone he died and agreed Tessie could take him away. She brought him to the farm with Noah. I knew after that raucous neither of them would be safe living under the same roof as Charles."

"What about you? Did you stay?"

"Of course. If I would've left him, Charles would've been publicly humiliated, and he'd have killed Tessie for sure. He could have strung her from a tree in front of town hall and no one would've questioned him."

"How did Henry...end up here?"

"He got a fever last year and wasn't strong enough. For three days he fought, but his little body couldn't win. Noah, Tessie, and I buried him here. Tessie said the prayers. Noah found this rock, and I planted the rose." Bella reached out and stroked the stone lovingly.

"I'm so sorry, Bella." Jack hugged her close, his face buried in her hair. "You were smart to divorce the bastard." He pulled away and tipped her chin up until she was looking at him. "I promise you this, we'll have more children. Children you won't have to sneak around to love. You're such a precious woman." Jack pulled her close, cradling as if holding her tightly would erase the memories, the pain. "And I'm gonna take you away from here. Away from all the bad memories. Today, sweetheart, this is the beginning of *our* life together. Two together, like God planned. Anyone tries to hurt you, they'll have to go through me to do it. You understand?"

Bella nodded.

He kissed her. When he pulled back, he wiped the tears from her cheeks. Bella smiled, her heart and body warmed by his promises. She fixed his collar as she whispered, "So, you understand why this truly is the best wedding day I could ever dream of?"

Jack closed his eyes and kissed her again.

Chapter 6

Jack and Bella arrived at the farm well before noon. It felt awkward to be back. Awkward to be carrying a wedding certificate without having a ceremony. Did a slip of paper really mean she was married? Bella couldn't decide. She was tempted to ask Jack, but somehow no words seemed right. She was worn out from crying, emotionally drained from telling her son's tale.

"I'll stable the horse, Bell. Why don't you rest?"

"I really should do the laundry. It's still cool after last night. Can you believe it got so cold? But it was a Godsend after planting the garden in that heat."

"It'll be hot within the hour, once that sun is full in the sky."

Bella looked to the rising sun. Within an hour it would be at its highest point. She looked across at Jack as he unharnessed the horse from the wagon. He looked up at her and smiled; she smiled back. Euphoria swept over her. Jack was hers. Legally.

She leaned against the wagon and watched him work. He unhooked Nero and brushed him with such care, talking to the beast like it had total understanding of human language. Bella swore the horse looked healthier already. And they had a garden growing. There wasn't anything Jack couldn't do. He turned to her. Bella blushed and looked away, feeling silly for acting like she had never been this close to him before.

Jack led Nero into his stall and latched the gate.

"I think he's looking better already, just having you around," Bella said.

"Don't know 'bout that, but he'll rebound soon enough. He's a fine stallion. One of the finest I've ever seen."

Bella nodded, but went silent. Her mind was too busy floating on clouds to make small talk.

He didn't seem to notice her awkwardness. He grabbed a pitch fork and tossed some hay into Nero's trough. "Give me a couple of days to fix a fence, old man, and we'll get you out to pasture. Fatten you up and you'll shine like the prize you are."

Bella stepped closer and stroked the animal's neck. "He's the last of Daddy's thoroughbreds. So sad really. The last of his line."

"He still has potential. With some good feed, you'll see. Maybe we'll even find a mare to stud. No sense letting his line die."

"Seriously?" Bella looked at Jack as if he were crazy.

"Completely serious."

"But he's almost twelve."

"He's in his prime. And soon as we get him some good food, he'll look it." Jack frowned. "Where ever you got that hay, it's poor as poor comes."

"I bought it from Vince Wheeler." Bella scratched Nero's ear. "Nero can really live that long?"

Jack nodded. "You never heard of Old Billy?"

Bella shook her head.

"Oldest living horse on record. Lived to be sixty-two years old."

"Why I never dreamed…but then poor Nero isn't being treated very well. Feeding him poor hay and making him drag a plow." Bella rubbed the silken bridge of his nose. "Poor Nero. The first time I hooked him to a wagon, my heart broke. He's too fine to pull a cart."

Jack laughed. "Bout like a princess planting a garden?"

"Well, she will if she wants to eat."

"Then Nero can earn his keep, too." He patted the stallion's neck. "Besides, Old Billy was a work horse, too. Spent his day dragging barges up and down a canal in England. Work won't hurt him. But we do have to get him something better to eat. Vince sold you weeds and he knows better. Barely any nutrition in it at all. He ought to be ashamed of himself."

"Well, times have been hard, maybe he didn't have anything else."

"I doubt that."

Bella sighed. "Hard to tell really. May as well think the better of him. If I dwell on all the people out to cheat me, it only makes me mad, and anger doesn't do any good."

"I s'pose you're right. God knows what they're up to. Guess I'll leave Him to judge."

"You're a wise man, Jack. I'm certainly glad I married you."

It was Jack's turn to redden and trip over his tongue. He took off his hat and rubbed the top of his head. "I'm a fortunate man."

Bella pressed her lips together wondering if Jack might kiss her. Her cheeks flooded with color as she realized she was hoping he would.

But he didn't.

Instead he took a breath and issued an order, "Now, I want you, since you don't plan to rest, to go into the woods and see if you can find any sugar maples. Do you know what a sugar maple looks like?"

Bella was tutored in horticulture. She should know this, but she didn't. All those days spent in study, she only half listened, never once dreaming her world would crumble and she might actually need to know one tree from another. "Of course I know what a sugar maple looks like. Why?"

"Thought we might make some syrup. Cold nights, warm days. That's what makes the sugar run."

"Really? We could have syrup?"

"Sure. If you can find the trees."

"I can." She started to walk away, then turned and asked, "They have the smoothish bark, right?"

Jack nodded. "Kind of, with vertical cracks. No needles."

Bella rolled her eyes. "I think I know the difference between a pine and a hard wood."

"Just making sure."

Bella turned with indignation and walked smartly to the house where she donned her trousers. "I'll show him." She muttered as she trudged to the attic and sorted through trunks of books to see if she had kept any old textbooks. "Yes," she said aloud to the empty room, proud of her triumph. She hugged the book of plants and trees to her chest. She would find a maple, so take that, Jack Byron.

She snuck out the back door, again unwilling to let Jack see her, this time headed to the woods with a textbook in hand.

Tessie clucked her tongue and shook her head, dropping the curtain back into place. "That girl will be out there all day holding the pictures up to those trees."

"Good. I want to do something special for her, but I can't with her hanging around. And who knows, she might find a couple."

"Sure would be nice. I suppose Missy wasn't so crazy to marry you after all."

"Well, thank you, Tessie, I think."

Tessie laughed. "It's a compliment. So, how did the wedding go?"

"There was no wedding."

"But…"

"The pastor gave me this certificate, signed and all. Told me to fill in the blanks and file it with Judge Fox when he comes back from vacation."

Tessie took the paper from him and studied it, her brows furrowed. "Now why in the world?"

"Says he won't marry Bella in *his* church. Says God wouldn't abide by it. She is a divorcee, thereby making me an adulterer if I marry her."

Tessie shook her head. "I suppose he's worthy of carrying out God's judgment?"

"Yep, he thinks so."

"I suppose most everyone would agree with him. Lord have mercy."

"I can't believe for one second anyone would expect her to stay with…with the likes of Stanley. She told me about Baby Henry. What kind of cold hearted son of a…"

"No need getting angry. It's over. He won't be coming back," Tessie assured him.

"The minister told me something else, too. I was gonna ask Bella, but I didn't want to make her think his words worried me."

"Mmm…well, what'd he say?"

"He says she ran away with a black buck when she was a teen."

"I suspected that's what it was. People in small towns don't forget a thing, Mr. Jack."

"Stop that mister business, Tessie." Jack shook his head and frowned at her. "So what's that all about? Or should I ask Bella?"

"No. It's more my business than hers." Tessie took a deep breath and cleared her throat. "Noah is the buck the man's talking about."

"Your Noah?"

Tessie nodded. "Well, Bella and Noah were always close, but when she found out he was her brother, she was even more protective of him."

Jack's eyes opened a little wider, though in reality, he knew he shouldn't be shocked. "I never thought Mr. Troy was that kind of man. I'm sorry. And I'm sorry I asked you about it."

"Oh no. Master Troy was a good man. We had a special relationship. I don't know if it was love, but we had a fondness for each other, and I guess a certain amount of loyalty. His marriage to Mistress Troy was little more than a sham. My, how strange a woman she was. But you lived there. Surely you remember her."

"I couldn't stand her."

"Few people could. I don't think Master Troy knew what he was marrying besides a beautiful face."

"She wasn't a beauty as I recall."

"Mistress Troy, before she had the twins, was a real beauty. Probably even prettier than Bella."

"I can't hardly believe that."

"Oh, she was a looker. But she was getting heavier and heavier as each year passed. And well, Mistress Troy knew she was losing her beauty. She was bitter and jealous of everyone, including her own child. She could barely stand the sight of her own blossoming daughter. Bell couldn't do anything to please her momma. I guess that's how her and I got so close. Mistress Troy only showed any real affection for her boys. She was so proud of them. They were handsome, intelligent, and charming. Ooh, were those boys charming. It was after their birth that Mr. Troy and I came to be more intimately acquainted. She didn't want any more children because she blamed the loss of her figure on pregnancy. And there's only one way to guarantee no more children, right?"

"Right," Jack agreed, mesmerized by Tessie's tale.

"Well, things went along rather smooth. Noah was born about a year after the boys. Why, Mistress Troy would hardly let Master Troy around *her* boys. She was always afraid they'd get hurt if she didn't watch over them every minute of every day. Which was too bad. Master Troy was a good father. He was even mindful to pay attention to Noah. He would take him and Bella on his daily rounds of the plantation. And Bella adored Noah. I think she thought he was a toy…her being four when he was born. She didn't have any baby dolls as interesting as him. Life at that time was peaceful, even happy. Mistress Troy had her parties and her boys. And…well, we had each other."

Tessie wiped at a tear. Jack turned his attention away while she composed herself. He turned back as she cleared her throat to finish her story. "Now, when Bella was 16, a fever spread across the plantation. Noah and Bella came down with it first and I doctored them both. Then the twins got it. I told Mistress Troy I would nurse them, like I did the other two, but she'd have none of it. Called me Hagar and told me to get Ishmael off her plantation. Accused Noah of making the boys sick in the first place." She sighed, thinking back on the memory with a sad shake of her head. "She hired doctors who tried every potion. One even tried bloodletting. I swear, she had them doctored to death. And when they died, she snapped. I begged Master Troy to let Noah and I leave, but he'd not hear of it. Thought he could deal with his wife. I knew better than to ever trust that witch." Tessie frowned, took a breath and continued. "I thought about running away. But the idea of facing the hangman's noose with my boy scared me stiff. Then Bella overheard her momma talking to traders about selling Noah. Bella didn't tell anybody, not even her daddy, she snuck away in the middle of the night with Sam Cleary, you remember him? The stock hand? Well, Bella talked him into guiding her and Noah north. She pretended she was visiting relatives and Sam was her driver. And lordy," she said with a laugh and fanned herself, "she dressed Noah as a girl and told everyone they met he was her maid servant. My gracious! That child is somethin' else."

"She didn't."

"She sure did. Left Noah with a preacher in New York, then came back. Mistress Troy told everyone Sam abducted Bella and stole Noah, but Bella wouldn't stand for it. She told the truth. Master Troy was disappointed in Bella; disappointed in himself for not listening to me before his little girl had to take matters into her own hands and ruin her reputation in the process."

"Sam's lucky he didn't get hanged."

"Master Troy vouched for him and he went on to be the town drunk and ne'er do well. Bella paid the heaviest price. Her reputation was ruined. She'd spent three weeks away from home with a young black man. A twelve-year-old boy, but still...she committed the worst sort of sins...she stole a slave and freed him. A beautiful young girl of sixteen and she was tarnished for life. Just trying to save her brother."

Tessie paused. Her shoulders shook and her face puckered. Tears rolled down her cheeks. "That's why Master Troy married her off so hastily. He wanted to save her reputation. So, he forced her to marry Master Stanley. He barely knew the man. And thank God he died without knowing he married his baby to a monster."

Tessie wiped at her tears. Jack handed her a rag on the counter. "Thank you, Mr....I mean Jack. It wasn't till after Master Troy died that Master Charles turned so ugly. He was a fool about running a plantation. And too stubborn to let the over seer handle things. A whole year's worth of crops ruined from neglect. Barely harvested enough to feed and clothe those that lived on the land. And if being a fool wasn't enough, he was also a gambler and a drinker. It wasn't more than a year after the firing on Ft. Sumter that Bella's Point went up for public auction. Mistress Troy blamed Bella for everything. The meanness I heard from that woman."

"What happened to Mistress Troy?"

"Died a few months after we moved off The Point. Can't say I miss her. God have mercy on me for feeling so."

"So Bella knows Noah is her brother?"

"Mmm, hmm. I let Missy slide in all her lessons, besides the ones on the Good Book. She knew exactly what her mother meant by Hagar and Ishmael."

"Does anyone else know?"

"That sort of thing isn't spoken of, child. You know that."

"But it would explain..."

"Bella doesn't care to explain anything to anybody. And if that bugs you, then you shouldn't sign those wedding papers. And as far as people around here are concerned, even if they didn't think she had *relations* with him, she still stole and freed a slave, be he her brother or not."

"And to think I always thought Isabella Francine Troy would never have any more serious a thought in her head beyond which shoes matched what outfit."

"I know. You'd tease her often when she was a girl. And boy would it make her spitting mad. She never quite understood why you didn't just fall under her spell like a good boy." Tessie chuckled. "Never dreamed of the day that she'd marry the likes of you."

"And I never dreamed I'd marry her either."

Tessie arched her brow and gave him a good, hard stare. "One good thing about war and hardship, it's a powerful equalizer."

Chapter 7

Bella found a grove of trees she was pretty certain were maple. She noted the location and ran back to the house feeling accomplished.

Tessie was in the yard, humming as she hung out laundry. Bella sidled up beside her, grabbed a shirt from the basket, and pinned it to the line.

"Lord have mercy," Tessie said pressing a hand to her chest. "You took a day off my life! How in the world are you done already?"

"Why do you sound so surprised?"

"Well, I figured...well, there's a lot of woods to go through."

"I found a whole grove of maples. Growing in a cluster waiting for me to find them."

"Did they match the pictures in your book?"

Bella rolled her eyes. "Busy body."

"You tickle me, child," Tessie chuckled. "But you're not supposed to be back so soon. Jack needed you gone for a while. He thought he was sending you on a wild goose chase."

"Why?"

"I can't say."

"What is he…" Bella couldn't imagine what he was doing without a penny to his name. Then an idea occurred to her. "He didn't go back to badger Bert, did he?"

"Go back? What did he do to Bert?"

"Long story." Bella pinned a pair of Manny's pants to the line. "But I think Bert will stop pinching my bottom while I shop."

"Well, bless Mr. Jack even more." Tessie pinned the last towel to the line and balanced the basket on her hip. "All I'll tell you is this," Tessie said and leaned toward her and whispered, "Jack is planning a special afternoon for you. You need to go hide yourself so you don't ruin it."

"Really?" Tears sparkled in her eyes.

"Really."

"I am the luckiest woman in the world."

Tessie gave Bella a hug. "Your luck certainly seems to be changing." She brushed back one of Bella's many wayward curls. "Now you go gussy up a bit and 'be busy.' Promise your mammy you'll be surprised when you bring Mr. Manteo home from school."

"I will. I better do something for Jack, too." Bella kissed Tessie's cheek and took off for the house. She went straight to the attic. Jack was right. The heat did rise with the sun. The air in the dusty room was oppressive, but Bella didn't care. She cared only about finding the right something for Jack. The sweat trickled down her spine as she rummaged through jackets, trousers, and shirts. She frowned. Jack wasn't the kind of guy to wear silk. And it was too hot for a coat. Digging to the bottom, she smiled with relief when she came across perfection. It was a fine blue cotton shirt with ruffles at the throat and on the sleeves. It also had Charles's initials on the cuff.

Bella frowned. It was far from Jack's taste. At least not without modification. But the blue was nearly as dark as denim and he could wear the shirt without fear of it looking dirty and worn too quickly.

Bella carried it to her room. She sat at her dressing table and worked, picking away the threads away until the initials were gone. She cut seams and dropped the shirt by two sizes. She removed the ruffles, leaving the sleeves straight. Finishing, she held it up in front of her. She was satisfied with the results. It wasn't fancy, but it had a certain quiet dignity.

Just like Jack.

Bella straightened up her mess, pressing the scraps and tucking them in the quilt bag. She tied up the folded shirt with a hair ribbon. To make herself ready for the occasion, she changed into a clean dress and adjusted her hair. The clocked ticked loudly in the silent room. She had plenty of time to get Manny, but a walk in the fresh air might calm her while passing the time till her 'surprise.'

She hurried downstairs where Tessie was busy in the kitchen. Tessie acknowledged Bella, though she kept her back to her as she continued her work.

"What are you doing, Tess?"

"Making more biscuits. Starting to run low."

"I'm headed to get Manny. Have you seen Jack?"

"Not telling you anything…don't even try."

"Oh pooh, I just wondered where he was."

"Mmm, hmm."

"Seriously. I'm more mature now. I don't even sneak peeks at Christmas presents."

Tessie's laugh was full bodied. "We haven't had any presents for years."

"And I've not peeked." Bella moved closer. "That doesn't smell like biscuits. What are you making?"

Tessie flogged her with the dish towel hanging on her shoulder. "Get! Get on out of my kitchen!"

"I want to see." Bella went to open the door of the oven, and Tessie smacked her hand. "Out before I turn you over my knee and spank you, like you was still in pigtails!"

Bella backed out of the kitchen. "All right. I'm going. Don't have to get so testy."

"You're real grown up. A fresh girl in a woman's body, that's what you are. I declare, I shoulda spanked your bottom more often when you were a girl."

Bella laughed as she left. Should have spanked her more…she couldn't remember getting spanked at all. But Tessie liked to threaten her with it often enough. Bella took a meandering path to the little white school. She waited at the edge of the schoolyard, leaning her back against an oak tree. She daydreamed until the bell rang. She stood and watched for Manny to emerge. The kids poured out of the double doors in clumps. They had the eager, active nature of foals set to pasture. They chatted and called to each other. Boys tugged on braids and girls giggled and squealed, feigning disdain. Happy chatter filled the air. Bella raised up on tiptoes trying to see Manny's dark head. She finally spotted it and smiled, but the smile faded.

Manny walked out alone. He hung in the back of the group hugging his books, his head hung low. His feet moved as if instinct, not sight, led him home.

Bella's heart broke for the boy. Not a single friend to call his own? No wonder he hated school.

Bella wrung her hands a minute debating what, if anything, she could do. Then Manny spotted her. A smile spread across his face and the energetic boy she knew appeared before her. "Miss Bella!"

She waved at him and smiled, though her heart felt heavy.

"Whatcha doin' here? I figured Miss Tessie would come get me, since you and Mr. Jack were getting married."

"Well, we did, sort of."

Manny looked suddenly nervous. "You ain't going nowhere are ya, Miss Bell?"

She brushed silky hairs out of his eyes. "Oh no, certainly not."

He looked relieved.

Miss Jobe stepped out of the school house. She waved to them as she headed to the flag pole, pulling on the string that held the faded flag in place. Bella took a deep breath. "You wait right here, little man. I need to speak with Miss Jobe."

"Why?" He eyed her with suspicion.

Bella shrugged. "I suppose if I make you talk to her every day, then I should, too."

Manny seemed content with her explanation.

Bella watched him settle himself under the tree, grabbing a stick and digging holes in the earth.

Bella approached the thin woman. Miss Jobe appeared to be in her thirties, though it was difficult to guess her age by her visage. She had the body of a twelve-year-old boy, the face of a mouse, and the hair of doll played with much too often.

She spotted Bella coming across the schoolyard, and waited, back stick straight, flag folded tightly in her hands.

"Excuse me, Miss Jobe?"

She gave a small nod. "Yes?"

"I...I'm Bella Stanley."

"I know who you are."

Miss Jobe's words were neither rude nor comforting, they were matter of fact, but Bella couldn't help but flush with embarrassment. She had no idea what to say, or what she expected Miss Jobe to do about the problem.

"Miss Jobe. I, uh, I'm worried about Manny. He doesn't seem to have any friends, and I don't really know why that surprises me considering I don't have any friends in this town either...because well, uh...oh shoot, I'll be frank, my reputation is foul as a dead bird in July. But poor little Manny! He's just a boy."' Bella's gaze dropped, and then she glanced back up at Miss Jobe and asked, her voice small in the open yard, "Shouldn't a boy Manny's age have friends to play with?"

Miss Jobe frowned. "I simply assumed he was studious."

"He keeps trying to quit school."

"Oh my. I never realized. He reads all the time. I thought he enjoyed it."

Bella shook her head. "I think he'd be happier if he was playing. But I don't know if people in this town want their children playing with him, considering he's under my care and all."

Miss Jobe contemplated Bella's words. The muscle in her jaw twitched. Then she looked at Bella and asked, "Why do you stay in this town?"

"Well, my, uh, my mammy's son left to find Manny's momma. I need to stay here at least until he comes back."

"Did you and Noah have a relationship like they say?"

Bella gasped. "Oh no, certainly not. Noah? Why he's my....why he's like my brother."

Miss Jobe's eyebrow arched and she stared at Bella for so long, Bella was about to confess her entire family history and then some. Fortunately, Miss Jobe asked, "And I hear you have a criminal living under your roof?"

Bella's cheeks reddened and her nostrils flared. "Jack isn't a criminal. He's a good man."

"Jack?" Miss Jobe asked with a hand motion that indicated to Bella that she answered the test questions with only half the facts.

"Byron." Bella supplied and Miss Jobe nodded her head with approval.

"Hmm, I remember Jack Byron. He wound up in jail? I always liked Jack. If I remember correctly, he was a real good student. At least when he had time off from work to come to school. Didn't he work at the Point?"

"Yes, ma'am. And Jack, why he's still a good man. He didn't deserve to be in jail. It was a Yankee jail. On trumped up charges….I'm sure."

"But still he lives under your roof?"

"I married him this morning."

"Oh my. Your life changes rapidly."

"I love Jack. I've loved him since I was a girl. If there has been any benefit to this whole awful war, it's that I got to marry Jack."

"I doubt the people of your *class* will approve."

"I don't think anything I do will shock a single soul. Honestly? I don't give two figs what others think."

Miss Jobe shifted her weight and sighed. "Decorum is necessary, Miss Troy. You can't expect people not to talk and judge when you feed them all the fuel they need to make a raging fire."

Bella crossed her arms over her chest. She wouldn't change a single choice in her life, all but one…and that was the one she made in an effort to be the proper lady everyone expected her to be. "I made my choices for good reasons. The only choice I regret is not running away from home instead of marrying Charles Stanley. And I did *that* out of *propriety*. No, I will trust my own instincts for all my choices now."

Miss Jobe nodded slightly. Bella could have sworn she saw a bit of a grin, but she couldn't be certain. Miss Jobe said in her usual somber voice, "Charles courted my sister, Maggie. Did you know that?"

Bella shook her head.

"Well, he did." She said nothing more. She looked across the yard where Manny sat under the tree. She looked as if she understood far too well how the child felt. She simply said, "I will look into the issue with Manteo." With that, she walked away. She was half way up the steps before turning to Bella and stating, "Miss, um, I mean Mrs. Bryon, most of my student's families invite me to dinner. You never have."

Bella's heart skipped a beat. "I, uh, will most certainly do that. We don't have much…"

"No one has much, young lady. No shame in that."

"Yes, ma'am." Bella answered red faced, but a feeling of hope fluttered in her belly. She had been judged and found innocent by one of the most spotless creatures in Troy. Who could throw a moral stone at Miss Jobe? No one. And she was willing to accept Bella socially. Bella felt such exuberance that she took off running toward Manny. She slowed down as she neared the tree, a smile plastered to her face. She dropped to her knees beside him breathless with excitement and exertion. Manny looked up at her, his face full of amusement. "Look, Miss Bell, an ant bridge." He lifted a stick out of a hole and showed her the little bugs flowing one after another across the stick.

Bella wrinkled her nose. "That's quite, um, interesting."

"Here, you can hold it."

Bella balked. "Oh, no. You keep it."

He grinned and acted like he might share it with her whether she wanted to or not. Bella hopped up and stepped away. "We best go. Better leave the ants here."

He let the ants crawl from the stick up his finger. He grinned at Bella. She cringed at the sight. "Eww. Manny drop it and come on. We don't want to worry Miss Tessie."

He dropped the stick and grabbed his books. "That's not my fault. Why'd you talk to Miss Jobe so long?"

"I invited her to dinner."

"What?!"

"It's the polite thing to do."

"It's a waste of time. I don't think she's human, so I seriously doubt she eats."

"Well, I thought she was nice."

Manny looked at her as if she lost her mind. "Going to school is bad enough. Now you're gonna make me suffer at home, too?"

Bella ruffled his hair. "Don't worry. As of right now, we don't have anything to offer for a dinner anyhow. I don't know that offering someone a bean dinner is very hospitable."

He pointed to a couple of deer in a meadow. "We could have some meat and gravy. That'd be good, wouldn't it? I'd even sit down with Old Jobe for that."

Bella grinned. How hungry must the child be to see animals prancing in a field and picture them on a plate? "That's an idea. Maybe Mr. Jack and you can go hunting."

"Really? I'd like that. I bet I'm the only warrior on earth who doesn't know how to hunt."

Manny's steps were quicker and livelier. He ran ahead, whacking at iron weeds with a stick. "Come on, Miss Bella." He called over his shoulder. "Mister Jack is waiting on us!"

Bella smiled. As the world turned green around her and the spring flowers bloomed in the field, Bella felt life's balance was finally tipped in her favor.

Elizabeth Seckman

Chapter 8

Bella barely kept pace with Manny on the way home. When he hit the last bend in the road and released his final reserve of energy, she gave up. She slowed to catch her breath while he sprinted down the dirt road, across the yard, and into the house.

Bella sauntered onto the porch with a grin, fully expecting to hear Manny getting an earful from Tessie for running through the house, banging the door, and raising his voice as he yelled for Jack.

But there was nothing. Not a sound. Her brow furrowed. Even if Tessie wasn't home, she expected to hear Manny calling for someone.

What could possibly make him completely still so quickly? Her heart constricted and her mind raced. More raiders? Damned carpet bagging thieves! Bella scanned the porch for a weapon. There was nothing. Not even a bench or a pot. Her eye caught on the warping floorboards. She chose a loose one and wrenched it free.

Ready to charge, she wielded it like a club and crept through the front door inching her way through the house. It was empty. Hearing hushed whispers on the back porch, she moved swiftly and quietly to the back door. With all the gusto she could muster, she kicked it open and charged. Weapon raised above her head, she let out a yell, fully prepared to smash someone over the head.

"Whoa, easy there, Paula Bunyan." Jack said, emerging from a corner of the porch and taking the board from her hands. "What in the world?"

"I thought..." Bella's words caught in her throat.

"Where did you get this?"

"The front porch." Bella took a deep breath as she calmed down.

"You dismantled the front porch?"

"I, uh, simply borrowed a board, which I will put back."

"Well, we'll see about that later." He leaned it against the house.

"Why are you guys back here?" Bellas asked. Tessie and Manny grinned from ear to ear standing in front of a table. Bella moved closer. "What is that?"

Jack wrapped an arm around her waist and pulled her toward him. "It's our wedding day, and with the help of Tessie..."

"I would've helped if you'd let me skip school," Manny interjected.

"And with Manny's help getting you away from the house, we were able to set you up a bit of a celebration." Tessie and Manny moved to reveal the new picnic table set with platters and plates for dinner.

"You didn't have to..." Bella's smile was broad, her heart light. She moved closer to the table. It was made of old barn boards, their rustic red color faded and chipped. Its patchwork quilt table cloth and mismatched dinnerware set a finer table than linen and crystal ever could. Bella, surprised to see so much food, couldn't stop her mouth from dropping in an unladylike O. There was a platter full of fresh flaky biscuits and another laden with fried meat. There were even bowls with gravy and collard greens. At the center of the table was a cake iced with fluffy cream.

"Where did you get all this?"

"Well, while you looked for maple trees," he grinned down at her, "I snuck into town to buy a bit of sugar for the cake…Bert agreed it was a wedding gift. Then I snipped some fresh greens, snared a couple of rabbits… left it all with Tessie to work her magic, while I went to work on the table. It'll come in handy this summer when it's too hot to eat in the kitchen."

"Where did you get the wood?"

"I found an old barn behind the garden. Looked about to fall in, so I stripped some boards and got to work."

"You were poking around the back barn?"

"Yes, dear, but don't worry, I was careful."

Bella looked pale. "It looks like it's about to fall in. I've been meaning to set it on fire, but I wasn't sure if we would need the wood this winter."

"I'll take care of the barn. Later. Today, we enjoy our wedding day."

"Of course." Bella placed a light kiss on his cheek. "Thank you, Jack. You didn't have to do this."

"Yes I did. It's a special day, even if the pastor is too busy to recognize it."

Bella looked over the table again and counted her blessings. Her ragtag family was the best she ever had. She started to sit when Tessie got her attention by clearing her throat.

"Just a minute, Missy." Tessie picked up the broom leaning against a tree. "Pastor Scott isn't the only one who knows how to do a wedding."

Tessie held the broom with both hands and raised her arms to the sky. She closed her eyes and began reciting words to a ceremony she had evidently done many times before. "Dear Lord, look down on your children. We thank you for your blessings that bring us comfort; we thank you for the suffering which brings us character. Bind your people, o' Lord, your people scattered and swept from their homes but stay bound together by the common bonds of love for the All Mighty, love for their kin folk, and a hope for a better future. Bella and Jack, in the tradition of my people, I invite you to jump the broom, to jump into a new life swept clean of the pains of the old." Tessie set the broom on the ground and stepped back.

A shiver ran down Bella's spine. She was overwhelmed by Tessie's thoughtfulness. Glancing at Jack, she recognized the same gratitude in his face. Her heart swelled with an absolute love for every curve and line of his face. Together they held hands and jumped over into a new life.

Bella ate until she was so full she thought she would explode. Manny ate himself into a near coma, his eyelids dropping, his head bobbing with the need for sleep. It was an hour before his bedtime, but Jack carried him off to his room rather than ask him to fight the sand man. Laying the boy on his bed, he snuggled into his pillow, a satisfied grin on his face. Jack tucked him in with a promise of hunting tomorrow.

Bella leaned against the doorway wondering when they would have their own children. She hungered for the feel of soft baby flesh. She wanted a child with Jack's blue eyes. He turned and she nearly jumped, embarrassed by her thoughts

"Tessie and I got the dishes done."

"That was fast."

"Many hands make work light. Is that how it goes?"

"Something like that." He closed Manny's door leaving a crack. He held her elbow gently guiding her down the darkening hall. "Take a walk with me, Bella?"

The sun would be setting soon and Bella could think of no better end to a perfect day.

They walked silently to a knoll which looked down over the farm. The tiny farmhouse was an eighth of the size of the home she grew up in, and though Bella had lived there for less than two years, she still felt more love for this place than she ever did for Bella's Point. The Point seemed like a dream, none of it real or lasting. This place symbolized her first days of freedom. And even if those days were marred by hunger and need, she was still free. No parents to make her decisions, no abusive husband to make each day a nightmare.

Jack sat down on the dew-covered grass and rolled a stump closer to him for Bella to sit on. She arranged her thin skirts and sat as graciously as if she were seating herself on a throne. The sun melted into the Smoky Mountains. The skies were awash in red, the thin clouds funneled a column of sun to the earth. "I always thought that was God," Bella said with a smile.

Jack looked at her and grinned. "Not an old man with a white beard?"

Bella shrugged. "He could be that, too. He could be whatever He wants."

"I always thought sunsets were God's way of promising us another tomorrow...or as a comfort for a bad day. Depending, of course, on what you need."

"Do you feel hopeful for the future, Jack? Or do you need comfort?"

Jack looked out over the fields and the woods and then turned to Bella. "Definitely hopeful. I can see a future in this place. Though I feel like I'm robbing Noah."

"I don't think he'd see it that way. Why, you're helping Tessie and Manny for him."

"This is a good place. We'll make money from it."

"That's definitely a blessing to hear."

"So, what I figured, and I'll discuss it with Tessie, is we'll take any profits and divide them in half. She can keep Noah's share."

"I think that's fair. What's the plan? Tobacco?"

"No. I have no intention of messing with tobacco. It's too hard on the soil."

"So, what will we plant?"

"We'll start with timber. It's selling high with all the building people are doing. The woods are thick with it, won't hurt to thin it out a bit. Next, we'll buy some goats. They're easy to tend and we'll have milk and meat without a whole lot of back breaking work, beyond trying to keep them fenced. And we'll want to get a few sows and a boar hog. Pork is easiest to store over the winter and we can make money on the piglets. Then, when we have enough money, we'll buy a well-bred mare and stud Nero ourselves. The Troy's have always been known for their horse flesh. Don't see why we need to break the tradition."

Bella's eyes glistened with the hope. She knew she could trust in Jack. Without thinking, she leaned over and kissed him. Jack kissed her back, his hands moving slowly up her arms, lingering at the base of her neck. She reveled in the feeling of closeness, the warmth of his body, the brush of his whiskers against her tender skin. She pulled back and looked down at him. He smiled at her; touched her cheek with the back of his fingertips.

"It's really going to be all right, isn't it, Jack?"

He took her hands in his and nodded. "May be some rough patches still ahead, but we'll get by."

He stood and pulled her to her feet. He wrapped her in his arms and held her close. "We're a team, Bell. You can trust me with anything."

She nodded, anxiety nibbled at her as she wondered what secrets he might know.

"Anything," he repeated.

She buried her face in his chest and nodded, but said nothing.

Elizabeth Seckman

Chapter 9

Jack escorted her to the bath barrel and kissed her forehead before leaving. Night fell and it was time for bed. She chewed on her fingernail.

"Save the water for me," Jack said from beyond the quilt wall.

"Oh, okay," she stammered.

She stripped with nervous fingers, fumbling with buttons and ties. Stepping into the warm water, she bathed quickly. The cooling night air and her fear of the wedding night, froze her to her core. Her body shook as she wrapped herself in a blanket trying to warm herself before slipping into her thinning night gown. She felt bare and exposed in the worn-out shift, so she wrapped the damp blanket around her shoulders.

"I'm done," she called to Jack as she dashed from barn to house. She went directly to her room and closed the door behind her. Trying to pretend it was a normal night, she occupied her mind with her usual bedtime ritual. As she brushed out her hair, her shaking hands dropped the brush twice. Her fear and anxiety grew with every passing second. She could hear her mother's voice as clearly as if she was standing behind her. "Marital duties never killed anyone. Just do it. Who knows, you may get lucky and supply him with an heir early, and then you can turn that duty over to a servant. Though knowing how well you perform your other duties, I expect you will have oodles of daughters before you get it right." Bella closed her eyes and shut out the voice. She would do whatever he expected of a wife. At least she trusted him enough to know he wouldn't hurt her. Not on purpose, anyway.

Bella put the brush down with a sigh. She reached back to plait the thick hair that fell nearly to her waist. Half way through, she felt Jack behind her. She looked up from her vanity and forced a smile.

"Leave it down," Jack ordered, his voice quiet and gravelly.

"It'll tangle."

"You look beautiful." He ran his hands across her temples to her hair where he wove his hands into the thick strands. "If you need help in the morning, I'll gladly lend you a hand."

Bella felt her cheeks flush then redden to a blaze. She hadn't thought of him still being here in the morning. Charles always kept his own room. Jack's fingers released the curls she managed to twist into the braid. He caressed the soft locks between his finger and thumb.

"The first time I saw you, it was your hair that caught my attention. In the light, it is as red as the sunset we saw tonight, inside it shimmers like gold. And when I separate it between my fingers I am amazed at how many colors it's made of. I don't think there's another woman so unique as you."

"I never thought you noticed me."

Jack grinned. "Of course I did. But I wasn't fool enough to think I'd ever be allowed to have you."

"Why not?"

"You were a Troy, and I was a stable hand."

"So?"

Jack smiled down at her. "You still don't get it, do you?"

"If I loved you, and you loved me, what would it matter?"

"It simply wasn't done. Why do you think your father sent me north, paid for my mother and sister to come from England? He wanted me off the plantation before you meant something to me that I could no longer resist."

"Father sent you away?"

"He relieved me of the contract he bought from Captain Newsome, sent for Mother and Agnes and recommended I move farther north. I took the hint."

"I missed you so much when you left, but father said it was your choice. He said he even tried to bribe you to stay."

"He was protecting a foolish daughter who thought she could marry a poor man because she fancied him."

"I don't see why not. Daddy was once a poor man."

"A poor lord. Big difference between impoverished nobility and a poor nothing."

"Oh pooh! You can't believe that." Indignation dispelled her worries until he took her hand and pulled her from her seat.

His arms circled her waist and he pulled her close to kiss the tip of her nose. "I suppose in the end, you were proven right. Never did know a time when Isabella Troy didn't get her way."

Bella tried to think of something witty and appropriate for the moment, but her mind was numbed by his closeness. She smiled up at him; a nervous half twitch that almost resembled pain. Her throat was dry. She liked his touch, enjoyed the feel of his hands in her hair. Felt her bones weaken as his fingertips grazed the skin of her neck. Still, fear kept an icy grip on her. She knew what was coming, and she felt nauseous. She only hoped that when it was all done, she didn't loathe him like she did Charles.

Jack tipped her head back and kissed her, his lips soft and patient. Bella tried to relax, fought to distance her mind, but she couldn't. On her first wedding night, Tessie provided her with wine. It had helped. A little. At least her memory of the encounter was vague. Tessie had recommended a glass or two, but Bella chugged the bottle.

Bella squeezed her eyes shut trying to block out the memory of Charles's hands, the pain from his haste and inconsideration, his harsh words of reprisal for her lack of knowledge and skill. The harder she tried, the more her body shook.

Jack sighed and stepped back. He caressed her cheek with the palm of his hand as he looked into her eyes. He looked concerned as he pulled her to his chest, nestling her cheek against his thumping heart. With lips so close they tickled her ear, he said, "Nothing will happen tonight, Bell."

"Nothing?" Bella felt ashamed at her relief. She should want to be with her husband, but she didn't.

"Nothing. Not until you ask."

Pulling away so she could see his face, she checked to see if he was serious. He looked disappointed, and she felt bad, but not bad enough to convince him otherwise. "What if I never ask?"

Jack frowned. "I guess it'll be a strange marriage."

"Not really. Many men have..."

Jack's words were harsh, "I'll keep my vows, Bella. I pledged I'd be faithful to you and I will."

"I'm sorry, Jack, I'll do my best. I promised and...and I can do this. Please, be patient with me." Her eyes burned. She didn't want Jack disappointed in her. She'd made him promises and she was already breaking them. With cold, shaking fingers, she untied her nightgown. Jack's hands covered hers, stopping her from undressing.

"Please, Bell, don't. Let me stay here with you. Let me hold you, be close to you. That's all I need."

"Are you sure?"

Jack answered by lifting her from her feet and carrying her to the bed. He placed her gently on her pillow and lay down beside her. He pulled the blankets up around her and settled in next to her. His fingers brushed through her hair.

"I'm sorry," Bella whispered.

Jack snuggled her in to his body, holding her close. "Don't apologize."

"You're upset with me. I can hear it in your voice."

His breath was warm against her neck with his sigh. "No, I'm not. I'm happy to lay here and hold you. It beats the floor in the kitchen."

Bella giggled and rolled to face him. "I offered you a bed."

"Yes, you did my sweet. Now go to sleep."

Bella nodded and Jack gave her a squeeze. She snuggled against his naked chest relishing, much to her shock, the feel of his warmth, the hardness of his body. She sighed in contentment. "I don't deserve you, Jack."

"Maybe not," he said with a laugh. "But I guess you're stuck with me."

Bella pinched him and he kissed her and said, "Goodnight. Pleasant dreams."

"You too." She kissed the hollow of his throat and breathed in his musky scent.

Jack groaned. "Ah, you might want to stop that or... hell... I may have to take a cold dip."

"Are you too warm? I could open a window." She started to move from his grasp, but he held tight.

"Stay, woman. I'll survive till morning."

Bella smiled and kissed his throat again, then snuggled closer and dozed right off. She hadn't felt so secure since she was a little girl and her world was unbreakable and pure.

Though Jack did his best to slip out of bed without stirring her, Bella woke. The sun had not yet risen, but the room was lit by the gray of early morning. She yawned and stretched. Jack tucked the blankets around her and whispered for her to stay in bed.

"Where are you going? To the privy?"

"Sleep, Bella." He kissed her forehead and she smiled, allowing herself to drift back to sleep.

She woke again when the sun was full. She sat up in bed with a start. She overslept. She tumbled from bed flustered from her laziness. Debating whether to wear trousers or a skirt, she quickly opted for the trousers. There was too much work to get done to worry about propriety. She tidied her room, pausing a moment to absorb the idea that Jack was her husband. Goose bumps rose on her arms, and a warming shiver ran down her spine. It was too good to be true.

A crow landed on her window sill. Its caw grabbed her attention and made her heart skip a beat. "A bad omen," she whispered. She crossed herself, said a little prayer, and reminded herself she didn't believe such foolishness. This was a new beginning. Nothing would stop her from living happily ever after. She frowned as she grabbed her brush and yanked it through her hair, plaited it, then twisted it into a bun.

She checked Manny's room before heading downstairs. Of course, Tessie got him off to school. Bella gave herself a scolding for allowing Tess to do her duties. Tessie had

104

enough to do. As Bella hurried down the steps she heard humming and pots clanking in the kitchen. She went toward the noise.

She found Tessie stirring a big pot, a kerchief tied around her head. The room smelled sweet, and Tessie looked pleased as punch to be stirring the brown liquid.

"What are you doing, Tessie, making gold?"

"Might as well be. Mister Jack tapped those trees and got some late syrup. He left me with instructions on how to boil it down and I've been working on it since. Did you know the sap isn't sweet? Not till you cook it, anyhow. Isn't that something?"

"Fascinating." Bella oohed and ahhed, dipping her finger in the pot. She sucked the sweetness and imagined sweet beans and hot cakes.

"Keep your fingers outta the pan. Heaven's sakes, how'd you end up with no manners whatsoever?"

Bella grinned and shrugged. Tessie sighed as she said, "Well, at least you can be useful, get those pans over yonder. Mister Jack said dump it as soon as it had tiny bubbles. Too early, or too late won't be good. Looks like now's the time."

Bella grabbed the pans from the counter and spread them out on the dining table. She grabbed a dish towel and helped Tessie wrestle the cast iron cauldron from the fire.

"Why did you let me sleep in? How would you have managed this yourself?"

"By God's grace, Missy. I always manage with God's grace."

Bella sniffed. "You would've been in a pickle if I hadn't shown up."

"But you did, so why you fretting child? Hasn't the world handed you enough problems to keep you from digging up more?"

"You could have gotten burned trying to pour that yourself."

"Shush. Don't lecture your mammy."

Bella couldn't resist attempting another taste, but Tessie read her mind and slapped her hand as it headed for the pan. Bella pulled her hand back and stuck out her tongue.

"So, how do you feel being a married woman again and all?"

Bella grabbed a biscuit and a cup of tea and sat in the chair, her mouth watering from the smell of the maple syrup cooling right under her nose. "No different."

Tessie sighed, her face relieved. "I was worried for you. Afraid you'd regret your decision once the sun set."

"No. Tessie," Bella leaned in whispering, her cheeks suddenly red. "He expected nothing of me."

"Nothing?" Tessie eyes were round in shock.

"Nothing. Said I needn't worry about it till I feel...you know...a need."

"What need?"

"I guess he thinks I'll get the desire to you know..."

"Is the man healthy? Do you think he's sick?"

Bella shrugged, her face worried. What if he was sick? She would have to watch to be sure he took care of himself.

"Where is he, Tessie?"

Tessie shrugged. "He got the ax and asked me for the matches, then he took off."

Bella looked out the window. He wasn't in the front yard or the horse barn. Maybe he was at the hay barn again. Bella stood leaving the final swigs of her tea at the bottom of the cup. "I better make sure he's not snooping around the hay barn."

"Oh, lordy. Have you told him about...well, about that night?"

"No," Bella answered sharply. Tessie gave her a look that Bella read as disappointment. Bella defended her silence by asking, "Just how do you bring that sort of thing up in conversation?"

"Best find a way. You owe it to your husband to be honest."

Bella thought a moment, then shook her head. "I just can't. If my lies catch up with me, then so be it. But I refuse to ruin what I have."

Tessie shook her head and frowned. "I think you can trust Mr. Jack."

"I *know* I can. I don't see the point in digging up the past."

Tessie snorted. "I'd think that statement was ironic if I didn't worry God would strike me dead for it."

Bella looked worried as if the wrath of God would split the ceiling and strike them both dead. *Foolishness,* she assured herself with a grimace, *and the crow didn't mean anything, either.* She cleaned up her breakfast dishes with shaking hands. "I'm not going to think on this right now. I'm married to Jack and I'm happy. That's all that matters." She folded the dish towel and laid it on the counter. "If you don't need me anymore, I'm going to find him."

"I'm fine. Get on out of here," Tessie said. As Bella headed out the door, Tessie stopped her by saying, "Come to think of it, you're probably right to leave the past behind you."

Chapter 10

It didn't take Bella long to find him. She simply followed the smoke. He stood guard over a raging fire, a rake in one hand, hat in the other.

"What are you doing?" Bella asked as she approached.

"Burning the privy."

"Oh," Bella said as if she fully understood. Her mother always told her to never nag a man about his business, but curiosity got the better of her. "Why are you burning the privy, Jack?"

"It's too far away. I made another one closer to the house. No need to go a damned half mile to use the bathroom. Manny could get lost trying to find this place at night. And the new one is tighter, less drafty. Though, I did add two windows we can open in summer for a cross breeze, and close em' up for warmth in the winter. Winking at her, he added, "Just trying to make things a tad better for my new wife."

Bella rubbed his arm. "That's sweet of you."

"Come sit by me and we'll enjoy the fire together."

"I should…"

"Sit with me. The timbers are old and it'll burn quickly."

"I really should…"

Jack dropped the rake and sat in the grass. Grabbing Bella by the hand, he pulled her down beside him. "There's nothing you need to do right now. The house is sparkling clean, the garden is growing, the syrup is in the hands of Tessie, and Manny doesn't come home for hours. Relax with me a while. Then, we'll go check the traps and see if we'll have more rabbit for dinner."

"That's how you got the rabbits?"

"Yes. How'd you think?"

"With a gun."

"I don't have a gun."

"There's one under my bed." Then she added, "But there aren't any bullets left."

Jack nodded. "Well, I talked to that Yankee in town the other day. Seems he plans to start a furniture business. He was interested in some of the cherry and walnut on the farm. Drop a few of those, get us some cash, then buy some shot and powder. Then I could go hunting, maybe find a deer."

"Oh, and be sure to take Manny. I told him you would teach him to hunt. I hope you don't mind. He looked so sad yesterday."

"He told me. I promised I'd teach him to make a bow, though I may want to start the hunting lessons with being quiet." Jack laughed as he plucked blades of grass and pulled them apart at their seams. "Took him to check the snares yesterday and he talked the whole time. Told me three different stories on how his dad died."

Bella smiled, then frowned. "You know it is sort of funny, but Wendy never speaks of the past, or the present...oh, my lands, the girl hardly talks about anything! I think Manny talks so much to fill the void." She looked across the field to the Smoky Mountains on the horizon. "I honestly have no clue about Manny's dad. I *assume* he's passed on, but who knows? Wendy has never even told me he's Cherokee, Manny did. She did tell Tessie she was Lumbee and she lived in Quallatown before coming to Troy."

"What the hell's Quallatown?"

"Poor Jack, did Daddy ever let you leave the plantation?" She gave him a smile before explaining, "It's a Cherokee village, though technically, tribes and Indians can't own land. Will Thomas, a white man adopted by the Cherokee, bought the land and holds the deed to hundreds of acres. The village has schools and houses, like any other town. They try to live as much like white people as possible, trying to fit into a changed world. That's why we are set on Manny going to school. If the Cherokee know they need book learning, then Manny does too."

"So, the story about his dad skipping the trail of tears and leading the people to the hills isn't true?"

Bella shrugged. "I suppose it could be true. Or it could be a young boy's fantasy. I really don't know."

Jack shook his head and sighed. "Got to be hard on a person not to know a damned thing about his lineage."

Bella thought a bit, her eyes vacant and lost in thought. Then she answered, "I suppose it doesn't always matter where you come from, as long as you know where you are going."

Jack grinned and whistled low. "I am mighty surprised. You do consider things beyond dresses and bonnets."

Bella's mouth dropped open and she was about to scold him, but his eyes were too merry to stay mad for long. Instead she harrumphed, crossed her arms over her chest and threatened, "See if I share any more of my thoughts with an ungrateful cur like you."

"You look lovely."

"Hah!"

"But you do." She sat with her lips pursed together, ignoring him as she studied how many birds landed and took off from the tree in front of her. His grin widened. "You're also sweet to take in a homeless man and an abandoned boy."

"I what? Oh, you and Manny. You had a home, a lice-infested rat hole, but still it was a place to stay. And Manny? He wasn't exactly abandoned."

"What the hell do you call it?"

Bella thought a while. She thought of Wendy, the quiet woman who dipped her head low when spoken to. Wendy earned a living washing laundry, often bringing the torn items to Bella and Tessie for mending. The first time she asked for their help, she brought a shirt and showed it to Tess, pointing to the tear. They assumed she either didn't speak English or was a mute. They knew her for three weeks before she talked to them...in perfect English.

"Wendy, Manny's mom, is odd, but she's a good woman. Wendy's mom hated being associated with anything tribal. She wanted to be white; she even went by the name Smith. And poor Wendy has the raven hair and olive skin her mother loathed so much, so she was treated harshly...by her own mother! Can you believe that?"

Jack bobbed his head and shrugged his shoulders.

Bella continued, "I mean I never got along well with my own mother, but she never hurt me. Wendy's mom would tie her to a tree in their yard and leave her out all night as a punishment."

"Wendy tell you this?"

Bella shook her head. "No, Tessie knows a lady who cleaned for Trudy, Wendy's mom, and saw first-hand how she treated her daughter." Bella grimaced "Though it was never much of a secret. Most people knew what was happening. They knew Trudy was hateful. When Wendy disappeared, Trudy tried to form a search party, but few helped. Everyone figured the girl was better off with her kin than her mother. They law checked Lumbee lands, but didn't find her. Seems the Lumbee were smart enough to take her to the Cherokee."

"That's why she's so odd?"

Bella nodded. "How could Wendy have a chance at being normal? Trudy Smith was crazy as a bed bug. I can tell you, the only thing Wendy said about her mom was that the woman saw visions that made her irate. Tessie says the woman was demon possessed. Maybe she's right, because Wendy has scars from her mother. Real physical scars." Bella leaned close to Jack. "She tries to hide them, but I've seen them. She has whip marks on her back. What kind of mother does that?"

Jack scratched his head. "A terrible one?"

Bella nodded. "And to think Wendy was the child who came back and cared for the old witch when she went blind. I don't think I'd have been that forgiving."

"And nobody knows where Manny's dad is?"

Bella shook her head.

"Did you ever ask Wendy?"

"No. She doesn't ask me my secrets. I don't ask for hers. If she wanted me to know, she'd tell me."

"I'm shocked. Curiosity and questions were once typical Bella."

"Well, I've come to find, knowing some things only makes me sad, so I'd rather not know."

Jack put an arm around her shoulder and pulled her toward him. He kissed her temple. "You certainly are a good woman."

Bella blushed. "Why thank you, Jack. I appreciate that and well, I also appreciate everything you've done."

Jack took her hand in his and gave it a kiss then held onto to it. They sat quietly watching the timbers burn. Once it settled into a small smoldering mound, Jack said, "I suppose it's about time I get started digging out a root cellar, so we have a cool place to start storing supplies."

"I'll help you."

Jack took her chin in his hand. "I never doubted that for a moment."

Bella smiled, pleasantly surprised he didn't tell her it wasn't woman's work. She felt herself being absorbed by his stare. She knew he was going to kiss her and her tongue flicked across her lips as if by instinct. It seemed an eternity before he made contact, but it was worth the wait. She relished the taste of him, welcomed the feeling of warmth that spread all over, even to the tips of her toes. Easing her onto the grass, he continued to kiss her. The weight of his body pressed against her brought a chill. She couldn't, try as hard as she might, get the feel of Charles's hands off her mind. Jack whispered in her ear. "Open your eyes, Bella. Look at me. I want you to know who's touching you."

Bella nodded and opened her eyes. She felt the immediate flow of contentment, the feel of safety when she looked into her husband's eyes. He would never hurt her. Her hands moved to the silky hair that was growing like stubble over his head. He kissed her lightly, then moved on to her ears, down the sensitive muscle of her throat, on to its sensitive hollow. She kept her eyes open, though her lids were heavy, her hands stroking the back of his neck. He looked up at her, his lips hovering at the cleft of her breasts. Bella enjoyed the feel of his lips on her skin. She didn't want him to stop. She surprised herself when she heard herself in a lusty, hoarse voice say, "Don't stop."

Jack's eyes squeezed closed and he took a sharp breath before he returned to his exploration. He unbuttoned the top button planting a kiss against the warm flesh where her heart beat pounded against his lips. He placed his ear over her heart as if to verify she was real. Bella watched as the sun glistened off hair so black it seemed to have a touch of blue. She watched in fascination as he slowly undid each button until only the thin undershirt separated them. Jack looked to her and she nodded her head. He lifted the shirt and revealed well shaped breasts. "You're so beautiful, Bella." He leaned on an elbow propped on his side as his fingers traced the sensitive skin around the breast causing them to respond and harden, though the warmth from the rising sun heated her flesh. "So beautiful." He breathed again, his head dipping slowly, taking one nipple in his mouth and rolling it against his tongue. Bella pressed him to her breast, ignoring the tears which fell down her cheeks. She thought a moment of her child, how he had suckled so gently and she felt the longing for another babe so deep in her soul she felt it would burn her. She stroked the top of his head, enjoyed the feel of him as his lips moved down her ribs, his tongue flicking in the sensitive dip of her belly button. Bella's body shivered as his attentions sent waves of need to the tops of her thighs. She would make love to her husband. But she couldn't bring herself to say the words. What if the full reality wasn't so good? What if the horrid act was still as bad as she remembered and then she would lose this intimacy? No, her lips remained frozen and Jack pushed her no farther. He kissed and caressed her until the crackling fire behind them stilled.

Jack pulled her shirt down and buttoned it up. "I suppose the time for work has come. Can't play all day."

Bella said nothing. She watched his features go from passionate to serious. "Ready to dig?" He stood and held out a hand to her and she took it without a word. She had no word for the moment besides regret.

Chapter 11

Jack showed Bella the new privy. It sat closer to the house and was built much sturdier than the old one. Bella voiced her appreciation. "So, when did you find the time? The wood?"

"Still busting up the old shed in the field. Structurally, it's not fit to put a hay bale in, but piece by piece, it's good as the day it was built."

Bella fiddled with her hair, her gaze moving to the direction of the old barn. "Seems the barn is a favorite spot of yours lately."

"Just using what we have to work with. Something 'bout that barn bug you? Any reason I should stay away?"

"Well no, I just…you said yourself it wasn't safe."

"I know how to move around it. But a little one like Manny wouldn't. And that's all the more reason to bring it down."

"That's true." Bella's voice was distant.

He took her by the shoulders and turned her toward him. "Trust me, all right? And remember, we're together now. Forever. Your problems are my problems. You don't have to fear telling me anything." His fingers lifted her chin until their eyes met. "Anything, Bell. Tell me…what bothers you about the old barn?"

Bella's cheeks flamed. "Nnnothing…it's just," she cleared her throat. "You're certain we won't need it later?"

"No. It's out of the way; it's structurally unfit. Whoever built it didn't even add support beams. They evidently lacked knowledge in farming too because they stuck the damn thing in the middle of a perfect pasture."

"The man who owned the farm was a blacksmith. He never farmed."

"Still odd, even for a smith. Even if you kept the hay barn for the horses and such, why set it so far from the stables?"

Bella grinned. "Tessie heard from some of her people that the mistress of the house was a real tyrant and her husband found tolerance for her in a bottle. Maybe it was his sanctuary."

"In that case…what a clever man. Maybe I *better* keep it."

Bella gave him a jab to the ribs. Jack laughed and gave her a hug. "I've no need to escape."

Bella smiled, her heart warmed by his compliment. Jack gave her a wink and ruined her good will toward him with the added observation, "I've had a couple of years in prison to harden my hide to annoyances."

"Ohh!" Bella gave him a punch, "I ought to…"

"Temper, Bell. Temper."

"I'll show you temper, you…you…"

"Come now. I'm teasing." She gave him another jab to his ribs. He laughed and pulled her close. She wriggled half halfheartedly. "You're an ogre. Why I ought to…"

"Kiss me?" he answered with a wink.

"Hah! Hardly. Why you don't deserve any kisses."

"Maybe not…but still…" Before she could utter another word, his lips found hers. His kiss left her breathless. He licked his lips, his flickering tongue so close she could feel it against the soft skin of her own. "So sweet." He dropped his forehead against hers. He kissed the bridge of her nose. "I shouldn't provoke you. You've been good to me. A man should never torment such a beautiful, tender wife who's willing to spend her gold on his freedom."

Bella adjusted his collar pretending to pout. "You're right. I did. Could have bought me a couple of pretty dresses. Least that would have been an investment I could enjoy."

Jack laughed and hugged her tighter. "Still as saucy as you were at thirteen."

"Because you were awful to me!"

"Come now, awful?"

"Well, you weren't very nice."

"I was always nice. I couldn't resist teasing you. You're so damned cute when you pout."

"You teased me intentionally?"

"Of course. I especially love it when you'd turn and storm off. Hell, I'd often wonder if you'd snap your pretty little neck twisting it in the air like you do." He imitated by flipping his chin to the sky.

"Jack Byron! That's just awful. I do *not* do that."

He rubbed his nose against hers. "You most certainly do."

"I am *not* a hoity toity princess."

"Hoity toity, no. But princess you most certainly are."

Her mouth formed an O.

"But now you're my princess." He stroked her cheek. "And I wouldn't change one bit of you. I think you're perfect in every way."

"I'm still not sure I like being called a princess. I think you're still teasing me."

He chuckled. "Not at all. I consider myself your loyal subject."

"Oh, well, if you put it that way."

She was feeling rather smug until he winked at her and said, "Besides, I also know as your subject, you have the power to tell what's his name I'm being bad and he'll send the cavalry to lock me back up."

Bella stomped her foot and stuck her nose in the air and twisted free from his embrace. "I was thinking I rather liked your kisses, but you've spoiled it. I would gladly go dig the rocky earth in the blazing sun than kiss you again!" She strode toward the barn to get a shovel. He called after her but she pretended not to hear. Offering only one word as she disappeared in the shadow of the barn, she called over her shoulder, "Swine."

Jack laughed and shook his head. He followed behind her catching her in the doorway. Grabbing her around the waist, he pulled her into him. "Never offer me a kiss and walk away."

"I don't recall offering," she said with a raised brow.

"I'm certain you said something about kisses. You should never tease me about those. And never storm away from a man while in your trousers. 'Cause when you're mad, your back side swings and screams, 'Jack, come catch me.'"

"It says that?"

"Oh, it says so much more than that, but I'd burn your ears if I was completely honest."

Bella opened her mouth to speak, but she was silenced by his kiss. Her body eased against his as if magnetically drawn. Jack kissed her, his hands holding her close, fingers digging into her flesh.

"Bella, Bella," he breathed, his lips brushing against her ear as he spoke. "We'll all starve to death if you don't stop tempting me."

Bella grinned, instinct telling her she had the upper hand. She caressed his cheek gently. "Why, I'd think a man your age would have better self-control."

Jack's smile spread across his face. He grabbed at his chest, "The princess shoots a barb right into my heart."

Bella laughed. "Come on, old man, we better start digging. We don't want to starve this winter 'cause you lollygagged all spring and summer."

He took her hand and led her to the hillside by the east end of the house.

The green mound looked suddenly like a mountain. "How long do you think it'll take?"

"Isn't going to be easy. Got a lot of rock to dig through. I suppose we'll know we're done, when we're done."

"Well, let's get started." Bella pulled on her leather gloves and picked up her shovel.

They dug for nearly an hour before all the sod was removed from the rectangle which would eventually be a door. "Why don't you get us some water, Bell?"

She nodded. The tender skin of her hands burned from the course leather gloves. She pulled them off. She looked at them top and bottom. They were red, but not yet blistered, though she could feel a few tender spots that were going to bubble soon. Jack took one of her hands in his and kissed it. "One day, Bell, I hope to have enough so you never have to labor like a man again."

"Oh, hush. You're just worried I make you look bad. I dig so much faster and all."

Jack gave her a soft look, one that told her he might love her, at least a little. Her heart soared, but she cautioned herself against getting crazy ideas. "I declare working hard to make a home, a secure one where we're not just scraping by?

Why that's worth every ounce of work." She added with an ornery smile, "I only wish I had some better company."

Jack laughed, his head thrown back, his chest reverberating with the sound. "All right, woman. Go get some water. I'm dry as a bone."

She brought him a canning jar full. He chugged it down and sent her for more. He swallowed it in a couple of gulps, and then told her to bring a bucket full. She was beginning to wonder if he was keeping her out of his way. She returned with the bucket and he told her, "Now go get Nero, hitch him to the wagon and bring it around. You can shovel this dirt onto the wagon and I'll dump it in the old privy hole later."

By the time she had Nero all hitched and brought around, the cellar was looking like a real cellar. "You work fast."

"Well, thank you. Still a lot left to do."

Jack went back to work. He worked the pickax to remove large rocks from the hill side, and then he grabbed the shovel and tossed shovel loads of dirt onto the wagon. Bella shoveled the loose dirt lying on the ground. They worked without consideration for the time. Tessie appeared with biscuits drizzled in syrup. After they ate, Tessie offered to relieve Bella. She refused, asking instead for Tessie to fetch Manny from school. Tessie agreed, though she grumbled, "Workin like a field hand. Gonna get you a mess of blisters."

"Oh, now, Tess. Blisters never killed a soul."

"Hmmph. Shows what you know. Blisters can bring on the fever. Don't go to bed without me checking your hands, child."

"Yes, Mammy," Bella chided.

Tessie sauntered off, tongue still wagging with admonishments.

"I declare that woman still thinks I'm a child. Like I don't know how to take care of a blister!"

Jack looked at her with a serious head to toe perusal.

"What?" Bella asked feeling his scrutiny.

"Tessie's right. You need to stop. You'd never survive the fever. You're too damned skinny."

"A few hours ago you seemed to like…"

"I'm not talking about whether or not you're pleasing to the eye. I'm talking about your health. You need more meat on your bones to get you through an illness."

Bella shook her head and returned to digging. "Don't let Tessie rattle you."

"You're stopping when she returns. Have her look over your hands."

"Now this is just…" Bella stuck the shovel in the pile of dirt and leaned on it.

"I'm stopping then too. I need to get some other stuff done today. Did you really think we'd finish in one day?"

"Oh. No, I guess not. But it's really looking good. I think you dug back at least three feet. Seems like if we keep this pace, we *could* have it done by dark."

"Nope. We'll work on it tomorrow."

"But if we…"

"Trust me. Don't need it for a while anyhow. I still need to figure out how to build a fence for Nero. Can't find an ax anywhere on this place."

"Oh, the ax…it's in my room."

"Planning renovations?" he asked leaning against his shovel handle.

"Funny, Jack. We ran out of bullets. We needed something for protection. There were raiders all over the place. I suppose I don't need it so much now that I have you."

"I'd gladly die than let anyone hurt you."

"I know." Bella's voice was quiet.

Jack leaned forward and kissed her cheek. His breath tickled her ear. He looked down at her with flushed cheeks. "Bella. I…well, we better get back to work." Jack grabbed his pick ax and went at the hill at a frenzied pace. Bella tried to match his pace, but her body wasn't equipped like his for hard labor. The pain creeping into her back made her ready to admit she was plum tuckered out. She was tempted to plop herself down on the grass and rest when she noticed the dirt on the road was stirred up. Her heart leaped. No one ever came down their road. "Jack. Someone's coming." She dropped her shovel. "Maybe it's Noah." Her belly fluttered with joy, and she took off running toward the road. Jack grabbed her arm. "Don't be foolish, Bella. Could be anyone." He pulled her back behind him, her wrist held securely in his grasp like she was a wayward child.

Bella's excitement died as she realized the wagon only carried two white people. She squinted against the sun, shielding her eyes with her hand. The driver looked familiar and as he came closer, Bella gasped and nearly fell over from fright.

Charles!

She covered her mouth with her hand. It was Charles. She recognized his red hair and beefy build. She tried to wrench her arm from Jack, but he held her tight. She needed to run. "Let me go." She hissed as she tried to escape. Jack let go of her arm, but caught her around the waist and held her tight against him. "What is it, Bell?"

She looked over Jack's shoulder, "It's…" As the wagon pulled closer, Bella let out an exhausted sigh. It wasn't Charles at all. Just a man who looked like him.

"Bell? You look like you've seen a ghost."

Bella moistened her lips and cleared her throat. "I thought it was Charles."

"Your ex-husband?"

Bella nodded.

Jack looked over his shoulder at the wagon. "That looks like...I'll be...it is..." He let go of Bella and let out a whoop and waved at the wagon. "Daniel Clemons. You old scoundrel. How the hell did you find me?"

"Jack!" The red-haired man laughed, his face wrinkled in relief and pleasure. "You don't know how happy I was to go visit your sorry hide in jail and hear you'd been set free."

"Yep, I'm free. Now I got myself chained to a woman." Jack touched Bella around the waist, propelling her forward till she was right beside him. "I'd like you to meet Isabella. She's the beauty who paid the bounty on my head. Bought me lock, stock, and barrel."

Daniel smiled and gave Jack a punch to his arm. "Never thought you'd be owned by any woman, old man."

"I guess Bella's not just any woman."

The woman next to Daniel snorted. She was a big, rawboned woman. Bella couldn't tell what her face looked like. It was shadowed by her bonnet. The way a proper lady went out into the sun. Bella touched her uncovered plaited hair which was probably awry, if not sticking out all over as if she had been struck by lightning. And her nose was slightly burnt; freckles probably covered her cheeks. She wiped at what felt like a clump of mud on her chin and cringed when she remembered she was wearing trousers. Bella covered herself as if she were naked. Looking nervously at Jack, she excused herself. "I better go. I need to check on...umm, see about..."

"Don't run off, Bell. Daniel is one of my best friends. I even let him marry my sister."

Daniel whispered to Bella, "Some days, I think he did it to spite me."

Jack laughed and the woman on the wagon said sternly, "I don't find you at all humorous, Daniel."

"Come now, honey, this is a happy day. Your brother is a free man."

"Nice of him to let his family know."

"Now, kitten," Daniel said and held a hand out to her to help her down, "come give your brother a hug."

The woman dismounted. She gave Jack a gingerly hug, scolding him for getting her dirty. She nodded to Bella, offering only her fingertips for Bella to shake. Bella felt like one of the house girls who would dip and curtsy to their mistress's visitors. Her distaste for her old life rose like bile in her throat. God must still be showing her how ludicrous she was to think she was above any other. Bella simply smiled and ignored the hand shake. "I'm filthy, ma'am. I'm sure you'll forgive me for my reserve. If you all would excuse me, I'd like to freshen up a bit." Bella didn't wait for permission. She simply turned and walked off, her spine twice as stiff as the aching muscles in her arms and back.

Chapter 12

Bella carried a bucket into the barn. She planned to at least wash up in a stall before facing anyone else. She couldn't blame Jack's sister for looking at her like she was a leper, but she was surprised it bothered her. She'd had plenty of opportunity to get used to shunning, with all the practice the good people of Troy gave her. But to be hated on sight by Jack's only family? Well, that made her eyes sting and her chest hurt.

Too worn out to stand and pull off her shoes, she plopped down in the hay. She pulled off one shoe, then another and set them beside her. She studied the cracked and worn leather and fiddled with the mismatched strings of her only pair of shoes. She remembered a time when she owned a closet full of them. A pair for every outfit and season. In those days, when she entered a room, people didn't just smile and greet her, they tripped over themselves to gain her attention. She leaned her back against the rough wood and closed her eyes, tears dribbling from closed lashes. People used to love her. Respect her.

No, the thought crept through her mind slow and painful...*they loved the Troy money*. Stripped of it, she was nothing. Without money and Daddy's power, she couldn't even protect her own child. Her breath caught in her throat and her heart squeezed in agony.

"Poor sweet baby," she whispered as she cupped her face in her hands and curled up in the hay. She lay there and cried, wishing a soul could just die of heartbreak so she could go on to Heaven and be done with this place.

The image of Tessie finding her dead in a barn stall gave her pause. Or if Manny found her. He already worried over his mother. She couldn't add the fright of finding a dead body to the child's worries. Or even Jack. He may not love her, but he would be sad if she was dead. No, she thought as she sat up and slumped over her knees, dropping dead wasn't the answer. She dried her eyes on her sleeve. She'd have to change Agnes's opinion of her. If that was at all possible.

She knocked the mud off her shoes, then stripped down to undergarments and began scrubbing her skin till it was pink and cool. She finished and was about to leave when she heard the barn door squeak open. She gathered her dirty clothes and hugged them to her chest as she stepped into the darkest corner of the stall. Bella couldn't step out half naked, nor could she re-dress in her filthy clothes now that she was squeaky clean. She heard Jack clear his throat. She breathed a sigh of relief. She'd ask Jack to fetch her some clothes from the house. She opened her mouth to speak when his sister's voice stilled her.

"Jack, you know I'm happy, even grateful that you're out of that jail."

"And you have Bella to thank for that."

"I didn't say I don't appreciate what she did. I'm just saying one kindness shouldn't tie you to her for life. We will pay her back."

"I can't pay her back; neither can you."

"So, you will walk away from Mary?"

"She walked away from me, Aggie." Jack's voice was harsh and brutal. "She gave up on me."

"Why do you say that? She still loves you. I talked to her before we left. I wanted her to come with us today, and she said she would next time, if you said you wanted to see her."

Bella could hear Jack moving around the barn. She pressed her ear closer to the cracks in the wall. "Please, Jack. Tell her you don't," Bella whispered.

Jack said nothing for a long moment. Then he sighed. "That part of my life's over. You can tell Mary I've moved on. I'm married to Bella."

Agnes's voice was sharp and biting. "You can't be serious. You've not even been free a week and you already married her?"

Jack must have nodded because Agnes continued, "Are you insane? You and Mary belong together. You can't mistake gratitude for something permanent enough to build a life around."

"I know Bella will make a good wife. I could do far worse."

"Why? Because she looks good in trousers? Which, I might add, is absolutely disgraceful."

"Bella understands that to survive times like these, propriety has to be set aside."

"What other proprieties has she set aside?"

"Aggie, don't disrespect my wife. I won't tolerate it."

"Stop calling her your wife. This is a farce. One that you will change. It is ludicrous to think you've made a lifelong decision based upon guilt. You deserve so much more than that, little brother."

Bella felt a tear slide down her cheek. She wiped it away, her stomach turning with a sickly feeling. "Please, Jack," Bella begged quietly. "Tell her you could love me. Tell her you don't love that other woman."

"Bella is a good woman. Get to know her before you judge her."

"Maybe you should do the same."

"I do know Bella."

Agnes harrumphed. "What for a week?"

"No, I've known Bella since she was a young girl. She's Henry Troy's daughter."

"Oh, that makes me feel so much better. Are you insane? The Troy's were the most stuck-up, greedy bunch of people to ever grace this land."

"Bella's not like that. And besides, if it weren't for Master Troy's money, you'd still be living in East End squalor."

"Mother paid him back for the fair, especially after the way he acted when she tried to thank him. You remember that, little brother? You tried to speak to him at the races and he walked away?"

"He released me from my debt to him, one which our dear father put on my head, and brought you two from London so I had family. I can't hold a snub against the man. I worked for him. I never expected to be his friend."

"So, you admit it. The Troys don't associate with our kind."

"Damn it. How can you be so thick? You saw her. She was digging right beside me."

"In trousers."

"She's simply willing to do what needs done to survive."

"Even marrying a man she barely knows? They have words for that. Words I won't disgrace myself by using."

"Tread lightly, Aggie. She's my wife for better or worse. I won't tolerate anyone, not even you, disparaging her."

"So, what about Mary?"

"What about her?"

"She still loves you. Are you going to tell me that means nothing to you?"

"Not enough to change my loyalty. I made a promise to Bella, and I will honor it."

"You and your honor! When will you make a choice that's best for you?"

"If I only thought of myself, Aggie, young Sam would have spent the last couple of years in prison and not me."

Agnes broke down into tears. "Oh, Jackie, I know. I know what you've sacrificed for us. That's why I want, no I need, to know you're making choices that will lead you to happiness. I want only the best for you. I don't want you to adopt this woman like some stray dog and miss out on true love."

Bella covered her mouth with her hands trying to block the sobs with a near strangle hold on her airway. If she didn't, they would surely hear her. And she didn't need Jack to pity her anymore than he already did. She fervently prayed they would leave. She had to get out of this place. Had to get away from the truth that she tried to deny. Jack married her out of pity. And the woman he loved still wanted him. He didn't say he didn't love her. How could she keep him for herself when he'd be happier with someone else? She needed to think and this closed stall was not the place for that.

"Pretty nice place you've got here, Jack." His brother-in-law stepped into the barn.

"Place doesn't belong to me. Belongs to a man up north. We're staying here till we get back on our feet."

"We?" Daniel asked.

"Jack *married* that woman," Agnes groaned.

"Well, congratulations, Jack." Daniel gave him a pat on the back.

"Not congratulations, Daniel. Jack is making a big mistake."

"Now, Agnes. I think Jack is…"

"Soft in the head after being in jail," Agnes finished.

"Agnes." Jack's voice rose, his words were clipped. "I've made myself as clear as I can without simply telling you to shut the hell up."

Agnes gasped and sputtered, "Well, little brother, I never. You never. I just…this woman is having nothing but a bad influence on you." Agnes turned and fled the barn sobbing.

"She cares too much for you, Jack. You are her little brother."

Jack sighed. "I know. I don't want to argue about Bella. She's off limits. I'd still be rotting in that hell hole if it weren't for her."

"Jack. I'm sorry." There was a long pause then Daniel took a deep breath and asked, "Was it that bad?"

"It's not something I'd ever wish on someone I loved."

"You know I owe you. If I'd been home…"

"Things worked out as they worked out. I'm not going to wallow in it. What I need Aggie to understand is that Bella heard where I was and she came for me. She finagled and bribed the guard to get my release. You don't know what that means to me."

"I'll talk to her. You know if there's ever anything I can do for you…"

"Are you sure you want to offer that?"

"Of course. Words can't say how grateful I am. I owe you my boy's life. One day you'll have yourself a child and you'll understand. Saving my own life wouldn't mean half as much. This gratitude you feel toward the girl? Well, double it."

"What I'm going to ask could be dangerous and is hardly legal, and I'd feel most at ease if we got it done sooner rather than later; without a soul but us two knowing what I got planned."

"Now's as good a time as any. Samuel joined the Navy and Agnes and I pulled up stakes, thought we might go west. Well, once she verified her little brother was safe." He gave Jack a wink. "So, what is it I can do?"

"I need to get an ax from the house. Then we'll head out yonder field and I can explain."

Bella heard them leave. Boy, she put herself in a pickle. Jack was in her room. She sat half naked in the barn. She crept to the door and waited until Jack came back out of the house with the ax, and he and Daniel disappeared into the meadow. Bella bolted from the barn and ran to the house, slamming the door and thumping up the steps. She tossed herself on her bed and cried. She tried to stop, but she couldn't. She couldn't steel herself against the hollow feeling of defeat, loneliness, and heartbreak. Why couldn't Jack have said he loved her, or even that he could learn to love her? And he never said he didn't love Mary! Her sobs reverberated off her pillow, threatened to rob her of her air. Now the woman had a name. Somehow that made her and his love for her real. She was no longer an idea easily dismissed.

Tessie knocked on her door. Bella couldn't answer, but it didn't matter, Tessie stepped in anyhow. She sat on the bed and stroked Bella's hair and patted her back. "What is it, child?"

Bella composed herself enough to say, "I'm tired."

"Seen you tired before. Never seen tears like this since Henry passed on."

Bella wiped away her tears and rolled over. "I miss him, Tess. I miss him so much. And I want life to be easier, like it was. I'm tired of struggling. So tired of worrying. I am so tired of everything."

"You've just plum exhausted yourself, crazy child. Women weren't meant to work like you do. You're gonna get under those covers and rest yourself." Tessie pulled her close and gave her a big hug. "And I promise you, it's gonna be all right. We've come this far and we'll make it these final miles. I'm going to go get salt and rub down these blisters on your hands. Then I'm going to bring you some dinner and you're going to eat it all. And finally you're going to go to sleep. I'll tend to our guests."

"I can't. It would be disgraceful to be so rude."

"You're gonna rest. I'll make your excuses. Besides, what I've seen of Miss Agnes leaves little worry that she's schooled in manners."

Bella nodded and offered no more argument. The idea of not having to face Agnes tonight was a blessing. She dried her eyes and blew her nose on the hanky Tessie handed her. Tessie smiled with relief and kissed Bella's forehead. "Now, that's a good girl. Thought I'd have to fight with you to get you to rest."

"I am tired," Bella admitted, not mentioning her heart ached.

Chapter 13

Tessie and Manny worked hard to prepare the spare room for their guests. She pulled together her and Manny's twin mattresses and covered them in a clean flannel sheet. It was the best they owned, so she hoped it got cold tonight so their guests didn't burn up. Manny was excited by the prospect of sleeping on Tessie's floor on blankets.

He informed Tessie as he helped unfold a quilt onto the mattresses. "Real warriors sleep on the ground Miss Tess. We'll pretend like we're living in a teepee and hunting bear."

"Well I'm glad you're so excited, little man, 'cause my old bones sure ain't looking forward to it."

Manny laughed. "You ain't old."

"Don't say ain't." Tessie scolded.

"But you just did."

"Well, I'm colored…folks expect it."

"I'm colored too, so I ain't gonna stop."

Tessie rolled her eyes and shook her head. "I'll be darned if you aren't the sassiest."

"That's 'cause I'm a warrior."

"Oh that's right. I keep forgetting."

He gave her a quizzical look. "How do you and Bella keep forgetting I'm injun, but no one else does? You guys blind?"

"You're not 'injun', you're Cherokee. Remember who you are and be proud."

"What tribe you from, Tessie?"

"Well, near as I can remember, I'm from the putting little boys to work on their homework tribe."

"That's a boring tribe. No wonder you're always so cranky."

"Why! I am!" She took the pillow she was stuffing into a case and popped him over the head with it. "You get about doing your homework...then wash up for dinner. And be quiet through the hallway so you don't wake Miss Bella."

Manny looked worried. "Can I check on her?"

"Nope. She's fine. Just needed some extra sleep is all."

"Like when I had a cold."

"Yep, like that."

Manny nodded and left, tip toeing through the hall.

Tessie peaked in on her and then closed the door, satisfied that she could hear the steady breath of sleep. She went to the kitchen and prepared a hearty meal that would have lasted the four of them three days. She wasn't happy about the waste, but she wouldn't disgrace Bella by demonstrating stingy hospitality.

Tessie laid a clean cloth across the paint-chipped table and set a glass filled with spring flowers in the center. She laid out a platter of biscuits, a bowl of white gravy, sweet rolls made from the syrup and bits of prized dried apples, and a crock of coffee. The smell of coffee made Tessie's mouth water and she longed for a cup, but she only used enough of the grounds to make a crock. Bella was raised well and remained mindful to keep small stores of luxuries in case of company.

Tessie called for Mr. Jack and his guests. As they came in and took a seat, Tessie requested to be excused.

"Sit and eat, Tessie."

Tessie's eyes were round. "Oh, no sir, Mr. Jack. I'll be in the pantry should you need anything."

"That's nothing more than a closet. Sit, Tessie. Where's Bella and Manny?"

"Miss Bella is plum exhausted, so I put her to bed. And Mr. Manny has already eaten and is washing up for bed."

Jack tossed his napkin on the table and jumped from his seat. "What's wrong with Bella? I better check on her."

"No. No, sir," Tessie said, grabbing his arm. "You need to eat. She's fine. I tended to her myself. She needs rest. I don't think she's ever worked so hard in her life. You go up now, you'll just wake her."

Jack considered her words, then settled back into his seat. "I guess…if you say so."

Tessie nodded and smiled and headed for the pantry.

Jack shook his head and frowned. "Sit, Tessie. And that's an order."

Tessie shook her head at Jack and clucked her tongue. "That's not fitting, Mr. Jack."

Jack turned to his guests. "Tessie hasn't yet realized she's a free woman."

Daniel laughed. Agnes clucked her tongue pitifully.

"Oh, I know I'm free, Mr. Jack. But I also know what's proper and what's not."

"Don't try to put on airs with me, Tess. I've seen you sit and break bread with Bella since I got here. My family not good enough for you to sit and enjoy a meal with?"

Tessie gasped and looked stunned. "Why, I…Mr. Jack…"

"It's just Jack. Now sit. Eat and relax. My sister and her husband aren't as bad as they seem."

Daniel bobbed his head and chucked again. Agnes's face puckered at the offense.

Tessie pulled a seat away from the table and perched her bottom on the edge of the chair. Jack offered her a plate. Tessie shook her head. "I already ate."

Jack nodded and began filling his plate, passing the food on to Agnes and Daniel. Tessie sat and listened, offering comment only when Jack prodded her. Agnes kept looking at her, though she did make an effort not to.

"Daniel and Agnes live in the new western Virginia. I don't think Agnes has ever come face to face with a black person before, have you Agnes?"

Agnes turned cherry red. "Why, of course I have. What a shameful thing for you to say."

"She just never talked to black folk before," Daniel said.

"Why, I!" she sputtered. "The two of you. You know my church was part of the abolitionist movement. Talk to me like I am some kind of…"

"It's all right, Miss Agnes. I can tell you're good folk." Tessie smiled.

Agnes pressed her lips together. "Thank you, Miss Tessie. If I may call you that?"

"Why of course." Tessie smiled.

Agnes stared at her plate. "Your food's mighty good too."

"Why, thank you, Miss Agnes. I wish we had better to offer you."

Agnes eschewed the idea. "Times like these, I'm ever so grateful to have a hot meal."

"This war has taken a mighty toll." Daniel sighed.

"Yes. And I hear they are NOT even going to hang Robert E. Lee for treason." Agnes shook her head in disbelief. "Even going to give the southerners back their right to vote. Why, they ought to be happy they get to live in this country after what they did to us all."

"Peace and healing comes through forgiveness. Have to quit fighting to get along. I think they're doing the right thing. You know what the Bible says about a house divided," Daniel said.

"If they're to pay their fair share of taxes, they have the right to vote," Jack said as he scraped a piece of biscuit around his plate to get all the gravy.

"Why, with your logic, Jack, you'd even have to let black people and women vote."

Agnes chided.

Jack shrugged. "Seems only fair. Why is anyone less a person than another? As long as they swear to be loyal to the union, they should get to vote."

"Not my business," Tessie said quietly. "But the whole lot of you better watch how you talk in these parts, or you'll all end up hanging from a tree. Not smart to blather on like you are. People are still angry 'bout all they lost. Fathers, brothers, homes…no end to it."

"All the more reason to give the south a voice. If not, the anger will continue to grow, on all sides," Daniel said.

"Seems simpler to simply leave this part of the country than worry about everything you say. Jack, why don't you forget all your crazy notions and come west with me and Daniel? Folks out there aren't so bitter."

"You know my reasons for staying, Agnes."

Agnes made a sound of disgust. "That's a mistake you need to rectify also."

"Agnes," Jack warned.

"Well, a sister has a right to look to protect her little brother. But I'll say nothing more. I suppose I owe you that much."

"No, you owe me more than that. But I know how you can repay me. I need you to let me borrow Daniel for a week or two."

Agnes nearly choked on her food. "You're joking, right?"

Jack grabbed an apple biscuit and shook his head.

"And what am I supposed to do?" Agnes argued.

"You can stay here."

"Oh, no. You cannot be serious."

"It's only for a week or two week, honey." Daniel rubbed her hand. She yanked it away.

"No way. No. Over my dead body."

"This is mighty important to me, sis."

"What could be so important you have to run off and take Daniel with you?"

"I have some business I promised I'd finish for a friend."

"So, I rot here?" She dropped her fork in protest.

"It'll give you time to get to know Bella. You'll see why I married her."

"Will I have to wear trousers and dig holes in mountains?"

"Only if you want to," Jack said with a smile.

"You are totally and completely insane." She shoved her plate away and blinked back tears.

"And it's a good thing he is, Ags, or Samuel might have been stuck in that jail."

"I know what he did for me, Daniel!" Agnes spat. "I didn't say I wouldn't do it. I'm just asking what's to be expected of me."

"Well, I'm glad you're going to be a sport." Daniel grabbed her hand and gripped it gently.

"You're my best sister," Jack said with a wink.

"I'm your only sister." Agnes wiped at her eyes with her napkin. His words made her smile a little despite her sour face.

"We'll leave in the morning," Jack announced.

"The morning!" she repeated.

He nodded. She harrumphed and asked, "Right after services, I assume?"

"No, at the break of dawn."

"And miss Sunday services?"

"It's like the ass in the well, Aggie," Daniel reminded her.

"I don't need a lecture on parables Daniel." Her frown deepened, but she said, "Fine. Fine. Do what you need to do. I guess I'll go alone. Maybe Bella? Miss Tessie?" She looked to Tessie.

Tessie chewed her lip a moment before saying, "Oh no. Neither the missy nor me will grace them with our presence. You can borrow the wagon and take yourself if you want to join the *good* people of Troy."

Aggie looked like she was about to ask more questions, but Jack interrupted, "I'm headed off to bed. Thank you for another fine meal, Tessie. Good night." He kissed Agnes's cheek. "Thanks for being a sport, Aggie. You really are the best sister." Her cheeks turned as red as her husband's hair. Jack patted her head and chuckled, then nodded to Daniel. "See you in the morning."

Jack entered the room quietly. He undressed and eased himself into bed, careful not to wake Bella. As his weight made the mattress sink, her body rolled toward him. He wrapped her in his arms and whispered her name. She didn't answer. He held her tight, tucking her body into his, and burying his face in the soft curve of her neck. His lips grazed the soft skin of her exposed shoulder. "No one will ever hurt you again." Jack squeezed her closer and closed his eyes.

Chapter 14

Bella felt Jack stir. Her eyes stayed closed, but she could feel him staring at her. She could feel his breath against her cheek as he leaned over her. She couldn't bring herself to open her eyes and face him. She lay awake most of the night, struggling over what to do. She felt a little guilty about feigning sleep when he came to bed, about ignoring his whispers of her name, but she knew she couldn't speak to him without tears choking her up. And now she dared not face him, her swollen eyes betraying the tears which rolled silently onto her pillow for most of the night.

Jack brushed her hair away from her cheek and kissed the soft spot behind her ear. Bella's breath caught in her throat.

"You awake, Bell?"

Bella burrowed a bit deeper into her pillow and pulled her blanket up over her shoulders. "Mmm, hmm," she answered, hoping she sounded sleepy.

"Are you all right, Bell?"

Bella nodded.

"You went to bed awful early."

"I was tired."

He sounded gruff. "Agnes say something to you?"

Bella shook her head. "No. Why, I hope she didn't think I was being rude to skip…"

"No, sweetheart, if you need sleep, you better sleep. Tessie said you were worn out. I'm glad she made you rest. You make sure when I'm not around, you listen to her, all right?"

Bella flipped onto her back. "What are you saying Jack? Are you leaving?"

He sighed and touched her cheek. "Just for a while."

The burning in her eyes returned. New tears accentuated the red puffy look from a night of tears. Bella bit her lip to stop it from quivering. He was leaving. Her heart felt like it stopped.

He leaned on a bent arm, looking down over her. He looked worried, seemed to be studying her.

"Where are you going?" Bella asked her heart beating a little faster.

"Daniel knows a guy who needs some help moving some cattle. He and Agnes are pretty much all the family I have left, so I hate to say no."

Bella nodded.

"But I suppose it can wait a while. I don't want to leave you if something is wrong."

Bella's voice was barely above a whisper, "Nothing's wrong."

Jack's eyes narrowed. "Don't lie to me, Bell. You've been crying."

"It's…it's just…I sometimes get down. I think about my dad and Noah, and the way life used to be." She sighed hard at her lie. "It's simply overwhelming sometimes."

Jack pulled her close. "Are you sure that's all?"

"That's all? Gosh, Jack, in a matter of a few years, I've lost almost everything."

"You're right." He kissed her forehead. "I'm sorry, sweetie. You've been so strong, so positive, I never thought of you being sad."

"Well, I'm not normally." She looked up at him innocently. "I guess I was worn out."

Jack frowned and shook his head. "I should never have let you dig all day. That's no work for a lady."

Bella groaned inwardly. She didn't mean to make him feel even sorrier for her. What kind of a ninny was she? "It's not that Jack. It's more like a monthly thing."

Jack looked confused then as her words made sense, he blushed and nodded. "I see. Well, then I won't trouble you any further. You rest, all right? While I'm gone, you take it easy."

"Where will you be?" Maybe he wanted to go see Mary. See if he would rather be with her. Bella felt her eyes burn with unshed tears. She blinked them away, laying back on her pillow and closing her eyes again.

"North. I'm not certain as to where. But when I get back, I'll be able to relax knowing all my debts are paid." He kissed her forehead. "We're doing it, Bell. We're buildin' the future we talked about. We'll have the cellar done by harvest time. Daniel and I fixed a corral yesterday, so now Nero can pasture and run. He'll shine within a month and we'll be able to stud him out for a fee. Use that money to buy the pigs, so we have meat come winter. Daniel's going to help me with the timber, so we'll have a bit of money put back." He stroked her cheek. "It's all working out. Together we'll have the best future."

She opened her eyes and smiled up at him. If she didn't know he loved someone else, she'd almost believe he was excited about spending their life together. "So Daniel asked you for the favor? Is that why they came? So he knew you were out of jail?"

"Oh," he stuttered, "well, he uh, didn't of course know I was out. This is, I suppose, something he was going to do on his own, but since I can help, I may as well."

"I see." Bella bit her lip. She knew she wasn't brilliant, but even she could see he was lying. It had to be Mary. Was he going to go say good-bye to her; would it break his heart because he foolishly married her? Bella opened her mouth to tell him he was free, but her mind wouldn't let her speak. One thought preoccupied her mind…Mary left him and no longer deserved him. She wrestled with her thoughts, then took a deep breath and said, "Jack?"

"Yeah?"

Tell him he's free to choose. But how could she say that? Just the thought of letting him go left her feeling totally hollow and hopeless. Instead of all the noble words she knew she should say, she simply said, "Please be safe."

He smiled and wrapped her up squeezing her body to his. "I'll be fine. We have a future to plan, right? Everything's gonna be fine, sweetness. I promise you that."

Bella nodded. She disliked herself for taking advantage of such a wonderful man. She gripped him harder.

"Give me a kiss, Isabella Byron, one that'll sustain me till I get back."

Bella gave him a nervous peck on the lips.

"Ahh, I need more than that." He gave her a mischievous grin and locked her against him for a bold, searching kiss. His body was hard against hers causing her body to heat up, melt, and become ever so pliable. Jack pulled away and smiled. He pushed the blanket down below her hips. His fingers traced the curve of her waist, across her belly, cupping a breast. "Now there's a memory to help me brave the cold nights."

"Jack." Bella was shocked.

"Good thing I'll be gone a while. If not, I might not be able to keep my promise of not making love to you."

"Really? It means that much?"

He closed his eyes and nuzzled her ear. "More than you'll ever imagine."

"Even though…you know…I've been shamed?"

Jack's face darkened, his voice was harsh. "I don't want to hear that. And I sure as hell don't want you thinking that. You're my wife, and no one speaks wrong of anything that's mine. Understand?"

Bella nodded.

Jack took a deep breath. He cradled her face in his hands as if he had more to say, but in the end, he grimaced and growled. "Now you're going to have to kiss me again. Make up for upsetting me."

Bella giggled in spite of her mood. He didn't fake hurt very well, but she apologized and gave him a proper kiss, which he quickly turned into a devouring that left her breathless. He kissed her again, then again, then with a long sigh he said, "Damn, but leaving kills me." He tucked the blanket close around her. "You stay here and rest. I want you happy when I get back."

"I'll be happy." She promised, her worries gone for the moment, wiped clean from his embrace.

He said good-bye, tipping his hat at her from the doorway as he paused, looking her over as if he'd never see her again.

Chapter 15

Bella hopped out of bed and watched from her window as Jack and Daniel left in the pre-dawn glow in Daniel's wagon. She waved good-bye, though she knew they couldn't see her in the darkened house, even when Jack took one last look over his shoulder before the wagon rounded the bend in the road. Bella dressed and headed downstairs. She was halfway down when she remembered — with Jack and Daniel gone, they were left alone with Agnes. Bella took a moment to pray for patience and the courage to face the woman who shattered her happy dream.

Pancakes sizzled on the griddle. Tessie offered her a smile as she came in the kitchen. Manny sat at the table, his face radiant from the promise of eating something other than a biscuit for breakfast. This week had been a smorgasbord compared to the winter.

"Morning, Miss Bella." Manny wiggled in excitement. "We're having pancakes."

"Mmm, pancakes? Wow, we're living like kings, huh, Manny?"

"Oh, yeah."

Bella ruffled the boy's hair. "Well, you wait till the garden is harvested and the fruit trees and berries will be ready to be picked and we'll have fresh fruit and pies. Won't it be great to have a fresh apple pie?"

The boy's eyes sparkled. "Oh, yes, Miss Bella. That will be sooo good. Do you think my mom will be back in time to have pies?"

Bella bit her lip and sat down next to Manny so she could look him in the eye. "I know Noah won't stop looking till he finds her. And I know she loves you, so when she can, she'll be back."

"I don't know how you can say a mother loves her child, but willingly abandoned him." Agnes spat from the door. "I don't think you should lie to the child. If his mother left him, she'll probably not be back. My church runs an orphanage and I've seen a mighty lot of it. People simply walking away and leaving kids to fend for themselves." She sat herself at the table and smoothed her skirt over her beefy legs. "It's despicable."

"Manny's mother didn't abandon him. She left him in our care. She has some things to work out. Then she'll be back." Bella shot Agnes a glaring look.

Tessie shook her head and tried to hide a frown. "Here's your pancakes, child." She handed him a plate of golden brown cakes and a crock of warmed syrup. Manny dug in and filled his mouth with food. He chewed and swallowed. He grinned at Bella. "Wait till Mr. Jack tastes these. He brags about getting biscuits without weevils? He'll love these."

"Mr. Jack had to go away on some business," Bella answered gently.

Manny's face fell. He dropped his fork on his plate. "Will he be back?"

"Oh, yes," Bella promised.

Agnes snorted. Bella pretended not to hear her. She took Manny's hand. "Mr. Jack left because he had some work to finish. He promised me this morning he'd be back in two weeks."

"He said two weeks?" Manny asked picking up his fork and poking at his pancakes.

"Yes, he did. As a matter of fact, he said, 'when I get back, I'm going to teach Manny to fish so he can earn his keep.'"

Manny's face brightened. "Did he really?"

Bella nodded, feeling very little guilt for her fib. She hadn't thought of how attached Manny had become in such a short period of time. She realized having Jack around was comforting to this little warrior as much as herself. She gave Manny a squeeze and a kiss, then ordered him to eat so he could do his Bible lesson.

"It's Sunday. Won't the child be going to Sunday service?"

Bella blushed and looked to Tessie for support, but Tessie dropped her eyes to the floor. Bella cleared her throat and answered honestly. "We worship at home."

"Well, that's just ridiculous. And you should be ashamed of yourself. Why, this young man needs to be in church. Why, you can tell he's a heathen."

"Manny is a little boy who probably knows his scripture better than any child penned up in Sunday school. And, sadly, it's Christians like yourself who make it uncomfortable for people like myself, Tessie, and Manny to go into a church."

"Why, I never. I can't believe you would be so insulting to a guest. I don't know what got into my brother to marry the likes of you."

"Well, that seems to be your brother's business, not yours." Bella was on her feet, her hands gripped protectively on Manny's shoulders.

"Maybe taking some time away will help him wake up. Make him understand that he isn't beholden to you. Pity and lust are no basis for a real marriage. My brother is a good man. He deserves a good woman. He deserves to be with the woman he loves. You should be ashamed of yourself."

Bella had no argument. Agnes's words hit too close to home. She swallowed hard trying to remove the lump from her throat. She nodded her head and spoke softly. "Seems you have some strong opinions. And I'll not take any offense since you obviously love your brother. But," Bella said and stared at the woman until she made her flinch. "Leave Manny out of anything you have to complain about."

"Why, of course. For that I do apologize."

"And if you would like to go to Sunday service, I suppose the cordial thing for me to do, is to drive you there."

"I can walk."

"No you can't. It's five miles and I won't have you blaming blistered feet on my lack of hospitality."

"I apologize for my rudeness." Agnes studied her hands. "I would appreciate a ride. I never miss a service."

"No apology needed, but you better get ready. Pastor Scott always starts on time."

Agnes turned and left. Bella sent Manny after his Bible, and then she sighed as she sat down to her own plate of pancakes. Tessie snickered. "Hate for her to miss a service. She might lose some of her Christian love."

Bella laughed and smiled, though her heart broke. She knew Agnes spoke the truth. Jack did deserve better.

As Bella drove Agnes to town, she wondered at the beauty of the day. The sun shined off the dewy grass. Flowering trees lined the road and wild blooms grew along the banks. The song of morning was sweet to her ears on this sour day. Bella took a deep breath of the fresh air and wondered how, on such a glorious morning, could her world be in such a terrible state? Yesterday, she was certain her life was steadying, that happiness was within her grasp. Now look where she was.

Bella sighed and tried to keep her thoughts from her troubles. She couldn't think of these things as she traveled through the town, heaven forbid she burst into tears in front of the vipers. Instead, as they came into the mile-long town, Bella pointed out the obvious sights, the mercantile, the post office, the saloon, the wheelright, the school, and beyond a short grove of pines the local church. Bella pulled up and told Agnes as she got out, "I'll be waiting out here."

Agnes's lips were pursed. "Are you certain you don't want to come?"

"Absolutely certain." Bella felt the color creep up her neck.

"Too bad." She turned, adding as she walked away. "It might have redeemed you."

"I'll leave my redemption to God Himself," Bella mumbled turning her horses toward the grove. The horses nibbled the tender grass, and Bella got out and sat against a tree.

Agnes settled herself in a back pew. The room was small, the pews nothing more than crude pine benches. The walls were painted a pristine white. The cross on the front wall was sanded smooth and glowed with varnish. The songs were unfamiliar to her. She was normally a Methodist, not a Baptist. But she sat and listened, fervently praying for God to speak some sense to her little brother.

Jack was indentured to the East India Company as a cabin boy at the tender age of twelve. Their father worked the docks where he picked up a cough that turned into a wasting consumption. He thought he needed some time to heal, so he talked Jack into signing into a temporary service, so their father could have enough money to get the family through until he could get back to work. Their father died two months after Jack left.

Jack signed onto permanent service with Captain Newsome, so he could send the money home to their mum. When he was fifteen, he calmed an absurdly priced Arabian horse that was being shipped to Henry Troy. The horse was delivered from Italy injury free. This so impressed the planter that he bought Jack's service from the company and put him in charge of his stables.

Then, of course, he sacrificed years of his life in jail for her family. And now he was sacrificing the rest of it to Bella. At some point in time, her brother needed to think of himself first. Agnes looked out the window. In the green of the trees, she could see the tip of Nero's ears. If only Bella were a God-fearing woman, she might be able to approve of the union, but what kind of woman refused to step foot in God's house? Agnes shook her head.

Mary, on the other hand, was as devout as they came. And Agnes knew Jack would never approve, but she asked Daniel to be sure Jack spoke with Mary while they were traipsing around the country with their *business*. Agnes sighed. Jack had himself a smal plot of land, a home, and a wedding a few months away when he was arrested. Now he was once again working borrowed land with his soul owned by a Troy. It was her fault that her brother was reduced to this.

Services over, the minister sent the flock out to face the world with a blessing. Agnes was barely out of her seat when two friendly women offered their hands in greeting.

"Good morning," a lady in a sober brown dress said.

"We haven't seen you here before," offered another lady in subdued blue.

"I'm visiting." Agnes smiled and offered her hand. "I'm Agnes Clemons."

They made some small talk as they made their way to the door. Outside, Agnes looked toward Bella. Bella waved and jumped to her feet to prepare the horse.

"Oh, don't tell me you know Bella Stanley?" the woman in blue admonished. Both women gasped. "Why, you realize she is divorced?"

Agnes's jaw dropped. Divorced? An adulterer and a harlot? Her heart thudded.

"Divorced?" Agnes's voice was barely above a whisper.

"Yes, she ran her husband off a year ago and no one's seen him since."

"Are you certain he ran off?" Agnes supposed it wasn't Bella's fault if her husband abandoned her.

"Well, I don't know. You know, Lucy." The woman in blue turned to the woman in brown. "What if Charles didn't run away? What if she killed him?" Both gasped and covered their mouths. "No one ever really thought her capable of murder, but have you heard? The brazen woman went and shacked up with a convict. Maybe she had him murder her husband. Now, I've seen him around town and I can assure you, he looks fully capable of murder."

"Well, you know Midge, I heard she had an arrangement with Bert for credit in the store, and her convict threatened to kill him over it. Almost strangled him. Some thanks Bert gets for his charity."

Agnes's head spun as she tried to keep up. It took her a few minutes to realize the criminal was her brother. "She's not living with a murderer," Agnes huffed.

"Yes, ma'am, she is. He murdered a Yankee."

"Well...if it was a Yankee..." Midge said.

"But still it was murder," Lucy added, her voice urgent.

Agnes was about to defend her brother, but her voice was lost. Lost in total shock. Her brother was being labeled a criminal?

Agnes only half heard them chatter on about Bella and Jack's marriage not being recognized by the church because of Bella's divorce and her, liaison with a black man. Agnes's eyes were round with total disbelief. She excused herself from her new acquaintances and walked to the wagon in a near trance.

"Enjoy yourself?" Bella asked.

"It was..." Agnes seated herself and fanned her perspiring face. "It was enlightening."

Bella snapped the reins and began their flight from town. "I'm sure you learned all about my history?"

"What makes you say that?" Agnes couldn't look her in the eyes. "Well, Midge and Lucy are not two of my biggest fans. My mother was quite the debutante in her day and they have always had a special loathing for her. So, of course, my family's fall from grace is one of their greatest pleasures."

"They did..." Agnes looked to the side of the road, her hand on her fluttering heart. "They told me you were divorced."

"That's true. My husband was a horrible man, though I'll leave his final judgment to God."

"They also said you had a bit of a tryst with a..."

"With a black man. That's true too. I ran away at the age of sixteen with one of my parent's slaves."

Agnes's head jerked around to face Bella so quickly Bella thought she heard her neck snap. Bella explained, "Noah is my brother. That's my father's shame, not mine. My mother would have killed him if I hadn't gotten him to safety. I took

156

him to a place in New York along the Great Lakes where he could be free, or at least close enough to the Canadian border if he ever needed to escape."

"Your brother is black?"

Bella nodded. "He's Tessie's boy. Don't be shocked. Happens a lot. The good folk don't speak of it. But regardless of our skin, we share the same blood and I wasn't going to let my brother die."

"Well then, why don't you tell them that?"

"Because I don't care about people like Lucy and Midge. I don't need busy body, pretend do-gooders in my life. The people who know me well enough probably have a good idea that Noah is my family."

"They said Jack was a murderer." Agnes's indignation was thick.

"Is he?" Bella asked her voice lowered.

"You got him out of jail and you don't even know what he was in for?"

"I trust whatever he did, he did for a good reason."

"How can you trust a man under your roof and not know whether or not he's violent?"

Bella shrugged. "It's Jack. I've always trusted Jack. So, did he murder someone?"

"Of course not!"

"Then how did he wind up in jail?"

"You didn't even ask?"

Bella shrugged. Agnes shook her head. "My lands girl, are you daft? And marrying him no less."

"But you said yourself, he wasn't in for murder."

"It was attempted murder!"

"Oh my." Bella breathed. "What could lead Jack to that?"

"Some Union soldiers were bullying my boy Samuel. They had him all fired up and then they told him they were

157

going to steal…well they called it commandeering our…pig…and Sam fought with one of them. And well, during the scuffle, Sam knocked him in the head with a shovel. When the man came to, Jack said *he* clunked him from behind. And Jack was arrested and not Sam."

Bella smiled "That sounds like Jack." She shrugged as she said, "See? I told you whatever he did? He did for good reason."

"And now everyone is calling him a murderer. Land sakes, they even accused him of killing your husband!"

Bella's mouth dropped open. She pulled up on the reins and turned to Agnes. "They what?"

"They say he probably killed your husband."

"Oh my." Bella felt cold and her hands trembled. "I think you're right. Jack's made an awful mistake in marrying me."

"Are you telling me you believe those wagging tongues about my Jack?"

"Oh please. Mrs. Clemons, I have loved Jack since I was a girl. I've never admitted that to anyone, not even myself. But that's the only way to define what I feel for him. I love him for his strength, his honesty, his dependability. Why there's nothing about him I'm not plum crazy about. But I suddenly realize all those things I love most about him are the exact things that are going to put him in a situation that may not be best for him. The people in this town never would have paid any attention to Jack's past were he not connected to me. I bring him shame. And I can't stand that. I don't want to hurt him." Bella's voice cracked, but she straightened her shoulders and took a deep breath. "I justified marrying Jack, though he loves another, because I told myself that she walked away from him while he was in jail. And I would never have done that. But I can't keep using that as an excuse to be selfish."

"What do you mean, 'she walked away?'"

"Jack told me she broke off their engagement because she didn't want to wait five years to get married."

"Well," Agnes let out a sigh. "He never told me that when I visited him."

Bella shrugged. "I don't know. Maybe he lied to me. Maybe he was trying to make me feel better, since I had already begged him to stay with me."

"But then come to think of it, she never did visit him."

"Well, none of that matters." Bella nearly choked on her words. She took up the reins and urged Nero forward. Neither said another word until they got home.

As Bella brought the wagon into the barn lot, she informed Agnes, "I'm going to leave before Jack gets home. Tell him I changed my mind. I don't want to be married anymore."

Bella jumped down and began unhitching Nero stroking the horse's sides, combing her fingers through his hair. Agnes dismounted and began to walk away, but stopped and turned to Bella. She paused a few moments, shifting from foot to foot, hands wringing.

"I can't let you leave Jack without talking to him."

"Why not? You'll be doing him a favor. He's your brother you know, you should look out for him."

"I know. I just don't know what's truly best for him." Agnes blotted the tears from her eyes.

"Well I do." Bella stroked Nero's firm neck. "Jack's too good for the likes of me. He shouldn't have to pay the price for my choices. And he will. If people start thinking he killed Charles and no Charles can be found. He could go back to jail or worse."

"But you seem to make him happy."

"He's grateful to be out of jail. Pity and gratitude can't replace love."

"I agree, but I just don't know anymore."

"Well, I do and I'm not arguing about this." Bella assumed Agnes would leave, but she stayed. Bella sighed and wished she would go so she could feel free to cry. Several long awkward minutes passed. Agnes still made no move to leave. Instead she stood next to Bella and patted Nero's side. "Jack loved working on your plantation. He was so happy there. He loved the horses. Said Mr. Troy had the finest eye for horse flesh."

"Hah! Daddy was good, but Jack was the best. Nero's father was the most high-spirited Arabian my father ever bought. Why, he was so full of vinegar that when he was brought here from Italy..."

"And that's why he hired Jack. Jack was so pleased to be off that boat. Truth be told, I think the sea scared him to death."

"That horse won the Phoenix Stakes on my father's first entry into the Kentucky Derby. That meant so much to Daddy." Bella ran her hand along Nero's back. "And look at old Nero here. To me he looks skinny and worn out; to Jack he's still a prize stallion. No. Nobody compares to Jack. He's wiser than any man I've ever known. And gentler. But brave enough to take on a wild Arabian. He truly is special, Agnes. I have to admit, it nearly broke my heart when he left Bella's Point. I was always so excited to run down to the stables, and then one day I went and he was gone."

"You really do love him."

"I love him enough to know what's best for him. Be truthful, Agnes, all the rumors about me, all the things I've done wrong, Jack will suffer humiliation for it. He doesn't deserve that."

Agnes shook her head. She no longer tried to hide her tears. They slid down her cheeks unchecked.

Bella took a deep breath and let it out slowly. "So, this Mary. She will love Jack and treat him well?"

Agnes shrugged. "I always thought she would. She comes from a very respectable family."

"That doesn't mean much to me. The Troy's were about as respectable as a family could get, and look at the daughter it produced."

Agnes blew her nose and took a breath to calm her tears. "I suppose you're not so bad. I can see many reasons why my brother married you. It was wrong of me not to give you two my blessing. I will…"

"I'm not changing my mind. I mean what I've said…I'm not staying married to Jack." Bella turned and walked away. She led Nero into the paddock and gave his haunches a firm pat. She watched the horse as he grazed on the green grass and remembered the hundreds of times she would lean against a fence and watch Jack work the horses. She brushed away a tear and latched the gate. She returned to Agnes and gave her a weak smile.

Agnes grabbed her arm. "You can't possibly be planning to divorce again?"

"No. Our marriage isn't legal yet. The papers haven't been filed."

"But in God's eyes…"

"Still not binding. When Jack gets home, tell him I changed my mind and you don't know where I went. Take him home….take him to Mary."

Bella looked to the sky, damn if it wasn't a pretty day. Just didn't seem right. It should definitely rain. Then she could go inside and curl up in bed and sleep this day away. "He deserves a wife without shame." Bella barely got the words out, her throat burned, a lump formed that threatened to shut off her breath. "Now," she cleared her throat, "you go on in the house and get out of the sun. I have some books in the parlor if you'd like something to read. I have some work I should get done."

"On the Sabbath?" Agnes gasped.

Bella sighed. "I forgot. Well, I think I'll go for a walk."

"I'll..."

"Please, Agnes, I'm not trying to be rude. I'd really rather be alone."

Chapter 16

Bella spent the next six days alone. She sat at dinner and made small talk, she finished her chores and helped Manny with homework, but only the shell of Bella was truly there. Her heart and soul packed its bag and left long before her body.

The day she chose to leave, she walked Manny to school, explained she'd be back in two weeks, and assured him she would return with a surprise for him.

"A puppy?" Manny asked with big round eyes.

Bella shrugged and feigned a shocked look that he was so clever and said, "Why, I wouldn't tell you what your surprise is?"

"It is a puppy!" He grinned from ear to ear. "But Miss Bell, why can't you get one in Troy?"

"Well, I'm not saying I am, but if I were, I would want to get a very special puppy."

He looked as if that made perfect sense. He gave Bella a hug, then went on toward the school. He turned half way there and said, "But hurry, Miss Bell. I'm going to miss you."

She waved good-bye and walked on into town. She didn't tell anyone her plans, not even Tessie. She couldn't trust them not to tell Jack. She told Agnes to tell Jack she was gone and it was over.

She went to Maggie's Boardinghouse. Like her sister, Miss Jobe, Maggie never married. Miss Jobe seemed committed to teaching. Bella never recalled her having a beau. She was always a bit too skinny, her face a bit too pinched, and she had a severe personality and a sharp mind. Just the kind of woman Bella's mother told her never caught a man.

Maggie on the other hand was prettier than her sister with soft curves and a friendly face. Bella always assumed Maggie would marry, but she had to be approaching thirty by now, so her chances were slim. But then considering the full joys of marriage, Bella decided Maggie's mind was probably as sharp as her sister's.

She walked through the dark hall of the house looking for her. The place was immaculate. Sparsely furnished but tastefully decorated. Bella felt hopeful that she could survive as a single woman. Maggie did it.

But then Maggie was an excellent cook. Bella frowned and kept walking through the house toward the kitchen. She called her name.

"I'm out here," Maggie's voice answered from the porch.

She found her sitting in a rocking chair reading a book. Maggie laid the book in her lap and smiled up at Bella. "Afternoon, Bella. Lydia told me you might be stopping by; to arrange for Manny to come play with Jada? You were looking to find him some friends, right? And Jada may be colored, but she is his age."

Bella wrung her hands. "Honestly, I had forgotten all about talking to Miss Jobe, but yes, I would like Manny to have some friends.

Maggie removed her spectacles and set them and her book on the floor. "Please. Sit." She indicated the twin rocker on the porch.

Bella sat. "I," she started and blushed, not sure how to ask a near stranger for help, "I need a place to stay. And I don't have any money, but I'm willing to work, and I don't need a room, maybe a corner in the pantry? Or if you have a store room?"

Maggie's brow furrowed. "Are you in trouble, Bella?"

She shook her head no. "Not really. I'm trying to undue a mistake. And I know my reputation around here is in shambles, and I don't want to bring any shame to your establishment, but I really don't know what else to do."

"I don't give a fig for public sentiment. I know I am laughed at for taking in an orphaned darkie, for teaching her to read and not just scrub floors. I'm sorely tired of people and their opinions! So, you need a place to stay, I have rooms."

"Well, I wouldn't want anyone to know I'm here."

"That so?"

Bella nodded. "No one. Even if they ask."

"Are you in trouble with the law?"

"No. It's completely personal."

"So you want me to hide you somewhere in the house?"

Bella nodded.

"Ah, Bella. I will gladly help you." She turned in her rocker and studied Bella for a moment. She sighed and asked, "But, I can't help but ask, why haven't you ever left this damnable town?"

"Noah. And Wendy. I guess Manny. And Tessie." Bella shrugged and studied her hands. "Though sometimes I think they'd be better off without me."

165

"Hogwash. I'm going to get us an iced tea." Maggie went into the kitchen and yelled through the screen door, "and I'm bringing you out some barbeque. My lands you're thin as a rail."

Maggie kept up the small talk as she made Bella a plate and brought it out to the porch. "You probably *should* stay here a while...let me fatten you up a bit." Maggie winked at her.

"This really is too kind of you." Bella looked at the plate. Her stomach growled. Even as sad as her life was, her mouth watered.

"You're doing me a favor. It's a new recipe and I need a taster to let me know if I should put it on the menu."

Bella nodded and took a bite. She closed her eyes and let out a moan. She barely swallowed it all before she opened her eyes and said, "It's perfect. Absolutely perfect."

"Not too much vinegar?"

Bella shook her head no. She swallowed and wiped the corner of her mouth with her napkin. "Don't tell Tessie, but this beats hers. But oh my, I'd get flogged for saying that."

Maggie laughed. "You're secret's safe with me."

Bella nodded and continued to eat. Then she took a swig of the chilled tea...so sweet she thought she might have died and gone to Heaven.

Maggie rocked in her rocker. She gave Bella a wide grin and said, "Charles Stanley courted me, did you know that?"

Bella's cheeks turned blood red. "Miss Jobe mentioned it."

"But my daddy had the good sense to run him off our farm with a shotgun."

Bella set her napkin on her empty plate. Tears clouded her vision. "I'd have to say your daddy was a wise man."

"Yes he was. I probably missed my opportunity to marry and have kids because I felt it was my duty to care for Daddy when he got crippled, but it was the right thing to do. Lydia wanted to so much to be a teacher and I didn't have the heart to make her forget her dreams. And I've always believed that if you do the right thing, in the end you will be rewarded."

"You're a good woman, Maggie. There's plenty of men..."

Maggie laughed. "Hardly any men left and you know it. The half that's left from this war are too old, too young, or too married already. No, I'll accept what I have and be grateful." She rolled her head on the back of the rocker. "So, tell me, any good come from any of your good deeds?"

"I've done as many things wrong as I have right."

"Well, I'll be honest, I can't help but thinking you staying here with me may be another good deed gone wrong."

"No, it's the right thing to do."

"Really? You and Tessie have a falling out?" Maggie asked and Bella shook her head. "Certainly it's not little Manny you're running from?" Bella snickered at the thought. Maggie sighed, "So, that leaves Jack. I heard he left town, but I assumed he'd be back. If you're hiding from him, then I think you'll regret it. I went to school with Jack. He's a good man."

"It's complicated." Bella looked to the sky as the clouds passed overhead. "I need a few days to think about what I should do with my life. A few days where no one knows where I am, so I can think in peace."

Maggie nodded. "Lydia asked me about Jada after she talked to nearly every parent in that school. She wanted to find a little boy Manny could have adventures with, but she said it appears people won't to let their kids play with a half breed who's being raised by a divorcee who runs away with a black men, then marries a convict."

Bella's shoulders sagged. She swallowed the lump in her throat. "I figured as much."

Maggie reached out and grabbed her hand. She held it tight. "So you understand how people are?"

Bella nodded.

"And you know staying in this town is like fording a raging stream? Now, I would never turn you away, Bella, but what you really need to do is get out. Go with Jack on up north. The talk in town is growing worse and worse as each day passes. I don't want to see you get hurt. I know what happened to Wendy. And I fear...oh why not be honest? I'm shocked it hasn't happened to you. You're a beautiful woman and any fool can see your time is running out. Especially now."

"Why now?"

"Jack's gone. And from what you're telling me, he won't be back."

Bella shrugged.

"Then you're totally unprotected and that's dangerous." Maggie leaned closer and grabbed Bella's arm. "Listen to me. Even if nothing comes of the rumors and chatter, you still don't deserve to be treated like a leper your whole life. And I don't see your standing changing in this town, bar a miracle. I have an aunt who lives in New York. I can give you a letter to take to her. She'll help you, at least offer you shelter until you can find a place to work. Take Tessie and Manny and get the hell out of here."

"You would do that for me?" Bella whispered. "That's ever so thoughtful, but I can't...if Noah comes back and we're gone."

"I'll keep an eye out, tell him where to find you guys. I won't let him lose touch. And if there's anyone you don't want to find you, well then, my lips will be sealed."

Bella thought the plan over. It could work. She could get out of here and Noah would still be able to find them. And Jack wouldn't. She sobbed. Maggie handed her a handkerchief and patted her back. "Thank you." She managed through her tears.

"So, what shall I do? Show you to a room or write the letter?"

Bella took a deep, shuttering breath and said, "Write the letter and I'll go explain to Tessie."

Agnes sat with Manny on her lap as she rocked on the back porch. She entertained him with stories from the Bible. Manny was familiar with the stories, but Agnes had such a wonderful gift for voices and exaggeration, the child was awed. "Tell me the one about Moses and the pharaoh."

Agnes smiled and started, "Well, you see his place as ruler would be in trouble if…" Agnes's story was interrupted by raised voices coming from the front yard. "You wait here," Agnes ordered Manny gently. "I'll be right back."

She pulled a candy from her pocket and gave it to him, brushing his bangs away from his eyes. "That's for assuming you'll mind me."

Manny nodded, his eyes wide with delight.

Agnes slipped into the house. She found Tessie trying to shove the front door closed, but two men pushed it open against her. Agnes let out a scream and looked around the room for a weapon. The near-empty room held nothing useful. Agnes lunged at the door, "Who is it, Tess?"

"Couple of town folk looking for Miss Bella."

Agnes leaned her back against the door. The added force held them back for a moment, but she felt her muscles growing weak against the pressure of two grown men.

"Why?" Agnes asked.

"Say they want to look around. Say she killed Mr. Stanley."

"Oh, my." Agnes's eyes were huge with shock. "Why would they say that?

"Say she's hooked herself up with a murderer and think she had him kill her husband. And now that man is gone too."

"Jack? They're still calling my brother a murderer?"

Tessie nodded. Agnes stood up straight as she ordered, "Move." She grabbed the door handle and yanked it open so quickly Tessie had to jump backward to keep from being trodden upon by tumbling men. Agnes planted her hands on her hips and locked eyes with the man closest to her. "Might I ask what this is all about?"

"We're here on official business. I'm Deputy Sands and this is Deputy Wills. We need to talk to Bella."

"I assume you have a search warrant?"

"We just want to ask Bella some questions," Sands said.

"But without a warrant, you're not here as an arm of the law, but mob rule," Agnes said.

"Look, lady, I been a deputy in this county for twenty years. I have a right to question suspects, without permission."

Agnes clucked her tongue. "Why I do believe you are sorely mistaken. Wearing a star doesn't give you the right to force your way into a woman's home without a warrant. And I presume if you had one, you'd have shown it. Why are we still under martial law? You working for the Yankees?"

He looked grim. "This don't have nothin' to do with you. We just have a few questions for Bella. People are talking. Some say she has a fresh grave in her family's cemetery and there ain't no death certificate to match. Some eager folks want to visit with her personal like, we're only here to figure things out before people get too hasty."

"Since when does this town have so much love for Charles Stanley anyhow?" Tessie asked.

"That seems an odd question, Tess. A human being is a human being. No one has the right to do away with him just 'cause no one likes him. Laws have to be followed."

"Unless you're dealing with a woman? Barging in here, making accusations. That ain't how a real officer of the law acts." Tessie glared at him.

"You sure gettin' a sassy mouth on you, Tess. I suggest you remember who the hell it is you're talking to."

Tessie eyes flashed anger, but her head dropped in submission. "I'm sorry Mr. Sands. You know how I get when I thinks people are mistreatin' my miss. I been her mammy since she was but a minute old."

"I understand, and I honestly don't aim to hurt Miss Bella. I just need to know what's in that grave."

"What grave?" Bella asked stepping onto the porch.

Deputy Sands and Will, turned their attention to Bella. "You have a new grave in your family's cemetery. Who's buried there, Bella?"

Bella's voice was barely above a whisper, "My son."

"What'd you say, Bella, speak up," Sands ordered.

"My son," she said a bit louder. "My son is buried there."

"What son, Bella? Your son died five years ago."

"No. Charles lied. Truth is Henry wasn't quite right, and Charles was ashamed of him. He told everyone he died, but he lived here with Tessie and Noah."

Mr. Sands looked at Tessie; she nodded.

"Now come on, Bella," Will said with a chuckle. "I know Charles could be a hard man, but to go so far as that?" He shook his head and spit on the porch. "And ain't no one in town going to buy that either."

"Well, that's the truth. You'll have to believe me."

"No, we don't have to believe you. Simplest way to find out who's there is to dig up the grave." Will's eyes were cold. Bella's face turned white as a pale moon in a darkened sky.

"You wouldn't…" She found it hard to breathe.

"Will's got a point. Seems like it's the only thing that'll solve the mystery," Sands said.

"Leave my baby alone," Bella hissed. She balled her hand into a fist and shook it at Sands. "Or I will…"

"Or you'll do what, Bella? We're the law here." He pointed to Will. They both sneered at Bella.

Bella launched herself at Sands's chest, fists flying. She got one good hit in before he grabbed her arm and twisted it behind her back. He gave it a yank and warned her, "Settle yourself down, Bella."

"Go to hell!"

"You sure do have a hot temper." Sands laughed and looked at Will. "You know what they say about hot-tempered women." Will chuckled and nodded.

"Leave my baby alone! Let him rest in peace, you bastard," Bella shouted, her voice raking from her throat.

Sands pulled her body close to his, her arm still twisted behind her. She panted and her breasts heaved against his chest. He looked down at her and grinned. "Seems that passion could be better spent, Bella. You could be friendly and have some friends in this town, right, Will?"

Will snorted and ran his hand up her thigh. "Easier to sort things out when everyone's friendly."

"So, what do you say, Bella? Want to work this out friendly like?" His head bobbed low, his lips grazed her cheek searching out her mouth. Bella tried to break free, but he snaked an arm around her waist and pulled her body tight to his. With one hand behind her head, he held her, his lips descending in sloppy, wet pressure. She could barely move or back away, so she bared her teeth and bit him, her mouth filling with the warm, iron taste of blood. He let go of her, but before she could flee, he struck her with the back of his hand. The blow knocked her off balance, and she fell to the porch floor. Her ear rang, and she wiped at her mouth. Her blood mixed with his. She hardly gained her composure, when he grabbed her by the arms, and yanked her up, shaking her until her teeth rattled. Tessie stepped forward, but Agnes pulled her back.

"Is this how the sheriff treats a lady around here, Mr. Sands?" Agnes asked, her voice quivering ever so slightly.

"Ladies and murdering whores are two different things." He squeezed Bella's arms until she cried out in pain. He pressed his nose against hers. "You should have done this the easy way, Bella. It's not like you're the respectable little debutante anymore. Spread your legs for decent men like you do for bucks and criminals and your life could be easier."

Bella couldn't think to speak. She stopped twisting because he only squeezed her tighter when she fought. And he was a big man. Her hands were going numb from his grip. Tears fell from her eyes. He eased the tension. "Now, I think you better come with me. We have to get to the bottom of this."

Bella grabbed his arm. "Please, leave the grave alone. I swear to you, it's my baby boy."

"You're word ain't good enough. We shoulda checked when Charles disappeared," Sands said.

"What if I told you I did kill him? What if I told you I could show you his grave, would you leave my baby alone?"

"Now, Miss Bella! How you gonna do that? Don't go sendin' Mr. Sands on a wild goose chase. You know they ain't no dead body of Mr. Charles. She tryin' to busy you up, Mr. Sands," Tessie shrieked, arms flailing.

"Let me go and I'll show you!"

"Sands, I'd say we better check out the grave yard. Seems she's fightin' awful hard to keep us out of there," Will said seriously.

"You're right. Come on, Bella. Don't want you running off after we find poor Charles three feet under."

Bella wailed, but her screams fell on deaf ears. He scooped her up and carried her to his horse. He mounted his horse grabbed Bella by an arm, hauled her up, and set her in front of him. Bella struggled and tried to get away, but he locked her hips between his thighs and pinched her waist mercilessly. "Be still, woman, or I'll throw you from this horse and break your damned neck. Understand me?"

Bella slapped him and kicked at the horse's sides. The horse reared and they were both tossed to the ground. Bella crawled through the dirt trying to get away, but he grabbed her by the foot and snatched her back.

Tessie and Agnes ran after them, but they were too late. Sands dragged her to her feet by her throat and with one swipe of his huge hand, she went limp. He threw her over his horse and rode off.

Chapter 17

Tessie turned and flew into the house. Agnes ran after her. They almost collided as Tessie charged down the steps, the revolver gripped in a two-handed clutch.

"Saints alive, Tessie! What foolishness is going on in your head?" Agnes screeched. Tessie didn't respond. Her jaw was set and her hands trembled from the weight of the gun. Agnes grabbed her by the arm and jerked her body around till she faced her. "Don't be a fool. They will lynch you for sure."

"They might...but those bastards, they'll..." Tessie couldn't hold back the tears. "You don't know...you don't know what my baby's been through. No one deserves so much in one lifetime. I swear, I'll kill 'em all if they touch her."

Agnes wrestled the gun from her hands. "No, you won't. You will stay here with the boy. I'll take care of this."

"I can't expect you..."

"She's my sister-in-law. I think I have as much right as you. Besides, a darkie going into town with a gun? Insanity. They'd shoot you on sight. Some good that does Bella. No, it only makes sense that I deal with them." Agnes took a deep breath and straightened her spine.

"I'm her mammy."

"I'm her sister. Unless you're saying you don't trust me?"

Tessie's shoulders shook as she broke into sobs. "You promise..."

"I'll do whatever I have to do to keep her safe. And there's no time to waste, so you got to promise me, you'll stay here?"

Tessie nodded then tried to give her the gun. Agnes looked at it and shook her head. "I won't be needing that. I have no intention of becoming a murderer." Her foot tapped and her face pinched as she thought. "Besides, Bella already told me there aren't any bullets left anyhow."

Tessie flipped out the cylinder, saw it was empty, and flipped it back into place.

"Told you so. Now, put that down and come help me harness up the horse."

"What are you going to do?"

"Please, trust me. There's not much time. And watch Manny. The child's been listening at the corner, and don't you think for one second he isn't planning his own assault."

Tessie burst into tears again. Agnes gave her a hug. "It'll be all right. I promise."

Tessie nodded, rubbed her eyes with her apron and followed Agnes to the barn. She was strapping in the bit when she caught sight of Manny as he snuck around the barn. Agnes saw him too. She shook her head. "Go get him. I can finish this."

Tessie tore after him. By the time she caught up to the boy, Agnes was on the road headed to town. Manny struggled and wailed as she dragged him to the house. On the porch, she emptied his pockets of the rocks he gathered from the yard. "But I got to help her, Miss Tess."

"We will, baby. We're going to light us a candle and pray. The Lord says He'll not deny us if we ask."

"Come on, Miss Tess. You sound crazy."

Tessie shook a finger at Manny and scolded him, "Don't you doubt the Word, boy. You have to believe with a pure heart and He'll always help you."

"I'd rather throw rocks at them."

"Can't say I blame you, child, but for now we'll fight on bended knee."

"What are we going to pray for?"

"For deliverance from evil."

Manny gave her a look. He'd been less confused if she asked for a feather bed. "Maybe you better be more specific, Miss Tess. I'm going to tell him to send Mr. Jack on home."

Agnes's knuckles were white and her hands were sore from gripping the reins. She prayed hard as she rounded a bend in the road at breakneck speeds. She had to get to town, but she didn't want to upset the wagon either. She took a deep breath and slowed the horse. Her heart pounded in her throat. She wasn't sure exactly what she would do, didn't really know what she planned, she knew if Bella was to survive this, she couldn't be left alone with those two men. Agnes's fears of what Bella might go through bordered on dread as she admitted to herself that no one in Troy may care to help. Was Bella's reputation sullied enough to hinder an outcry from the public if she was sorely treated? As the town drew near, Agnes admitted with a frown that Bella could be killed today and no one in this town would likely care. Humanity was another casualty of the war.

And what of Jack? What would he do if this woman was abused and murdered? Agnes shivered at the thought. He would never accept it without executing fitting retribution. If they hurt Bella, Jack would undoubtedly return to prison. Agnes's burden pressed heavier on her mind. She left her wagon in the road and nearly ran down the boardwalk to the sheriff's office. She was nearly out of breath and unable to formulate exactly the right words. She found the sheriff tipped back in his chair, feet propped against his desk, arms crossed, and snoring lightly. Agnes's shrill greeting nearly made him topple over backward. "Please! You have to help! They came and took Bella and they're going to hurt her. You have to help!"

He rubbed his eyes and shook the sleep away scratching the back of his neck. "Now slow down, ma'am. I barely understood half of what you said."

Agnes gathered her thoughts. "I need your help. Some men, they said they were deputies, came to the farm and took Bella away."

"Isabella Stanley?"

"Yes." Agnes breathed a sigh of relief.

"I know. I sent them."

"Well, you need to stop them!"

"Look, ma'am, I assure you, Will and Sands are acting on behalf of the law. They just need to question her."

"Well, if slapping her and, and making untoward advances...lewd suggestions...why I have never seen...and I *don't* consider that acting on behalf of the law!"

The sheriff looked her over for the slightest moment, then took off his hat and mopped his bald head with a handkerchief. "I'll speak with them when they return."

"When they return?! When they return?! Are you totally insane? Why, where can I go to find a federal marshal? Someone who knows how to be a real officer of the law?" Agnes huffed; sweat broke out in beads above her lip and across her forehead.

The sheriff stood so fast his chair landed behind him. "Look, lady, when you walk in this office you better come in with some respect. Seems like maybe you've spent too much time with Bella already. And if she gave them as much sass and lip service as you are here, then maybe my deputies were forced to get a little rough with her. Maybe it's about damn time Bella Stanley was taken in hand. Her daddy let her run wild. And if she thinks she can kill a man and walk away, well, she has a lot to learn about justice."

"Justice? What do you know about justice? Just because she's a woman…"

"Lady, you better shut your mouth right now and get the hell out of my office before I decide to arrest you for causing a public disturbance."

A public disturbance? Agnes wanted to scream; to grab the short stubby sheriff and throttle him. But she was never a stupid woman.

Agnes dropped her gaze. She thought of Tessie's modulated attitude. She felt as if she herself were being stripped of every shred of decency as she stared at the floor and simpered, "I am so sorry. I know this woman probably isn't even worth your time, but she is one of God's creatures." She raised her eyes with the best amount of tears she could muster. "And I hate to see anyone get treated so harshly, even if she did bring it on herself. I didn't mean any disrespect. I was just scared. So scared." She hiccupped and let out a sob.

"Now. You settle yourself and don't worry. I'll look into the situation. Women shouldn't get caught up in men's business. It makes them too excitable. Now why don't you go somewhere and rest?"

"Yes, I should rest. All this…" Agnes fanned her face with her hands as she said, "excitement has just drained me. If my husband weren't busy running cattle, I'd have had him to guide me, but with him busy, I guess I panicked. I hope you won't judge me too harshly?"

"Of course not, ma'am. I understand the tender nature of women. No harm will come to Bella. I assure you. Sands and Will have been…"

Agnes wanted to yell, "*I know, I know, they've been deputies for twenty years. Probably all of them acting as crooked as a dog's hind leg, but you're too damned blind to see!*" Instead she interrupted with a sweet, "I'm sure they're good at what *they* do, but still, would you check on her? And if they are being a little too rough with her, you'll stop them?"

He strapped on his gun belt and nodded. "Of course. But slapping her for running her mouth isn't exactly abuse."

Agnes reddened ready to slap him, but instead she took a breath and asked, her flushed face disguised as embarrassment, "I have heard soldiers, union soldiers of course, take certain liberties…"

"That doesn't happen here in Troy. Even harlots like Bella are safe from, um, ungentlemanly behavior."

"Oh, good. Thank you. You don't know how relieved I am."

Sheriff Clark took his gun off his desk and slipped it into its holster.

"They took her to the cemetery."

"The cemetery?" Clark scowled.

"Said they were going to dig up her baby's grave."

"What the blazes? They know they'd need a warrant."

"I'm telling you, sheriff, Bella bit the one man and he got right angry with her. I don't think those men are thinking clearly."

Sheriff Clark stormed from his office, pushing the door open with a bang. Agnes followed behind him.

"Sir?" she asked as he saddled his horse, "is there any place open? I just can't return to that farm. Why I never dreamed Bella was such a...disreputable person."

"There's Maggie's down yonder. She serves dinner. It should be about starting." He pointed down the dusty street as he snapped the reins and rode off.

Agnes went directly to the boarding house. There were about twelve people seated at the long dining table. She apologized for her intrusion, and then she said with much face fanning and high drama, "I just needed a place to go. I have had the worst afternoon. I came here to visit my brother, who just got out of jail after protecting my honor from a Yankee, to learn he was living with that...that harlot Stanley woman." Agnes cast a furtive glance to assure herself everyone knew who she was talking about. They did, she admitted sourly. "And then I come to find out her husband disappeared. Disappeared? So, I ask them, did he really leave or could something bad have happened to him? Then the deputy comes and arrests her and drags her away kicking and screaming to the grave yard. They're going to dig up a grave and see if her husband is there. Oh, Lord help me, have I been staying with a murderer?"

The room broke into discussion, and the jury was mixed. Some thought Bella capable, a few doubted, but all wanted to go see for themselves.

The first to voice concern for Bella was the prune-faced school marm. "You all should be ashamed. Bella isn't violent."

Miss Jobe was shot glares, but she shrugged them off.

Then another voice of support surfaced. A skinny man with the wrinkles of a sixty-year-old and the body of a twenty-year-old stepped forward. "Bella fed me when she had nothing much to spare."

"Was Charles still alive then, Sam?" One of the men asked.

Sam waved a dismissive hand and shook his head. "No sense talking to the likes of you, Tim, go on, go be part of the spectacle."

Tim laughed and took off, as did everyone else, all but the teacher and Sam.

Even the woman serving the food tossed her apron on the table and said, "Tell Maggie I'll be back to help clean up."

Agnes followed the crowd to the porch and had to nearly holler above the din, "That's the Bella Point Cemetery."

Agnes smiled and was about to leave when the man approached. "You proud of yourself, lady?"

"Of course," she said with her chin held high. "I realized very quickly that hardly a soul in this town would lend a hand to help Bella, but I fully counted on their curiosity. Our tragedy gawkers will provide an ample audience. And unless there's a man's body in that grave, Bella will be fine."

"And if there is?" Sam asked with a sneer.

Agnes's mouth dropped open. "You defended Bella. How could you think she's capable of murder?"

"You ever meet Charles Stanley?"

"No," Agnes said slowly.

"Meaner man never existed. He'd sell his own mama into slavery if he thought he could get a nickel for her. I worked in his family's fields when he was a young man. And on that plantation there was a pretty little thing, no more than thirteen. Mr. Charles had his way with her, didn't care that she didn't want his attentions. He used her till he got her pregnant. Then he fired her from her job and sent her packing. Thank a merciful God for the likes of Mr. Jobe who took her in."

The prune-faced woman nodded her head. "Sam, Daddy was just happy to see Charles for who he was before he allowed him to court Maggie."

"And I tried to warn Mr. Troy when he agreed to marry Bella to Stanley, but after I helped the gal get Noah outta town, he weren't giving me the time o' day."

"What is it Lydia?" the proprietor of Maggie's stepped outside. "Where did everyone go?"

"Seems they're at the cemetery. They think Bella killed Charles and buried him there."

"Oh, poor Bella. I told her to leave this place." Maggie put a hand to her lips and stifled a sob. "I don't want to hear anymore. I'm tired of it all!" She pulled a hankie from her pocket and swept into the house.

"If'n she kilt him, she did the world a favor," Sam said.

Agnes's mouth dropped open. Just because someone was bad didn't make it all right to kill them.

"Sorry to offend you, ma'am," Sam said. "But that little blue-eyed lass was all the family I had in this world. And God help me, but I have a hard time finding any forgiveness for that man. Everyone in this town knew Stanley was beatin' her. She was always bruised up, but no one cared. People ignored it, said twerent none of their bizness. Hell, I heard him bragging over cards that he'd kill her if'n he ever caught her with Noah Solomon again. Acted like she was jezebel when he knowed full and good that Noah's her brother. Hell, he looks exactly like a Troy for crying out loud. All them people ignore her sufferin', ignore her, and now decide to run on out for the hoopla? People make me sick. Ain't no one offerin' to support the girl."

"Well, that stops today," the prune-faced Ms. Jobe said. "Bella has kept little Manny at her home and made sure the child attended school. We all know what happened to his mother. We all know the good sheriff has allowed his deputies to walk all over him and allowed the scum of this town to run wild. He never should have deputized his in-laws. They are fly brained little men with an ax to grind. I don't trust either one of them. They find a body, they'd likely lynch her just to show off for a crowd."

"Oh? Oh my. I better get to the cemetery. Oh, dear Lord, what have I done?" Agnes was nearly to her wagon when she stopped. She realized she had no clue where the cemetery was. "Sir, would you mind showing me the way?"

"I don't own no horse no more."

"I have a horse and wagon. I just don't know how to get there."

"I kin show you." Sam gave his hat a tug and nodded.

As they bounced along the dirt road, Agnes asked, "So, the girl you spoke of, was she your sister?"

"Mmm, hmm."

"Is she, well, is she all right now?"

"She and the babe died."

"I'm so sorry."

Agnes opened her mouth to say something comforting, but Sam interrupted, "Might want to use your breaths talking to the Lord. Pray that grave don't have no man in it."

Chapter 18

Bella huddled in the grass. She closed her eyes and tried to pretend none of this was happening, but it was impossible to deny. The grate of metal against dirt gave her cold chills and a queasy gut. They were undoing what Noah had so carefully done. She rocked back and forth with her hands pressed over her ears. Will stabbed the shovel under the rose bush and in one scoop it was uprooted and ruined. Bella moaned and dropped her forehead against her knees. It was too much. She couldn't watch as they carelessly destroyed her.

"Please...God...make them stop..." she whispered, but her plea was lost in the gusty wind that blew across the waving grass and over the cliff of Bella's Point. Bella imagined chasing that wind right off the edge. How sweet it would feel to let go of all the pain and allow her body to drift into oblivion. Then as if her soul stepped out of the confines of her body, she moved through Will and Sands as if they were mere apparitions and wandered to the cliff. Two hundred feet below, the waters sped white over rocks. A crow screamed overhead. The sun glistened on the water like diamonds scattered across the surface. She felt free; her body light as if it floated along the edge.

Henry called to her. His voice carried in the wind. "Mommy."

She called to him. Tried to see him through the fog that gathered before her blocking the waves and the bright blue beyond. She squinted trying to see into the fog. Slowly emerging as if carried on a ray of light, there was her baby boy.

"Henry!" she called.

"Mommy. I'm over here."

"Where baby?" The fog covered him again.

"I'm right beside you, Mommy." A chill ran up her spine. She looked around to find nothing but cold, wet fog.

"Right here." She felt his chubby hand in hers. She burst into tears and knelt before him. He was bigger than she remembered. His eyes sharper, his smile more vibrant than they were in life. He reached out and hugged her. She buried her face in his tender neck. He smelled like fresh air and sunshine. He patted her back. "Don't cry, Mommy. It's going to be okay. I'm watching out for you."

Bella shook her head. "I don't want to be okay. I want to be with you, Henry."

He shook his head no. Kissed her cheek and floated back into the fog. She called to him, but suddenly she was ripped back to reality. She was still sitting on the damp ground. She opened her eyes to see Will knee deep into the grave. She looked toward the cliff and her heart raced. Her baby was over there, a few feet away. Both men had their back turned toward her. She rose slowly, quietly, and then sprinted for the jagged edge. Excitement bubbled through her body like a child at Christmas. After years of pain, she was going to be free!

Her legs carried her swift as the spring wind to the ledge. She raised her arms, feeling the freedom within her grasp.

She smiled as she leaped, but instead of life ceasing liberty, Sands grabbed her, his arms like a vice around her middle, instantly forcing the breath from her body. She couldn't even scream as they tumbled to the ground. Her head hit a stone by the cliff. Her world went black.

"Bella! Bella!"

Someone touched her forehead gently. Brushed the hair from her face. "Jack?"

"No, sweetie, but Jack will be home soon." Bella opened her eyes slowly to find Agnes. Agnes pulled a hanky from her sleeve and squatted beside Bella. She helped her sit up, holding her by the shoulders to keep her steady. She wiped her eyes and removed a smudge of dirt from her chin. "I'm taking you home, Bella." Bella gasped at the size of the crowd gathered around the cemetery fence.

Agnes said as loud as she could without cupping her hands and hollering, "This sort of barbaric spectacle isn't supported by any of these decent human beings."

Bella couldn't think straight. Her head ached and her thinking was blurred by the pain and confusion. Agnes tried without any luck to hoist her off the ground and drag her home.

Will and Sands kept digging. They were in too deep now. Sands looked around at the crowd and whispered to Will, "Better be a damned body in here, or we're sunk."

"Your fool idea to begin with."

"Mine?" Sands shot back.

Will looked over his shoulder at the gathered crowd and groaned, "And you're the one that plum near killed her in front of God and everybody. That wasn't me."

"She was escaping! How was I supposed to know she'd hit her head on a rock?"

"You coulda just grabbed her."

The argument continued as they made their way waist deep into the grave.

"Listen to them. Scared as little boys caught with their hand in the cookie jar," Agnes whispered as she wrapped her arms around Bella. She tucked Bella's head against her shoulder as if she were a child and wrapped a hand protectively over her head.

Agnes surveyed the good people and smiled. Then she frowned as she touched the bruises on Bella's cheek and the welts rising on her wrists. "No one will hurt you anymore, not with this many people watching. And if they try, those demons will have to go through me. You relax, now, darlin'."

Bella looked over Agnes's shoulder. The crowd murmured among themselves. Bella couldn't make out any one thread of conversation. Half watched the men dig; half stared at her. She felt like a sideshow freak, but she no longer cared. She no longer had the energy to care. She allowed her head to rest on Agnes's shoulder.

Agnes tried again to pull her to her feet, but Bella shook her head. "Please, Bella. This is barbaric. Let me take you home." Agnes's words were drowned out by the sudden clamor of the crowd. A shovel hit wood; a hollow echo filled the air. People pressed in to the cemetery, trampling the graves of generations of Troy's as they peered into the yawning earth.

"Should we pull it up?" Will climbed out of the hole and looked down over the grave.

"That'd take all damn day," Sands answered. He sat on the edge with his legs dangling into the hole. He lifted his shovel above his head and brought it down with a smack splintering the wood. A second crack of the shovel and the wooden casket shattered. He got on his hands and knees and started pulling away shards of wood. It only took three boards to reveal who rested in the casket.

The crowd squeezed in peering over one another's shoulders. Reality must have registered with Will first as he tripped over Sands fleeing the hole. He fell to his knees and groaned, "Oh, Jesus. Oh, Jesus forgive me."

A collective gasp brought words of defense from Sands, "How was I to know?"

The townspeople backed away from the sight, heads shaking. Sheriff Clark stepped forward. "What the hell were you two thinking?"

Neither answered.

"Give me your badges and get the hell out of here before that crowd decides to lynch you up."

He turned to Bella and said, "I'm sorry, Miss Bella. This will be set to rights."

Bella nodded, but her face held a vacant stare. She looked at Agnes. "I want my baby."

"No, Bella. Best we go home."

"He needs me." Bella wrenched herself away from Agnes. Sheriff Clark grabbed for her arm, but her wild cry made him drop his grip and back up.

Bella moved on bent knees to the grave. She gripped the edge of the hole and dug her nails into the earth. She closed her eyes and promised herself he wouldn't be there. She saw him by the ledge. He was whole and perfect, playing on the clouds, not rotting in a hole in the earth. She knew in her heart, when she opened her eyes, the grave would be empty. Her baby was fine. She let out the breath she was holding and opened her eyes. Her screams pierced the air as she sat eye-to-eye with the decaying body of her child. Someone grabbed her around the waist and tried to pull her away.

"Don't touch me!" she screamed and swatted. "Don't ever put a hand on me again, do you understand?" She screamed at no one and everyone. Tears fell fresh down her cheeks. "Why are you all here? You don't care. You don't give a damn about me. About my baby." She let out a sob. "Just go. Let me put him back to sleep. He doesn't deserve this." Bella wiped at her tears, the earth from the grave smearing her cheeks. "Tessie was right. He is better off. He never had to know what lousy creatures human beings are. Didn't have to be scorned by a town that isn't worth one hair on his precious head."

Murmured apologies and condolences rumbled through the crowd. Bella shook her head and turned to the grave. She brushed away the grass from the blanket she had wrapped him in, plucked out clumps of dirt, and tucked his teddy bear closer to his body. She tried to right what was wrong, but the dirt kept rolling into the casket. She looked to the sky and let out a moan. "Why couldn't you leave him be?" No one answered.

She reached for the boards with shaking fingers.

"Stop, Miss Bella. Let me fix that proper for you." Sam's eyes overflowed with tears. He held Bella's hand, and gave it a gentle squeeze. "Ya know I never been harsh with ya. Ya know how I felt about Mr. Charles."

Bella searched his face as she remembered. "You're a good man, Sam."

"That's right, Miss Bell. So, kin ya trust me to fix the boy's restin' place?"

She nodded and handed him the boards.

"Now, if'n ya don't mind, I'm gonna fix this right proper, all right? Gonna go to town and get some nails and fresh lumber. Ya trust me to do that?"

Bella looked at him blankly.

"You go on home with Miss Agnes."

Bella shook her head no.

"Yes, Miss Bella. I'll come git ya when I have it done. You'll be right pleased."

Bella dropped her chin to her chest and cried, "I can't leave him like this. I can't leave him." She sobbed, her hands covering her face.

"Bella." The voice in her ear made her heart stop. Strong hands gently gripped her shoulders and pulled her to her feet. Her heart wrenched from the pain, but the arms wrapped around her held her securely. "You're going home, Bell. Agnes will stay. She'll watch over Henry."

Bella looked up at him and thought no human ever looked so beautiful. He wiped the tears and smudges from her face. He frowned and kissed her forehead, then lifted her off her feet and carried her like a child to his horse.

She nestled her face in his chest. "I missed you Jack."

"I missed you, too, sweetie."

She rode home cradled across his lap. He carried her to the house placing her gently in bed. He took a basin of water and washed away the dirt and the tears. Her eyes were swollen and heavy. He kissed her and ordered, "Rest, Bell."

"I need to talk to you, Jack."

"Not now. We'll talk later."

"I have to tell you the truth about Charles…"

"Hush, I said." He lay down beside her and pulled her in close.

Bella sighed and placed her cheek on his chest, her ear over his heart. She closed her eyes and felt herself lulled to sleep by the beat of his heart.

Chapter 19

Bella woke with the rising of the sun in a room cast in the shadows of dawn. She yawned and started to roll out of bed. Jack grabbed her round the waist and snuggled her into him. She lay on her side with her back to him. He laid his chin on her shoulder and kissed her neck. "Stay here with me, Bella."

Bella sighed and allowed him to hold her. She thought of her plan to leave him, but caring about it dissolved as she relaxed against him. His body was warm. And solid. She felt safe, content, and blessed beyond human worthiness. She gained strength from him and slowly realized she was strong enough to deal with anything. The fears that gripped her yesterday were a distant memory.

Jack was home.

She gasped and turned her neck till she could see him. "Why are you back so soon? You're not supposed to be back for another week."

Jack wound his fingers through loose curls. "You disappointed?"

"No, of course not. But did something happen? How'd you get done so early?"

He didn't answer. He planted small kisses against her neck totally ignoring her question.

"Jack?"

"Yeah?" he answered softly, then returned to her silky flesh.

"Why are you back?"

He paused and smiled. She could feel it against her skin. "I missed you."

"Seriously, Jack. Why are you back?"

He rolled her over to face him. He stroked her cheek and kissed her forehead. "Why is it so hard for you to believe I missed you? I felt like I was gone for months instead of days. And I had this incredible fear I couldn't shake that if I didn't get home, I'd lose you."

"Would that be so bad?"

Jack's eyes narrowed and he scowled down at her.

Bella pulled at the buttons on his shirt. "Wouldn't you rather have...you know...that other woman?"

"You trying to get rid of me, Bella?"

Bella's eyes flashed open. "Oh, no! I just don't want you to feel like you have to take care of me. I know I seem pathetic, especially after yesterday. And you probably missed me because you feel worried and obligated."

"Ah, Bella." He pulled her tight and pressed his cheek to hers. "I do feel obligated to you. I do want to take care of you. But not for any of the reasons you think." Jack's voice was a low whisper. "I want..." Jack began, but Bella interrupted.

She took a deep breath and rushed through her statement before she lost her nerve. "I want you to be happy, Jack. I want you to have the best life you can have. I love you. I have since I first met you. And sometimes loving someone means letting them go, so they can be with the person they love. I..." she lost her nerve a moment. The blood rushed to her cheeks and she had to swallow all her fears and force the words from her lips, "I think you might be better off with Mary."

Jack shook his head. "I don't love Mary. I love you. I don't want her. I want you." He kissed her gently and stroked her cheek. "I love you, Bell. You're the most amazing woman I've ever met. My hesitance at the start had more to do with you than me. You deserve better than me. You deserve a gentleman who can give you the life you had. I didn't want to ruin your life by marrying you. But I guess I'm a selfish man, 'cause it no longer matters. I love you and I'll have you 'cause I don't want you to love any other man."

Bella's smile stretched across her face, and she could barely speak from the feeling of breathlessness that suddenly overwhelmed her. "Oh, Jack," was all she could muster. She wrapped her arms around his neck and squeezed.

"I've always thought you were beautiful, inside and out. Even when you were a young girl. But I knew better than to ever dream of having you. Our worlds were way too different. Your father would have had me strung up. There was no way a Troy could marry a stable boy."

"But you're perfect for me. You make me happy. I can't ever imagine loving someone else."

He kissed the tip of her nose. "And I agree. I am the luckiest son of a gun. This war ruined so many lives, but it saved mine."

"Do you really think that?"

He nodded. "I want you with me till the day I die. I want you with me each and every day. And each night I want you right here in my arms. This is where you belong. This is where I belong."

Bella felt fresh tears slide down her cheeks. She closed her eyes and burrowed herself into him. "Oh, Jack. Tell me again that you love me."

"I love you." He showered her with kisses. "You're more precious to me than you'll ever know."

She looked up at him and her smile wavered a little with a niggling of fear and an overwhelming desire to make their marriage a real one. She licked her dry lips and whispered, "Make love to me, Jack. I should be close to you. You are my husband."

Jack closed his eyes, his neck tense. "We should wait. I want you to feel completely comfortable. I never want you to regret my touch."

"I won't. I know what I'm asking."

He shook his head. "Not yet, Bell. I also want to make sure you're healthy enough too. Just in case."

"In case what, Jack?"

Jack settled his cheek on her shoulder. "In case you would get pregnant."

Bella's heart raced. She really, truly could have another child. Her body warmed all over, the area above her thighs tingling. "I'm healthy, Jack."

"You're too thin."

"You think I'm ugly?"

Jack laughed, his breath ruffling her nightgown. "I think you're beautiful. So much so that you're driving me crazy."

"Really?"

"Ah, Bell. For a woman who's been married, you're very naive."

"What do you mean?"

"I mean I would like nothing better than to take you and make you all my own."

Bella lifted his chin until he was looking at her. "Then do it." She ran her hand up his shirt to feel the warm firm flesh of his chest. He had filled out quite a bit in the last couple of weeks. He was as handsome, if not more handsome than he was in his youth.

Her hand reached the tender skin of his nipple. She pulled gently at the hair that dusted his chest and smiled as she felt him harden under her hand. He took a sharp breath, then let out a strangled moan and collapsed on her. His lips sought hers; his hands explored every inch of her body, the warmth of her skin teasing him through the thin fabric. He lifted her nightgown slowly, inching it up her thigh as his hand trailed up her satiny flesh. His breaths grew more ragged as her perfection was revealed beneath him. He pulled her gown above her head and halted his exploration. He leaned on an elbow and looked down at her. He was quiet several minutes before his fingers traced the curve of her hips, and brushed reverently across a pink nipple. "Sweetness, you are so beautiful. I am a lucky…no a blessed man, to get a woman like you. Thank you, Bella." He nuzzled into her neck kissing the tender skin below her ear, down her neck, and across her collar bone.

Bella felt the first flutter of nerves as he stared down at her nakedness. She wasn't used to being bared of all clothes. She tried to pull the covers up, but Jack stopped her. "You cold?" he asked.

Bella shook her head.

"Then let me see you." He smiled down at her. Then kissed her until she forgot what worried her in the first place.

His hands moved slowly and deftly across her body until they reached her feminine core. Bella gasped and pushed at his hand. His hand retreated to her inner thigh, stroking the sensitive skin, his fingers brushed against her essence until she forgot she should be humiliated to be touched there. It wasn't until she felt him inside her body that she felt the alarm again. "Relax, Bell. I won't hurt you." She bit her lip and nodded. She closed her eyes and nuzzled her face into the thick muscles of his neck. He was her husband. The reality of the thought made her heart swell. She closed her eyes and allowed his hands to roam.

Her anxieties remained at bay until Jack stopped to remove his clothes. Bella closed her eyes and took a deep breath. He kissed her shoulder and continued his caresses. He moved so slowly, Bella felt herself relax, closing her eyes and enjoying the feel of his touch on her flesh. His hands and lips moved lower, slowly. Nibbling, touching. She felt her heart speed up, not with fear, but excitement.

She wanted to belong to this man. Wanted his scent, his heat, his touch to totally wash away every ounce of pain. Bella closed her eyes and pulled him close. She kissed him opening her body to him. Jack resumed his explorations until he was satisfied she wasn't just ready, but eager for more. He placed himself between her thighs and cradled her head against his chest. He felt her body stiffen ever so slightly as his manhood pressed against her. He kissed her, drawing back until he could see her face. "Look at me, Bell. Open your eyes and look at me."

Her eyes fluttered open. Her cheeks blushed from the intimacy, but each time she closed them he encouraged her to keep them open. "I want you to know it's me. I only want you to think of me, all right?"

Bella nodded. She looked into his eyes, felt the love and the safety of his embrace. Felt her body open and accept his. She thought her heart would explode with the tender feelings, the love that swelled in her. "Oh, Jack." She cried. Tears fell down her cheeks. "I love you, Jack. I love you."

He let his body rest against hers, his lips nuzzling her ear as he claimed her with loving words and assurances. His body moved slowly in hers in a deliberate deep grind until he felt her body respond. He heard her gasp, her hands digging into his biceps. His rhythm increased until he felt her tighten around him, her body stiffened under him, her thighs squeezed his hips as she held on as his body responded to hers moving in harmony until they had reached that place of peace collapsing together. Neither spoke, neither moved an inch. They lay together, still locked in an embrace. Neither wasted the breath to speak.

Chapter 20

Bella woke the second time to a fully risen sun. She smiled and stretched her arms above her head. Her muscles were sore, and the memories of how they got that way made her blush. She let out a sigh of pure contentment. She looked across at Jack's pillow and frowned. Where did he go? She propped herself up on her elbows and looked around the room. His clothes were gone.

She missed him more than a few hours of separation called for, but it didn't matter. She wanted him, needed him. She sprang from bed, dressed and tidied her room with never before experienced haste. Bella flung her door open and moved swiftly down the hall, but after a few steps, she nearly came to a stop.

Voices drifted up from the parlor. She and Tessie never used the parlor. Of course, they kept it tidy, the sparse furniture always dusted, floors always swept and mopped. But that was in case of company. And Bella knew better than to expect friendly callers in this town. Even Agnes gravitated to the kitchen during her stay.

Bella resumed her descent, slowly, cautiously. Her heart pounded erratically, and her mouth went dry. Her hand gripped the rail. Voices coalesced into a gentle hum. An occasional trace of laughter met her ears and raised her curiosity. As she reached the bottom of the stairs, she stopped. Bella placed a hand over her heart and her breath caught in her throat. The parlor was jammed with people. From the divan to the needle point chairs, all the furniture held bodies. Manny came in carrying a chair from the kitchen, Tessie directed him to set it in a corner. Then Tessie ushered Mrs. Flannery, old and fragile, to the seat. Bella hadn't seen Mrs. Flannery since her father's funeral. Her eyes scanned the rest of the room. There, jammed shoulder to shoulder, were so many of the people she grew up with. People she once considered friends.

Tessie said something to Manny and the boy scooted off toward the kitchen again. Agnes held a pot covered with a dish towel. She peaked under the towel and smiled at Miss Jobe, who blushed. Sam stood next to her, he added a comment to Agnes, which made Miss Jobe, dare she say, giggle? Was Sam flirting? Bella couldn't help but smile. And hope. She wanted everyone to be in love and be happy.

The front door opened and in walked Maggie. Tessie swept across the room and took a platter from her. Tessie's head bobbed with gratitude.

Manny arrived with another chair. Tessie pointed, and the boy dropped the chair, then took the platter from Miss Maggie. Maggie kissed his cheek and ruffled his dark head. If Manny's skin was pale, Bella was certain it'd be scarlet red.

Tessie moved from person to person, accepting gifts and speaking cordially. So many people Bella had known her whole life, who for the last two years spoke to her only if necessary. Bella wondered what could have changed their minds.

Bella adjusted her skirt, smoothing it over her hips. She wished she had put on her better blouse. She turned to run upstairs and change, but she was spotted. Sam's gravelly voice broke above the racket, "Miss Bella!"

All eyes turned to her. A collective hush blanketed the room. Jack stepped out of the crowd and took her hand and escorted her down the last few steps into the room. He wrapped an arm around her waist. "Bella, darling." He kissed the top of her head. "It seems some people have come to console you."

"Console me?" Bella sounded confused.

"Miss Bella," Sam said, wringing his hands. "I finished little Henry's restin' place. I think…well, I hope you'll be pleased…I mean, I hope it gives you some comfort."

Bella's eyes filled with tears. She closed the gap between herself and Sam in two quick steps. She grabbed him and gave him a bone-crushing hug. "Thank you, Mr. Sam. Thank you so much. You'll never know how much it means to me."

Sam turned scarlet from his chin to his once red roots. "Mr. Joel, he offered up a right beautiful headstone. So's no one will ever question who's restin' there."

Bella turned to the current owner of Bella's point. Mr. Joel was a carpet bagger and a Yankee with few friends in Troy. He nodded shyly at Bella. Bella covered her mouth and nodded in return, her eyes filled with gratitude. She wanted to say thank you, but words wouldn't come. Every time she tried to speak, she felt she would cry, so she smiled, nodded, and hugged her guests in gratitude.

Miss Jobe, stepped forward and said, "Oh, Bella. I was so stuck in my own worries that I never even gave thought to what you were going through. I heard all those tales, and while I never believed them, I never stood up and told anyone it was all balderdash." She squeezed Bella tighter. "Can you forgive me?"

"Of course," Bella managed to squeak. "Miss Jobe, you didn't do anything."

"That's what I'm saying, dear. And please, call me Lydia. We are friends." Miss Jobe separated from her, holding onto Bella's arms, looking her over. "I'll never again abide any bad words about a friend."

There was a murmur of agreement. Bella moved from one person to another on a tide of apologies and good will. She kept looking back at Jack, who would wink and smile, his steady gaze holding the promise of unity and protection.

She made her way back to Sam. His cheeks still stained red. "I can't thank you enough, Mr. Sam. I can't wait to see what you've done. And I will never be able to express how much it means to me."

Maggie cleared her throat and offered, "Sam told me he was finished, and I told him I wanted to go, then Lydia said she did too, then Mr. Joel...and before I knew it, there was half a town of people who wanted to comfort you and make amends for what happened."

"I don't know what to say. I'm, I'm speechless."

"I also took the liberty of speaking with Reverend Lloyd. I asked him if he would offer Henry a proper blessing."

Bella looked to the short portly man. He had baptized her as a baby and married her to Charles and then retired from the cloth. He nodded his head as if she needed encouragement to do this. Maggie smiled, then continued, "Afterward, I'd be honored if everyone would come to the boarding house for dinner. There are just as many folk there cooking up a storm as there are here."

Bella searched Jack out and leaned into him. He smiled down at her. "You up to this, Bell?"

She nodded, still too shocked to speak. Jack took her by the hand. "Well then, let's go." They led the crowd out of the house to the many wagons and horses on the front lawn. Manny, Tessie, and Agnes climbed into the back of the wagon. Bella looked back at their smiling faces and at the crowd behind her and wondered that President Lincoln himself couldn't have felt grander at his inauguration than she felt right now. Jack snapped the reins and Nero set off. He looked down at Bella and winked. She wrapped her arms around his arm and hugged it tightly. He kissed the top of her head and sighed, a happy contented sound.

As Nero crested the hill that led to the cemetery, Bella almost didn't recognize the place. Sam hadn't just repaired Henry's grave; he spruced up the whole graveyard. Even the picket fence had a new coat of white wash and once-broken boards were replaced. It looked as fresh and whole as it did in the days of Bella's Point's glory.

Inside the gate, the grass was freshly cut, all the weeds growing against the fence trimmed. Bella stroked her father's headstone as she passed to her sons. She knelt beside Henry's new headstone. The granite was freshly cut. *Henry Troy Stanley, loving child, darling angel 1860-1864.* Tears rolled from her eyes. It was perfect. He was once the loveliest child. He was now healed and perfect with the strength of an angel. She looked across at Mr. Joel. He bowed his head and stuffed his hands in his pockets. Bella would speak with him in private. She doubted he would much appreciate public gratitude.

The wild rose bush Noah planted was gone. In its place was a real rose bush. Bella wondered at the expense of such a flower. She touched a tiny bud that promised to bloom soon. Mrs. Maude, her old Sunday school teacher, spoke from her wagon next to the cemetery. "It's a white rose, Bella. As pure as snow. I only had the one, but I thought it was a fitting tribute to a little boy."

"Oh my." Bella's words nearly choked her. "I can't thank you enough. You all have been so kind."

Bella stood and took Rev. Lloyd's hand. "Thank you, Rev. Lloyd, for offering to say a prayer for my baby. I hate the thought of his peace being disturbed."

Rev. Lloyd gave her hand a squeeze. "He's been at peace since the Lord called him home, dear, but let's hope this puts his momma's heart to rest."

Bella covered her eyes with her hankie. Jack wrapped her in his arms and held her while Rev. Lloyd said his words of prayer and consolation. He finished with amen and it was echoed all around them. Then he extended Maggie's offer of dinner. The crowd dispersed.

Agnes and Tessie stopped and hugged Bella. She kissed them both. "Oh where would I be without you both?"

"I'm expecting you'll never have to know, 'cause we're like family," Tessie offered.

"We are family," Agnes assured. "And I dare anyone to mess with my sister again."

Bella laughed and hugged her tight.

Manny slipped a hand in hers, but said nothing. Bella looked down at him and smiled. She reminded herself to have Jack take the boy fishing this evening. His whole world turned on its ear again. It was a positive turn of events, but still, it had to be confusing.

Jack touched her cheek. "You need more time with Henry, Bell?"

She looked at the grave and shook her head slowly. "No. I believe Rev. Lloyd is right. Henry has been in good hands since he left us." She bent down and kissed the cold stone. "But it does make me feel better to know he has a proper place."

Jack nodded.

"But now we better get to Maggie's. It was so nice of her to offer." Bella looked at the dust stirred in the road as all the people headed to town. She couldn't believe how many people called on her today. She turned to Jack. "I don't know how I will ever repay these people."

"I don't think they expect you to repay them. They felt awful for how they treated you, and this alleviates their conscience. Let them have that for free."

Agnes, thinking of high debts to pay suddenly asked, "Oh my Jack! With all this excitement I forgot to ask you exactly how long Daniel thinks he'll have to run cattle....was he mad that you left him?"

"No, Ags, he understood. He's always been one to trust his gut and when I told him mine wouldn't be still, he told me to go. Said he could finish the job on his own."

Agnes smiled. "I do have me a good man."

"That you do, sister, that you do."

Agnes smiled and said no more.

"I prayed you home, Mr. Jack." Manny scrambled to the front looking up at Jack with a big grin.

"You did?"

"Yep. I did. Now I'm going to pray my mom comes home."

Bella turned and kissed the boy's forehead. "Some prayers take more time than others. Your mom will be back as soon as she can. Until then...now that Mr. Jack is back...why don't we go have lunch, then when we get home, you guys can get us some fresh fish for dinner."

Manny looked to Jack. Jack nodded, "Yep. The pond is chock full of catfish. Why, I think I hear my stomach rumbling. Fried catfish. Now that sounds good."

"How we gonna fish? We ain't got any poles."

"We'll make poles."

"You can do that, Mr. Jack?"

Jack chuckled and nodded. "Yep. And I'll teach you how to later. Right now, we better get to Maggie's. So," he said as he lifted the boy off the ground and spun him till he squealed, then dropped him in the wagon, "you sit and we'll go have us some eats."

"Can I just eat all desserts, just for today?"

"Sure," Jack answered, then caught a look from Tessie and clarified, "Right as soon as Miss Tess says you can."

Manny's eyes opened wide, thrilled and delighted, then rolled them with an, "Oh."

He turned and began negotiations, though they did little good, with Tessie.

He finally managed a promise of behaving and clearing his plate, and then he could eat as many desserts as Miss Maggie offered. His top-notch behavior was rewarded with not one, but two slices of chocolate cake.

Bella picked at her food, too excited by the day, and interrupted too often by well-wishers to chew. Hours passed when Jack touched Bella's arm and whispered, "You look tired, Bell. I think I should take you home." Manny, who was slumped in a chair, evidently from boredom, not exhaustion, let out a whoop that would have made his brave father proud. Then he flew out the door to the wagon. Bella chuckled; Tessie gasped. Bella shook her head at Tessie and said, "Let him go, Tess. He's feeling spirited. I think it's good for him."

"Hmmmph," Tessie grunted and shook her head. "Everyone will think the boy has no manners."

"Well, I don't think that much matters."

Tessie shook her head and clucked her tongue.

Bella thanked them all, then offered her hand to Jack, who escorted her home.

When they arrived, Jack was barely off the wagon before Manny was right on his heels. "When we going fishing, Mr. Jack?"

"Got a few chores to do first."

"Today?"

"Yep, today."

Manny kicked a rock.

"Do them later, Jack," Bella offered.

Jack frowned. Bella kissed his cheek and whispered, "It will wait till tomorrow. It's a special day."

Jack looked down at her and smiled. He touched her cheek. "I suppose you're right. But it's not right that we play while you work."

"Oh, there's only a few things to put away. Then I'll rest like you said."

Manny turned to Bella. "You ain't coming with us?"

"No, I think I'll let you men take care of the fish. Do you have any worms yet?"

He shook his head, then turned to Agnes as she climbed out of the wagon. "Miss Agnes? You said you know how to fish."

"Oh no, I need to help…"

"Go with them, Agnes. I can take care of the pantry. Besides, you came here to visit your brother and you've barely spent ten minutes with him," Bella said. "Please, go."

"Well…" Manny's eyes were round and bright. Agnes smiled as she looked down at him. "Now I can't think of anything I'd rather do."

Manny grabbed her hand and dragged her off toward the barn. "We're gonna turn over some rocks to get some worms."

"Hmm…maybe I'd rather go with Bella."

"Oh, I'll pick up the worms, Miss Agnes. And I won't even throw 'em at ya."

"Oh my, I must be special."

"Well, you are old, I wouldn't want to give you a heart attack."

Agnes frowned and shook her head. She turned to the giggling Tessie and Bella and rolled her eyes. "Aren't children delightful creatures?"

"Enjoy yourself, Agnes." Bella gave Jack a kiss on the cheek before she sauntered to the house.

Bella and Tessie put away the food with happy chatter and light hearts. Bella lifted a bag of salt and tripped on her way into the pantry spilling half of it on the floor. Tessie gasped. Bella scooped it up and poured it in a crock. She laughed, admonishing the open mouthed Tessie, "Oh pooh, Tess, it's just salt."

"Bad luck's comin." Tessie held a hand over her heart.

Bella paused a moment and chewed her lip. "It really is silliness, Tess. I have everything. What could possibly go wrong now?"

Tessie looked toward the back field and shrugged.

Chapter 21

A year and a spring passed. Summer was in full bloom and so was Bella. Her cheeks bore rosy splotches and her heart beat light as a feather. Not only was the spilling of salt *not* an ill omen, but it marked the beginning of four hundred and one of the most perfect days on record. Bella rubbed her swelling belly as she swung on her garden swing and sighed. In fact, she didn't even remember spilling the salt. Life was courteous, the days ticked by with the smoothness of perfect fate.

Last year, Bella feared they would starve to death or worse. By the end of the 1865, they weathered a winter with a surplus food. And thanks to Jack and Daniel's hard work, they had enough wood for the entire cold season without having to shut off a single room. They also had friends, and Manny had playmates. The lonely life of the ostracized ended without another apology said. Relationships resumed like the insults never happened.

By spring, Nero was as fit and people were eager to use him as a stud, just as Jack predicted. With that money, they purchased pigs and chickens. Agnes and Daniel built themselves a small home on the property. They saw little need to head west when their family lived in the South.

The seasons passed. Christmas arrived with real gifts and a belly bulging feast. They rang in 1866 with the wonderful news that Bella was pregnant

By the end of June, they had a letter from Noah. He and Wendy were on their way home and would be there in about a month.

By July, Bella felt blessed beyond all human comprehension. She was so giddy with thoughts of baby and her brother coming home that she could barely offer an ounce of assistance to Maggie and Lydia Jobe as they planned a double wedding for the end of August. Maggie and the Yankee found love once Frank Joel realized Maggie's was the best place in town to get a hot meal. And Lydia was ending her days as spinster school marm and beginning her life as Mrs. Sam Cleary. And Sam was happily sober and working hard at Mr. Joel's fledgling furniture business. Frank Joel hoped to put Troy, North Carolina, on the map as the place to buy furniture.

Bella swung with her head tipped back. The crickets hummed, oblivious to the soggy heat that made a body sweat just from thinking. Bella felt a bead of sweat trickle down her back and she shivered and thought of poor Jack, cutting hay in this sun. She missed him during the days now that she was banned from any work in the fields. He wouldn't even let her follow along to keep him company for fear she could burn and harm herself or the baby. Bella offered little argument. She caressed the growing lump. She could be happily bored to tears if it guaranteed a healthy baby.

"Bella?"

Bella turned toward the voice. She smiled and waved to Maggie. She started to stand, but Maggie hurried off the porch. "Stay still, Bell. Just scoot over and make room."

Bella slid over, and Maggie joined her on the swing. She gave Bella's belly a pat. "So, how is my God child?"

Bella smiled. "Making his momma very lazy. Or maybe it's the heat."

"A bit of both, I'd gather."

Bella laughed. "All I do is sleep. I'm lucky to get a bit of needle point done in a day."

Maggie squeezed her hand. "Well, you take it easy. I know how much this means to you."

Bella nodded. "And maybe one day, you and Frank…"

Maggie blushed. "I can't get my hopes up. I'm nearly thirty!"

"So? I'm twenty-six."

"But you've had a baby already."

Bella giggled. "So, how does that make any difference?"

Maggie shrugged. "I don't know. I just…goodness, Bella, I have to pinch myself every now and then to prove this is real. My life has changed so much in a year. And Frank is so…so perfect! This sounds awful, but I thank God every day for that fiasco with Wills and Sands. If not for that day, I would have lived in the same town with Frank and never knew how perfect he was for me."

"Well, I suppose it's good there was some benefit to all that."

"For Lydia too. Why, I never would have guessed she would find love. She's so persnickety!" Maggie gasped. "I mean her and Sam! I wouldn't have thought the Pope himself would ever be righteous enough for my sister. But, oh! Don't ever tell her I said that!"

Their heads leaned together in conspirators' giggles. Bella wiped tears from her eyes as she assured, "Your secret's safe with me."

"But seriously, have you ever seen such an odd pair?"

"I think they're adorable together. And..." Bella burst into giggles yet again, "...she makes Sam shave and take his hat off in-doors. Why, I didn't even know he was going bald! I never saw him with his hat off."

Maggie smiled, "I suppose there is someone for everybody."

"Hmm...wonder if there's anyone for Tess..."

"I hear ya jabberin'. And I warn ya both, I got enough dirt and gossip on the two of you, you better not slight me or you'll regret it." Tessie dropped a basket of clothes in front of Bella. "Here's the basket of mending you wanted. Figured you best do it outside where it's cool." Tessie fanned herself. "Well, cooler than in the house."

Maggie winked at Bella. "I hear Curtis Jones is going to be working for Frank. If I recall, he's a handsome man."

"A field hand." Tessie harrumphed.

"He's a free man now, Tess, a working man," Bella added.

Tessie shook her head and planted her hands on her hips. "The heat's gotten to the both of you. Foolish girls twittering on. Why, the birds in the trees make more sense than the two of you."

"Me think she doth protest too much," Maggie whispered.

"Hah!" Tessie answered. "Using Shakespeare against me. Why, Miss Maggie, I always thought you were nice folk."

"I am nice folk. But I'm also so happy. And I want everyone to be happy."

"Trust me, child, I couldn't be happier. Noah's on his way home to stay. Miss Bella is gonna have a baby. We got food for the winter and some money in the bank. Why, I couldn't ask for anymore."

"What will we do with Curtis?" Bella wondered aloud.

"I assume he's fine on his own. I got enough people to care for. Need a man? Hmmph…having a man is like having another child, no sir, I don't need that," Tessie said.

"Even one as handsome as Curtis?" Bella giggled.

"Oh, you. I swear. I AM not talking to you when you're acting silly. I got better things to do."

"Oh, come on Tess, what could be so important? We're having fun."

"You're having fun, Missy. I need to be making some dinner."

"Dinner is forever away," Bella said.

"Actually it isn't." Maggie sighed. "I should be going too. I still have a duty to my boarders. I can't wait until it's my own home, my own…well, my own family I have to take care of."

"Have you given them all notice? Where will they go?"

"Well, I have made it clear the place closes the end of August, so I mostly have people who stay a night or two. Which reminds me…" She turned her attention to Bella. "Kelly Stanley rented a room. I asked him how long he'd need it and he said all arrogant like, 'Indefinitely.' I told, 'well, you got till September here, then you'll have to go somewhere else.'"

"Kelly Stanley? Charles's brother?"

"Mmm, hmm."

Bella looked at Tessie and figured if her skin wasn't so dark, she'd be pale as a ghost. Bella took a deep breath, "Did he mention why he was in town?"

"Just said he had business."

"I didn't know any of the Stanley men actually worked," Bella said.

Maggie laughed. "All those Stanley's were such big-headed, spoiled pigs. I hear the youngest is in prison for robbing an old lady. In the street! The poor old woman drove into Macon for supplies and he robbed her as her wagon was passing through Purgatory. Gave the old gal a heart attack and she died."

Tessie gave Bella an *I told you so* look, but said nothing.

"Well, anyway, he complains about everything and pinches Mindy's bottom like she's working at a brothel instead of a boarding house. Whew! Couple more days with him and I'll shut the place down earlier than planned."

Bella gripped the swing to still the tremble in her hands. Maggie hugged her, then rose. "Oh, don't you worry over the likes of him. He's not even asked about you. Spends all his time drinking and playing cards with Sands and his cronies. Besides, I'm certain Jack wouldn't put up with any of his shenanigans."

Bella nodded. She felt queasy, and she doubted it had anything to do with pregnancy.

"You got yourself a good man, Bella."

Bella nodded and her throat tightened. She forced out the words, "I certainly do."

Maggie looked confused, but Tessie rubbed Bella's shoulders and explained, "Miss Bella is long past need of a nap."

Maggie smiled and nodded. She bent down and kissed Bella's cheek. "Take care. I'll stop by in a couple of days."

Bella smiled, it felt weak, but looked convincing. "Bring the muslin sheets. I'd be more than happy to monogram them for you."

"Are you sure?"

"Of course. What else do I have to do?"

"You do have beautiful handiwork. I'd be most grateful."

Bella smiled and hugged her good-bye.

216

Tessie walked Maggie to her wagon. Bella stayed in the swing and rubbed her belly as she thought about Kelly. She barely knew him. He came to her wedding and stayed at their home on several occasions, but Charles was intolerably jealous, even of his own kin, so she didn't mingle in the company of men. Tessie emerged from the house with a cloth-draped basket. "I have Mr. Jack's lunch finished. You need to take it to him and send Manny on home."

"Me?" Bella asked.

"You need to talk to Jack. Tell him about Mr. Kelly…" her voice dropped to a whisper. "…and about Mr. Charles."

"Now?"

Tessie nodded. "Sooner the better."

Bella's eyes stung. "I can't."

"You have to."

"But what if he hates me?"

Tessie shook her head. "He'll understand."

"If he doesn't?"

"Well, you're carrying his child. He won't let nothing happen to you."

"He could," she started but the words stuck in her throat, "stop loving me."

Tessie shook her head. "You got to trust him. You and I both know Mr. Kelly isn't here by chance or to play cards. He's here for his brother. And what are you gonna say when he asks you where he went?"

Bella nodded slowly. "I'll talk to Jack."

Chapter 22

Jack removed his hat and mopped the sweat from his brow. He frowned at Bella as she made her way through the high grass. She waved at him, and he shook his head.

"Manny," she called as she approached, "Miss Tess needs your help at the house."

Manny looked up at Jack. Jack nodded, and the boy ran off.

"It's high noon, woman. You'll burn yourself to a crisp."

Bella sucked in a breath and placed a hand over her heart. The heat seemed so much more oppressive with the added weight of a baby.

"What the hell were you thinking?" he lifted her from her feet and carried her across the field to a grove of trees. She'd have been impressed with his chivalry, but he nagged the whole way. "You have to take care of yourself. It's too hot. You'll pass out. Damn foolish woman. Hard headed as a damn mule." He kicked a few sticks out of the way before settling her in the grass. He brushed the hair back from her face and looked her over as if he were a licensed physician doing a check-up. He shook his head and sighed. "Don't know what could be so all-fire important that you have to half bake yourself…"

"Oh shush, Jack. You sound worse than a mother hen. I just..." She couldn't put the proper words together.

He sat beside her. "Something wrong?"

He took her hand and squeezed it gently.

She smiled and bit her lip to stop her eyes from filling with tears. "I brought you lunch."

"Manny runs for lunch. You know that."

"Oh, well, of course. But, um, Tessie needed him."

"So she knew you were coming out here?"

Bella nodded. Her cheeks flushed, and her heart felt like it was lined with lead. This wasn't a conversation she ever wanted to have.

"What the hell's going on at the house that she needed Manny so bad?"

"She wanted me to talk to you," Bella whispered.

Jack's brows knitted together. Bella reached out and touched his cheek. It was browned by the sun and fully fleshed out from full meals and hard work. He was more devastatingly handsome with each passing day. And he was hers...for now.

Jack cradled her cheek in his hand, his thumb stroked her skin. "What's wrong, Bell?"

She bit her lip. She felt faint, so she rested her head against the tree.

Jack's eyes widened. "Is it the baby?"

"Oh, no. He's fine." Her hand cradled her belly. Jack pressed his against hers. The birds chirped in the distance; the wind passed through the trees, offering a small respite to the heat.

Jack tipped her chin until she looked him in the eye. "Talk to me."

"It's...it's..." She looked around the field. "Where's Daniel?"

"He forgot his straw hat and had to go fetch it."

Bella twisted her hand in his glossy black hair. "You need a haircut."

He took her hand in his and held it, squeezing it gently. "What do you need to tell me?"

Bella's eyes were wide and blinked rapidly. She knew what she needed to say, but the words still wouldn't come.

"Did something happen today?"

Bella nodded. "Maggie came."

"And did she say something?"

Bella nodded. She gulped as she said, "She said Kelly Stanley was staying in her boarding house."

"A relative of Charles's, I s'pose?"

Bella nodded.

"So, what does that have to do with you?"

Bella's hands trembled. She looked out over the waving grass and wished beyond all wishes that she had married Jack at sixteen and could have foregone all the pain of Charles.

Jack's voice was gentle, but firm. He wrapped Bella tight, pulling her onto his lap, tucking her head against his shoulder. "You have nothing to worry about sweetness. I'll deal with any Stanley who crawls out of whatever hole they come from, all right?"

Bella shook her head as she focused on the strength in her husband's neck. The thick muscles lined each side of his throat. They seemed so firm, so capable. But tears of understanding burned her eyes. There were some problems not even Jack could fix.

His arms tightened around her. "It's all right. Trust met? Not Charles, or anyone else will ever hurt you again."

"I'm not afraid of Charles. I..." A sob broke loose and choked off her words.

Jack rocked her and kissed her temples and cheeks. "It's all right. I know everything. You can trust me, all right?"

Bella couldn't stifle the sobs long enough to ask him what he was talking about.

"Jack!" Daniel hollered from the field. Jack kissed Bella, her face cupped in his calloused hands, before setting her back in the grass. He stood and waved to Daniel. Daniel rode his horse down to the grove, pulling up short. The horse whinnied and balked at the quick stop. "Jack. You gotta come quick. Bella, you stay here. I'll send Agnes back for ya."

Bella grabbed at Jack's hand as he stood. "Is it Manny? Did he hurt himself?"

"Everyone's fine," Daniel answered. "I just need to speak with Jack. About cattle," Daniel stuttered. Daniel always flushed red when he lied, and right now he looked burnt to a crisp and nervous as a tax collector in the bayou. He led Jack out of her earshot and kept moving until he was certain Bella could hear nothing but chirping birds and swaying winds. Jack listened intently, his eyes glued to Bella as Daniel told him whatever secrets he carried. Jack rubbed his chin, and his face wrinkled with worry. This wasn't farm talk, Bella decided. She had a right to know what was happening. She struggled to her feet, using the trunk of the tree to hoist herself up, then charged forward, huffing and puffing with the exertion it took to reach them. "You tell me what's going on, Daniel Clemons! I have as much right to know as anyone!"

Daniel retreated with a mumbled apology, but no explanation. Jack gripped her shoulders gently and said, "You've got to promise me you'll let me deal with this in my own way."

"Your own way? I don't even know what's going on!"

"You have to think of your health, Bella, and the health of the baby," Jack reminded her.

Bella's jaws quivered, "I'd never hurt my baby...but, I still have a right to know what's going on."

Daniel took off his hat and scratched his head. Jack looked to Daniel, who shrugged and nodded. Jack sighed and said, "Seems Noah's been arrested."

"Arrested?! For what?"

Jack paused a moment, he took a deep breath and gave her shoulders a squeeze. "This is the part where you listen to me. I'm going to go into town and find out what's going on. You're going to go back to the house and stay there with Tessie and Agnes."

"But..."

"Wendy's back too, Bell. And I," Daniel said quietly, "I think you ought to be with her. She sure looked plum scared to death."

"Wendy's back?" Bella felt a small swell of relief.

"She's the one who told us he was arrested."

"You're serious? I can't believe it. Arrested? Why?" Bella whispered.

Jack forced her to look at him. "Now you listen to me. You got to trust me. Let me deal with this, all right?" Jack looked pale as a ghost. Bella stroked his cheek. He looked so worried, and yet he hadn't even met Noah. She gave him a little smile. "I trust you, Jack. I'll be patient. I promise."

"You'll stay put?"

She nodded. He breathed a long sigh of relief. "Good. I thought I'd have to argue with you more."

Bella smiled up at him and shook her head. She did trust him. If Jack said he'd deal with things, he would.

She waited in the field for no more than twenty minutes before Agnes arrived with the wagon. Manny rode beside her until he spotted Bella. Then he stood in the wagon seat and waved hollering as they approached, "Miss Bella! Miss Bella! My momma's back!"

Bella felt his excitement wash over her and she felt light as a feather as she waved back. The wagon stopped, and he leaped out and gave her a bone-crushing hug. "I wanted to tell ya first."

"Oh Manny, that's wonderful. I can't wait to see her."

"Well come on, she's back at the house." He practically dragged Bella to the wagon. Agnes stood and scolded with a wagging finger. "Now, careful, you'll trip her and hurt the baby. Land sakes alive, be gentle would ya?"

Bella climbed in the back with Manny. He offered her a hand, his mouth moving a mile a minute as he shared the good news with her. "I was runnin' back to the house, like you told me and I saw a rider." Bella situated herself against the back of the wagon seat. Manny scooted in next to her. "It was the sheriff and at first I was scared, 'cause of what they done last time they come. But then I saw her. I recognized her from way off. My momma was riding on the sheriff's wagon. I was so excited I ran all the way down the road and met up with her. Can ya believe it? My momma came home!"

"The sheriff brought her?"

Manny nodded. "And he wasn't mean this time. He gave me a licorice whip. Miss Tessie says I can eat it after lunch."

Bella looked at Agnes who cast her a tell-you-about-it-later look over her shoulder.

Bella felt the trepidation return, but Manny was so exuberant, she plastered a smile to her face and asked, "So, did you give your momma a big hug?"

He nodded. "Just the biggest in the whole world."

"I bet she liked that."

"Nah, made her cry. But I'm gonna get her flowers later. Girls like flowers better than hugs I think."

Bella's eyes misted. "You can get her flowers too, but you keep giving her those hugs. I'd say she liked it more than you'll ever know."

"But she cried."

"Happy tears."

Manny snorted. "You ever heard a' such a thing, Miss Agnes?"

"Most certainly," Agnes answered without looking back.

"Girls are just plain weird," Manny proclaimed with a shake of his head.

Bella grabbed him and gave him a hug. She spotted a cluster of daisies. "Hold up a minute, Agnes." She pointed them out to Manny. "There's some pretty flowers over there. Why don't you go pick them?"

"Sure. They are pretty. "Manny hopped out and starting yanking at whole clumps tearing them from the ground roots, dirt and all. Bella shook her head and leaned back against the wagon. "Is she all right, Agnes?"

"Who?"

"Wendy."

"I don't know. She was real quiet. I mean real quiet, barely answered the questions we asked her with more than a few words."

"She always was quiet like that."

"Seriously? Here I was worried the girl was in shock, seeing as how our young Manteo will jaw your ear off, I figured his mom to be a talker too."

"No. She doesn't say much. But surely she said something to Tess? About Noah?"

"Not while I was there. What I know I overheard from the sheriff while he was talking to Daniel. Seems the good man is done dealing with women," Agnes chortled.

"Did he say what Noah was arrested for?"

Agnes's cheeks reddened. "I think you better ask Jack."

Bella moved closer and grabbed her arm. "If you know, you have to tell me."

"Well," Agnes said as she twisted the reins in her hands, "I don't know. It's pretty bad, and you're carrying my niece and…"

"Please, Agnes. You know I'm way stronger than anyone gives me credit for. And if this was reversed, would you want me to hide information from you about Jack?"

"Certainly not."

"Then tell me."

"Well," Agnes started reluctantly, "it seems Kelly Stanley went to the prison in Macon to visit his little brother. You know, that Edward, the one arrested for robbing the old lady? I still can't believe that. How despicable can a person be?"

"Horrible," Bella answered impatiently. "Now what about Noah?"

"Well," Agnes continued, "seems while Kelly was visiting, he spoke with a guard. The guard asked him about your and Charles's divorce. Well, I guess Kelly didn't believe that Charles would ever get a divorce, so he came to town and told the sheriff he hasn't heard a word from his brother for over three years."

"And?"

"And well, he told the sheriff he suspected something bad had happened to his brother and demanded Sheriff Clark investigate. Sheriff said he was reluctant, but then his *former* deputies swore something was afoul and threatened to call in a federal marshal. So…" Agnes stopped and fanned herself. "You really should wait to speak with Jack."

"Finish the story, Agnes." Bella's words were firm.

Agnes sighed. "Well, the sheriff said he was on his way to the farm to talk to you when he ran into Noah and Wendy. Noah asked him if something was wrong. The sheriff told *him* the story and then…"

Bella grabbed the back of the seat and gripped it hard. "Then what?"

"Well, seems Noah confessed to murder. He told the sheriff that Charles was gone because he killed him. Said he hit him over the head with a shovel and then shot him and buried him behind the barn."

Bella clamped a hand over her mouth, but nothing could stop the taste of bile. She leaned over the side of the wagon and emptied her stomach.

Chapter 23

Agnes called for Manny. "Get in the wagon, son. We got to get Miss Bella home."

Bella leaned her head against the wagon wall and covered her eyes with her forearm. Agnes handed her a hanky and stroked the top of her head. "Jack and Daniel will get to the bottom of it. Oh, Lord, I never shoulda told you."

"No, you did right. I'm fine."

"You don't look fine. You're pale as a ghost and your breakfast is bird pickings."

"What's wrong, Miss Bella?" Manny asked as he clambered into the wagon. As a second wave of nausea washed over Bella, she covered her mouth with her hand and shook her head at Manny.

Manny's eyes widened, and he turned to Agnes and whispered, "Miss Agnes?"

Agnes swiped at her tears and sat straight in her seat clutching the reins and firming her jaw. "Don't fret none, son. Morning sickness is to be expected. She'll be all right, we just need to get her on home. She needs to rest till Mister Jack comes home."

Manny took Bella's free hand and cradled it. He gave it a sympathy pat. "Babies must be horrible creatures. Too bad ya can't just have an already grown boy."

Tessie met the wagon as it pulled in front of the house. Bella flew at her for a hug. Tessie squeezed her back, clutching her tightly. Tessie's tears dampened her shoulder, and her sobs brought a sense of calm to Bella. She had to keep a level head. Tessie and Noah needed her. Bella promised her trembling, incomprehensible friend, "I'll take care of this, Tess."

"Shh, Tess, you have to breathe, you're gonna get vapors. I know what needs to be done. You just need to calm down."

"My baby..." Tessie finished as if she didn't hear a word Bella said.

Bella turned to the silent Wendy who hovered near the porch. "Why did he do it? Why did he tell them he killed Charles?"

Wendy shrugged and shook her head slowly as if it weighed a million pounds. A tear rolled down her cheek.

"Well, I suppose if no one knows, I'll have to ask him myself."

"But he's in jail," Agnes said.

"So? You visited your brother in jail."

"Daniel escorted me. It's completely different. You must consider propriety with the babe and all."

"Then I'll speak with Sheriff Clark."

"Most certainly not. After the last run in with 'the law'? Hmph." Agnes shook her head. Her hands were firm on her hips, and she looked downright menacing. "You'll stay put till Jack and Daniel get home. They'll know what to do."

Bella nodded. She wiped her brow with the back of her hand. "I suppose you're right."

"Of course I am."

Bella took a step toward the porch. "I think I will lie down. This heat is getting to me a little. Agnes?"

"Yes, dear?"

"Would you be so kind to make me a cool drink and a little something for my stomach?" She turned to Tessie. "I'm afraid the heat and the news got the best of me."

"Of course I will." Agnes's bulk moved swiftly to her side, wrapped an arm around her waist, and practically dragged her into the house.

"I'll rest on the divan. It's so hot upstairs in the middle of the day."

"Manny, fetch Miss Bella a pillow. Miss Tess, you stay right by her while I get some cold lemonade. That'll make you feel better. Maybe a cracker or two." Agnes situated Bella with a mighty lot of fuss. She stood and surveyed her handiwork and sighed.

Bella looked up at her and smiled a weak, worn out grimace. Agnes frowned, patted her cheek, grumbled about the insanity of Troy then disappeared into the kitchen. Bella sprang to her feet as soon as Agnes was gone. Tessie gasped and covered her heart with her hand.

Bella grabbed Tessie by the shoulders and pulled her close and whispered, "Go slow her down. Tell her Wendy is caring for me."

"What in the name of the All Mighty?"

"Shush, Tess! You want her back in here, fighting me?"

Tessie looked confused. Bella leaned close. "I have to go speak with the sheriff. Tell him the truth."

"You...oh no, child, you can't. The baby."

"They'll hang him. You know it, and I know it. He'll not get a fair trial. Of that I'm certain. At least I'd get some mercy."

Tessie collapsed on the divan. She buried her face in her hands and her shoulders shook as she sobbed. "I can't let you do this."

"I'm not asking your permission. I'm asking you to help me escape Agnes. If she gets wise, she'll carry me off like a sack of flour and lock me in my room."

"Maybe she should."

"And let Noah take my blame? I think not."

Tessie looked up at her with the lost look of a petrified woman faced with an impossible choice. Which child did she let die? Bella knelt before her. "It'll be all right, Tess. They won't hang a pregnant woman, and it'll give Jack time to get me an attorney. You know Noah wouldn't get a decent trial or any sympathy. I stand a much better chance of surviving this."

"No, no, no." Tessie shook her head back and forth. "I can't do this." Tessie clutched Bella's hand to her heart. "I love ya like my own. You are my baby as much Noah. I can't send you to the hangman's noose."

Bella scowled. "Nonsense. You aren't doing anything. I *am* the guilty one. You know it as well as I do." Tessie opened her mouth to speak, but Bella put a finger to her lips. "Shush. If all else fails, I can count on Jack busting me out and we'll run away...maybe to England. He has family there, and I hear it's beautiful."

Tessie groaned. "You and your half-brained plans."

Bella patted her belly. "Seems they've served me well so far." She hugged her close. "Trust me, please? It'll be all right, but I have to go now. Before the warden comes back."

Tessie started to weep again. Bella hugged her. "Please, Tess. Trust me. We've gotten through it all together. We'll get through this too. I swear, it'll be all right."

"I don't know, baby. I just don't know. Maybe the luck has run out."

"Oh hogwash." Bella frowned and shook her head. "Now stop with the blubbering. Up off the couch and into the kitchen. I gave you a job to do and I expect it done."

"Boss yer mammy. Child's lost her mind and her manners." Tessie wiped her eyes and took a deep breath. "Wendy?" Tessie turned to the quiet woman. "Go with her please? So you can witness, get help if need be?"

Wendy nodded.

Manny moved quietly next to Bella and slipped a hand in hers. Bella leaned over and whispered in his ear. He nodded, then went to Tessie's side and wrapped an arm around her shoulders. "I'm gonna be here, Miss Tess. I'll keep you safe."

Tessie's face broke into a weak smile, and she wrapped the boy in a hug. Bella slipped out of the house while Manny had her distracted. Wendy followed tight on her tail.

As they rode into town, Wendy asked, "What are you going to do?"

"I'm going to tell the truth...I killed Charles Stanley."

Chapter 24

Wendy said nothing in response to Bella's confession. She nodded and looked forward. The silence unnerved Bella. As much as she told herself she was brave, honestly, she was shaking in her newly bought boots. And her baby stirred and kicked as if the little one knew his (she was certain he was a boy) momma was about to do a very foolish thing. She wasn't at all certain the law would be any more forgiving of her than they would be of Noah, but she was certain they'd allow her child to be born before hanging her. Hopefully, God willing, they'd even allow her a day or so with him before…her heart raced. She gave her head a quick shake and took a deep breath.

"That little man of yours sure has come out of his shell. Well, he was always a chatter bug with Tessie and me, but he was so quiet at school in the beginning. But he had his scrapes and run-ins with the bullies, and now he does real well. Did he tell you he wrote a story about his dad? Or at least a story about what he thinks he would have been like? Manny says he was a Cherokee warrior?"

Wendy nodded and smiled. The smile seemed to take a great amount of effort and looked extremely awkward on her face. Wendy looked away and gripped the edge of the wagon seat.

Bella planned to give Wendy a minute to add something to the conversation, but when she didn't, Bella had to fill the space, she couldn't endure the long silences. She gave the reins a jiggle and propelled the horse to move a bit quicker. Then she launched into a one sided conversation about Manny and his progress in school, with friends, and on the farm. It was only as the simple town rose before her that her chatter quieted. Cold hands held the reins. Pulling back without realizing it, she stopped the horse. Wendy reached across and took her hand.

"It will be all right," Wendy said quietly.

"From your mouth to God's ears," Bella mumbled, then gave the horse a snap and moved toward the sheriff's office.

Bella hopped off the wagon. Her legs felt weak, and she feared for a moment that she might pass out right there in the middle of the dirt road. Wendy wrapped an arm around hers and walked with her into the office. It was nearly black inside after coming from the blazing sun. Bella swallowed and opened her mouth to confess, but no words came. Her legs trembled, and her hands shook. She wrapped an arm around her belly as the baby kicked and rolled, setting off a cramp that started below her naval and spread toward her back. She leaned against the edge of the sheriff's desk. The new deputy, Bo Miles, leaped from his seat and took her hands.

"Holy cow, Miss Bella. You better sit down. A lady in your, um…condition…shouldn't be on your feet, or out in the sun. What you thinking, ma'am?"

"I need to speak with the sheriff," Bella whispered as she gratefully took the chair Bo dragged her toward. He was a young man, unscathed by combat as he just recently turned eighteen. His round face was smooth and free of the harsh lines and whiskers. He filled her a glass of water and offered her a hanky. She dabbed the sweat from her forehead and drank the water, hoping it could wash away the sick feeling.

Bo knelt before her. "You ought let me take you home, Miss Bell."

Bella shook her head. "No. No. I have to talk with Sheriff Clark."

"I can send him out to your house when he's done. He's arresting...oh, I see. Noah used to be your family's darkie, wasn't he?"

"He's like family," Bella said rubbing her cramping belly Wendy knelt beside her grabbing her hand and clutching it tightly. Young Bo looked pained. He told them he'd get the sheriff and bolted from the room.

"It'll be all right," Wendy whispered. "Try to relax. For the baby."

"I'm trying to."

"Deep breaths," Wendy said as she rubbed Bella's arm. Bella clutched her belly, closed her eyes, and took long, deep breaths.

That's how they found her. Sheriff Clark, Daniel, and Jack. The muscle in Jack's jaw flickered, and he looked at Daniel and shook his head. "Shoulda known, dammit. Shoulda known she'd find out." He closed the space between him and his wife, almost spinning Daniel as he brushed past. Squatting beside her, he held her hand in his. "Doggone it Bell. You said you'd let me deal with this. Now, I want you to go on home."

"Sheriff Clark, you arrested the wrong person."

"Hold your peace, Bell." Jack's words came in a harsh whisper. He stood and addressed Sheriff Clark. "I need to take my wife home. You want to meet me at the farm? You're free to search wherever you want. If Charles's body is there, then Noah has some explaining to do. But I assure you, Sheriff, he only confessed to protect his family. I believe there was a fight at the farm. I also believe Noah struck him with a shovel. He was done seeing the abuse and fought back. Men like Stanley are cowards, and once he knew he couldn't kick Bella and Tessie anymore, he headed out of town.

"Jack! What are you saying?" Bella jerked herself away. "How can you set Noah up to be hung?"

"The law is the law, darling."

"Don't darling me!" Bella's voice was shrill, her face red as a ripe tomato. The pains in her belly strengthened, her whole stomach tightening. It only made her madder. She should have known Jack would send Noah to the gallows. He'd do anything to save her worthless hide. "You know damned good and well Noah didn't kill Charles."

"He told us the whole story, Bell. Charles was drunk and beating you and he shot him. That's why he ran north and he only came back because he thought the heat was off. He told us everything," Sheriff Clark explained.

"Well, it's a lie. I shot Charles. He was beating on Tessie…he was done beating me. He was going to kill her. Noah hit him with a shovel, but it didn't do anything but make him angry. So I shot him. I killed Charles Stanley, not Noah."

Jack looked fierce in his anger. His eyes were arrow slits as he shook his head at his wife. "She's lying. She would do anything to protect her family, and it's no secret that Noah is her brother. I should have expected something so stupid and irrational from a woman in her condition."

"My condition?" Bella felt the rage. If he wasn't holding her arm so tight, she would have slapped Jack Byron. "I assure you, my condition does nothing to my sensibilities."

"The hell it doesn't. You're standing right before an officer of the law committing perjury. That screams addled in the head to me."

"I am NOT lying!" Bella pulled away, putting a half a room distance between her and Jack.

"Yes. Yes she is lying," Wendy said as she stepped toward the sheriff. "I know she's lying, because I killed Charles Stanley."

"You?" Sheriff Clark took off his hat and scratched his head.

"This is absurd." Bella leaned against the desk. "She never even met Charles."

Jack moved to Bella's side. He tried to hold her, but she slapped his hand away and glowered at him. Jack shook his head and sighed.

Wendy cleared her throat. Her olive skin hid the flush of nervousness, but it was evident in her voice. "I did too know Charles. He visited my home, as many did. Everyone knows my shame, must I say more?"

Sheriff Clark shook his head. "No, ma'am. I think we all know what you mean."

"I want to know more," Bella said. "You're saying you not only killed my husband, but you slept with him too and I never knew a thing about it? Hogwash. Besides, I put the bullet in him. I saw it hit; I watched him die."

"Stop lying, Bella." Wendy looked her square in the eyes. "You have to stop protecting Noah and me. The sheriff knows Noah is your brother and that you'd say anything to save him." Wendy looked at the sheriff. "Bella thinks Noah killed Charles, so she is lying for him. Noah knows I killed Charles and he is admitting to the murder because I have a little boy."

"This is absurd." Bella grabbed Wendy by the arm. Wendy looked at her. Bella whispered, "Stop this. Manny needs you."

Wendy shook her head. "I can't lie. No matter how much you want me to." Wendy closed her eyes a moment, then looked at Bella as she continued. "Bella told me her plan as we rode here. She thinks Noah killed Charles and that him being black will get him killed. She said she would claim the murder 'cause she would get the most leniency, being pregnant and all. Isn't that so, Bella?"

Bella's cheeks felt scorched with emotion. Her mouth dropped open. Jack's shoulders relaxed. His relief was only momentary, however, as Bella announced to them all. "I killed him, Sheriff Clark...and I can prove it. He's buried in the field behind the shed. Go dig him up. He has a bullet in his forehead where I hit him with a slug. The only thing Noah and Wendy are guilty of is loving me."

Wendy shook her head. "Bella is lying. She found his body and buried him. That's how she knows these things. But I am the one who shot him. He couldn't accept that I didn't want to be bothered by him anymore. I wanted to be with Noah, and he wouldn't keep his filthy hands off of me. That's why I killed him. I left his body in the barn. I didn't care if the dogs ate him. I didn't think he deserved a proper burial."

Sheriff Clark sighed and shook his head. "Well hell." He turned to Bo. "Lock 'em both up till I can get to the bottom of this."

Chapter 25

Sheriff Clark motioned to Deputy Bo, who responded with a blank look. Clark jerked his head toward the door that led to the holding cell. Bo looked like a pup who didn't yet know not to pee on the floor. He knew he was supposed to do something, but exactly what eluded him. Sheriff Clark shook his head, "Lock 'em up, dammit! Damn the wife and her mess of family. Gonna give up this job, I swear to God."

Bo wrung his hands. "Seriously, Uncle Pete? You want me to lock up ladies? Even..." He nodded to Bella. "...them kind?" His cheeks turned scarlet. "She's, you know..."

"I know what the hell she is, dammit. But she's also confessing to murder and telling me where to find the body. Seems like I'm obligated to hold her until I check things out."

Jack's hand snaked around Bella's waist and squeezed. He looked down at her, stroked her cheek. "Will you be all right here for an hour or so?"

Tears soaked her cheeks. She nodded her head. He pulled her close and held her tight. She tried to explain, but her throat was dry, and her mouth felt full of cotton. Jack put a finger to her lips, silencing her. Once she stopped trying to explain, he smiled and kissed her forehead. "There now. You be still, and I'll be back in an hour to fetch you."

She nodded as her stomach hit the floor. Jack was going to be so shocked when he found Charles's body buried in the field.

He kissed her, tucking the wayward hair back behind her ear. "I don't want you to worry over anything. Do you understand me? Nothing. I love you, sweetness. You have to trust everything will be all right."

Bella nodded. Of course everything would be all right. Even if she hanged, she could trust this man to take care of the baby that kicked and squirmed so much he made her back ache and her belly sore. Jack rubbed her belly as he pulled away. He put his hat on and opened the door to the glaring sunlight. Looking back at her as he left, Bella gave him the best smile she could muster. His eyes moistened, but he returned her smile with a tip of his hat.

When the door closed behind him, Bella felt as if her world ended. He would ride out to the farm, find out the truth, and then the life, the happiness they shared would be over. Bella firmed her resolve and looked to Bo and offered her wrists. "You were told to lock me up?"

Bo shook his head. "I ain't putting irons on a lady, especially not one in your condition. Come with me, the both of you."

He led her and Wendy through the door that separated the sheriff's office from the jail cells. He held open the first iron-barred door they came to like a gentleman, waving them in like he was offering grand accommodations, not a cold stone square with a single iron cot. Bella could smell the iron bars; she could taste their bitterness. They reminded her of blood.

"Bella? You shouldn't have come here." Noah stood and met her at the door for a hug. "But I won't lie and say I'm not happy to see you." He sighed. "For sure, you are a sight for sore eyes. Is Momma all right?"

"She's fine. Worried, but managing. Why, Noah? Why did you do such a foolish thing?"

Noah paced the room and rubbed the top of his head with his hand. He was a thin man, with small features and short stature. He and Bella shared the gray blue eyes. "What else could I do? Charles was my fault to begin with. If you hadn't rescued me, Master Troy would never have arranged that marriage. All this began with me."

"Phooey. It all began with my hateful mother. And that dreadful beast of a husband." Bella shrugged. "But none of that matters. The only thing that matters is that I am the guilty one. I can't deny that to save my hide, especially when it puts you in here."

Noah took her hands in his, "You aren't changing my mind. My story stands."

Bella stomped her foot, then squealed in agony as pain shot through her. "Oooh," she yelped and clutched her stomach.

Wendy grabbed her arms and led her to the cot.

Bo stood at the open door. "Should I get something? Hot water? Towels?"

Wendy scowled at the boy.

Bo asked, "Water?"

"I'm fine. I'm fine. Just need to sit.

Bo looked skeptical, but swung the door closed and locked it. "Well, if you say you're all right."

"She needs to go home," Noah said.

Bo shook his head and shrugged. "I'm sorry, Mr. Noah. I can't. I done told Uncle Pete I didn't want to lock up ladies, but he said I had to."

"Ladies?" Noah looked at Wendy. She looked at the floor.

Bella grimaced and hugged her belly. She looked at Noah. "I need to lie down. My back is hurting something awful." She suddenly felt nauseous. She rolled onto her side and pulled her knees into her belly. Bella closed her eyes and groaned.

Wendy sat beside her, her hands strong, yet gentle, massaged Bella's lower back. "When is your baby due?" Wendy asked.

"Not till next month."

"Are you sure?"

"Pretty sure."

"Oh Lord." Noah looked back over his shoulder. "Bo! Hell fire and blazes MAN, get her out of here."

"I can't go anywhere, Noah. I'm not visiting. I confessed."

"You what?" Noah spun from the bars to kneel by his sister. "Why? When Jack showed up and told me you two were married and expecting a child, I trusted you'd do the sensible thing and keep your mouth shut."

"And hang my brother?"

"And save your child. Jesus, Bell, what were you thinking?"

Bo reappeared. "Need something?"

"I need you to take Bella and Wendy home."

"Well, I can't. They're prisoners. Sheriff says they are to stay here till he checks the grave at the farm."

Noah's mouth dropped open, and he looked at Bella.

"I told them where to look," Bella said.

"Oh Bella," he sighed. His thin frame slid to the floor. He cradled his head in his hands. "You're such a fool."

"Shush. I don't want to hear it." Bella closed her eyes and concentrated on making the pain go away. Wendy kept massaging.

"You will most certainly hear it." He looked back at her. He looked scared, almost shaky. He turned to Wendy. "At least you were smart enough to come with her. I thank you for that Wendy."

"She ain't visiting either. She confessed to murder, too," Bo said. He wrapped his hands around the bars and pressed his face between them like a child watching the circus from a hiding spot.

Noah glanced at Bo, but said nothing. He laid his head against the cot and addressed Wendy "This is foolishness. You never met Charles, who would ever believe you killed him?"

"Her story sure sounded good," Bo said.

Noah didn't comment; he turned to Bella. "And you. You've saved my life too many times already. I don't expect you to do it again."

Bella opened her eyes. She smiled at her brother and patted his shoulder. "I'm not letting you die for this."

"Who said I would die?" Noah argued.

"You'd hang for sure."

"In America...a man is innocent until proven guilty," Noah said.

"Well, now...I'd have to agree with Miss Bell, Noah," Bo chimed in. "Not to say I'm pleased to say it, but if I were a betting man, considering how mad Charlie's kin is, 'cause they are, woo wee, HOT under the collar! You'll hang. And you can't be an innocent man if you've confessed. Seems pretty obvious," Bella pulled herself back into the seated position. The pain had subsided considerably. Must have been the stress, she decided. She poked Noah on the shoulder. "You see? You see why I have to do this? Bo knows."

"Bo is barely a Homo Sapien." He glanced over his shoulder. "No offense, Bo."

"None taken. I'd be the first to admit I've only been at this job a couple of months. I don't know all the laws."

"See what I mean?" Noah grinned. Bella couldn't help but return the grin. Noah sat beside her. "So, enough of this nonsense. Tell Mr. Bo here how Charles attacked you and I shot him."

"I won't lie. I'm going to tell the truth and trust in however the Lord works it out."

Noah stood and paced the cell. "Don't be a fool! You wanting to hang? Is that it?"

"Well no, I'm thinking me being a woman and all, they will offer me more leniency. I know they won't hang me while I'm with child...and maybe Charlie's brother will calm down and leave town knowing I'm in jail. Then when I go to trial, cooler heads will assess the situation." Bella thought a minute. "Why, they'd probably let me have a year, seeing as how I'd need to nurse the baby." Bella sighed and rubbed her temples. "Besides, I'm tired of hiding it. I have nights I can't sleep worried someone will find out, and even if they won't, I feel like God is waiting to punish me for all my lies. I can't, *I won't* do it anymore."

"She makes good points," Bo said with a head nod.

"She makes absolutely no sense!" Noah's voice reverberated off the cell walls. "Have a baby in jail? Are you a fool? Look at this place. It's dark and dirty and cold. A baby could catch any number of diseases here."

"Oh." Bella chewed on her lip.

"Oh is right. You need to start using the brain God gave you. You cannot be guilty of Charles' murder."

"But I can." Wendy spoke up. "I shot him and Noah is trying to protect me. Like you always protect me. And Bella is trying to protect you. But I am the guilty one."

"YOU NEVER MET HIM!" Noah gripped his head and looked to the ceiling as if God would drop a solution from the boards above his head.

"How do you know I never met him? I knew quite a few men before I met you."

"That is truth. Wendy…" Bo began.

Noah grabbed the bars on either side of Bo's face and came nose to nose with the lawman. "Finish that statement and I will add your death to my guilt."

Bella grabbed his arm and pulled him back. "He's not serious Bo. He's distraught because Wendy is obviously lying. Which is foolish considering she has a boy who needs her."

"He's better off with you. I've never been a good mother."

"Oh bull," Bella said.

"I abandoned him. I've lied to him his whole life. He waits for his father, but I know he's dead. I let Manny run wild because I don't want to make him hate me. Honestly? He couldn't even read till I left him with you. You are the kind of mother he needs."

"You're his mother. You only left him because you had to," Bella snapped.

"I left him before. When he was a baby, I couldn't get him to stop crying. I didn't know what to do, so I brought him to my grandmother. Then I left. I didn't come back till he was three and my grandmother could no longer care for him."

Bella looked at her, first shocked, but then thought of her own son, whom she sent to live with Tessie. Sometimes a mother does what's best for her child, even if it means leaving him. "Well. He needs you now."

Wendy shook her head. "No. I have brought nothing but shame to my child."

"Nonsense." Bella rolled her eyes. "If my tarnished reputation can be repaired, so can yours. People thought the worst of me, and I survived and recovered....well till this."

Wendy shook her head.

"I hafta say, I think Bella makes a good point. Running away with a darkie, getting a divorce, and marrying a criminal...I never would have guessed my momma would ever speak to her in public, but she did. Don't know what Momma'll think once she knows you're a murderer. That is if you are. You people sure are confusing me." Bo scratched his head, wagging it back and forth slow as a lazy dog's tail.

"Astounding," Noah said. Bella pinched his leg.

A new voice interrupted the tete a tete. "They're all fools, Deputy Bo. I killed Charles Stanley and they all know it."

Noah stomped his foot as he recognized figure in the doorway. "Momma, what the hell?"

Chapter 26

Tessie poked Bo's arm and pointed to the door. "Come on, young un', open the door and lock me up. I'm confessing to the murder of Charles William Stanley."

"But Miss Tessie, we already got three murderers."

"Seems Charles had a lot of enemies. But *I* am the one who pulled the trigger. These foolish kids are trying to keep my neck from being stretched."

Bo opened the door and waved her in. "What's one more added to the party? I'd offer you another cell, but we only have two and seeing as how you all are still fighting over who gets to be the killer, I don't see any reason to tie up the other. Might need to lock up a real criminal."

Bo closed the door and turned the key in the lock.

"Mama. Have you gone insane?"

"Not at all. I'm old. My child has done been born." She shook her head at Bella. "And raised." She gave an eyebrow-lifted nod to Wendy. "Seems fitting that I killed the bastard."

"But you didn't," Bella said. "All of you in here know damned good and well I fired the bullet that lodged itself in Charles' skull."

Tessie shrugged. "That don't mean it killed him. Hogs have thick skulls, tough to kill one of those. Probably just squealed him."

"He was dead."

"You ran off like a sissy girl. I had to whack him over the head with a shovel to finish him off," Tessie said.

"You lie," Bella said.

"Calling your mammy a liar? Pregnant or not, I can still toss you over my knee and switch you."

Bella's mouth made an O, but before she could speak, Noah jumped in. "Well, then, if this is the way it goes, then neither one of you killed him. I was the last to see him. Momma, you were overwhelmed with worry, so I sent you to check on Bell. Charles opened his eyes, said he had a headache, so I strangled him until his eyes bulged and I was certain he had no pulse."

"Damn boy. Them scrawny arms of yours must be stronger than they look. Charlie was a big man. That'd be a tough neck to grip," Bo whistled.

"He's lying," Bella scoffed. "The bullet killed him and he's making up the story about strangling him. And as for Tessie and the shovel, she whacked him with the shovel before I shot him. All the shovel did was make him angry as a runaway bull." Bella rubbed her temples. "You all mean well, but your stories are insane. Especially yours, Wendy. You need to go home to Manny. He has waited for you as anxiously as he waits for his father. That boy loves you. You can't leave him."

"What about your baby?" Wendy whispered.

"He'll have Jack. And all of you. I'm sure he won't be wanting for love."

"He deserves to know *his* momma," Wendy said.

Bella paced the floor with her hands on her hips. "You all are assuming I would hang. Have you ever considered I would get leniency? That the years of abuse, the drunken rage he was in…how he attacked Tessie…and threatened to kill Noah…why, all of that…and you guys are my witnesses."

"She has a point. I'd take that into consideration," Bo offered with a head bob.

"You are forgetting, Bella…I fired the first shot," Noah said. "If I hadn't missed, you wouldn't have had to fire another shot."

"So," Bo said, "you shot him twice and whacked him with shovels and strangled him…heck how will you ever know who really did him in?"

The group erupted. Each told their version of the death of Charles Stanley. Each tried to outdo the others by raising their voice, hoping their story was the one best heard. As the volume in the cell grew louder and louder, poor Bo shook his head against the bars.

"What the hell, Bo? You having some sort of riot in here? I could hear the ruckus from the office."

Bo yelled above the din, "They're arguing over who's guilty, Uncle…I mean Boss."

"Step aside, boy." Sheriff Clark pulled the keys from Bo's pocket and opened the lock. He held the door wide. "Y'all are free to go."

None of the prisoners heard him over their arguments. He stuck two fingers between his lips and whistled so loudly it echoed off the walls and made each person jump toward the sound.

"If you all would please. Just. Shut. Up!"

They nodded. Wordlessly.

"Seems you're all confessing to nothing. I searched the entire property. Not a body to be found."

"I don't understand." Bella looked at Noah. She looked confused, like she was about to ask him how he hid the body so well.

Noah cleared his throat and grabbed Bella by the hand and nearly gave her whiplash as he strangled her with a hug. "The sheriff knows his business, Bell." He looked down at her with big round eyes. "And if he says we're free, I say we leave."

"Now, you're not exactly free, but I am going to release you on a personal recognizance bond. You can't leave the county of Hickory and you each have to give a deposition regarding what you know about Charles and explain your confessions…all four of them."

"That's bullshit. Absolute bullshit and you know it." Kelly Stanley stood in the doorway, his voice echoed off the station walls. "You're letting that slut off the hook because your deputies dug up her little bastard and you feel sorry for her."

Jack's hands clenched into the flesh of Kelly's neck before Bella could fully register the insult. He lifted his body with a single hand and smashed him into the wall. It took Sheriff Clark, Deputy Bo, and Daniel to peel him off the rasping man.

"Arrest him," Kelly croaked. "Arrest him for assault."

"You need to calm down. You can't speak of a man's wife like that and not expect to be tossed around," Sheriff Clark said.

"I want him arrested," Kelly said as trembling hands adjusted his cravat. "And I want my brother's murderer," he said as he glared at Bella, "to know she will hang."

"There's no body, Mr. Stanley. No body. No murder," Sheriff Clark said.

"And I'm supposed to take your word for it, Sheriff? You witnessed this man assaulting me brushed it off as nothing. I think you're letting the whore walk too." he said and shoved a finger toward Jack.

Daniel had Jack by both arms as quickly as a gunshot, and Noah stepped between Kelly and Jack.

Sheriff Clark shook his head and said, "Listen, mister. I understand you're upset over your kin, but you best watch what fights you start. Some people are glad to end what fools begin."

"You threatening me, Clark? Sounds like a threat to me."

"Mr. Stanley. I suggest you go and have a drink. Cool yourself off a bit."

"Me? Me cool off? You crooked son of a bitch. I knew better than to trust the local law, and it seems I was right. Well, Sheriff Clark, I want you to know I've hired John Union. The best Pinkerton agent in North Carolina. He'll find where she hid the body. Then she'll hang and you, sir, will be in jail for aiding a criminal."

"Do what you gotta do, Mr. Stanley," Sheriff Clark said with a sigh. He scribbled a note on a piece of paper. He handed the paper and a pen to Bella. "You sign this swearing you won't run away and will remain in Troy until this situation is resolved. Then, of course, the rest of you three will have to sign it."

"Bullshit! She'll stay locked in jail!"

"No she won't. I'm not keeping a woman, a pregnant woman, in my jail while you chase a trail. You do all the investigating you want, Mr. Stanley. I'll even call in the Federal Marshall since you don't trust me. But, until I have some proof..." Sheriff Clark scribbled a few words on a piece of paper, stamped it with his seal, then handed it to Bella. "Here, dear, sign this and pass it on." He then looked Kelly square in the eyes and said, "Until that time I'm trusting them on their word."

"She confessed to murdering him!"

"Seems there's a lot of that going on."

Bella felt the pain return and wrap down the side of her belly. She also felt the pain of guilt. She did shoot Charles. "Sheriff Clark, if it would make things better, I could stay here. Till the Pinkerton reports."

Jack shot her a look that made her want to wilt Jack opened his mouth to say something, but Sheriff Clark interrupted, his voice weary, "Mrs. Byron, go home. Listen to your husband and shut up." He turned to Stanley. "From what I gather, and what will go into my official report is that Bella shot at him, and from what I gather, he damn well deserved it. But who's to say her bullet hit him? I did find a slug in the barn stall. I'm guessing Bella shoots like my wife...with her eyes closed...and she only thinks she shot him. Then Charles ran away."

"You're helping her! Your story is bullshit and you know it."

"Do I now? Seems like a plausible explanation." Sheriff Clark glanced at Jack, and Jack nodded ever so slightly, but Kelly didn't miss the communication. His skin reddened and his nostrils flared. "So you *are* in on it. What are you doing? Giving her enough time out of jail to run away? To get away with murder?"

"I'm not doing anything!" Sheriff Clark slammed a fist on his desk. "I AM NOT keeping a pregnant woman in jail just to satisfy the likes of you. IF I find a body, I will investigate a murder. Until then, as far as I know, Charles Stanley left town, and quite frankly, good riddance to bad rubbish. Now get the hell out of my office. I have work to do and I've already wasted a whole afternoon digging up an empty field." Sheriff Clark took his seat and wiped the sweat from his brow. "Jack. Get your wife home and make her get some rest. She looks pale as a ghost and I'll not have her swooning in my office to add to my goddam bad day."

Jack put an arm round Bella's waist and escorted her out. The rest followed. No one spoke. Tessie and Wendy climbed into the back of the wagon. Daniel mounted his horse. "Meet you at the house, Jack?"

Jack nodded and waved him off. Then turned to Noah and asked, "You mind driving the wagon? I need to speak with Bella."

"Of course," Noah answered with a bob of his head. His eyes glistened ever so slightly as he reached out and grabbed Jack's hand and pulled him close and whispered, "I don't know what the hell you've done or how you've managed it, but I thank you."

Jack nodded, and the easy smile that started to play across his face halted with the sound of pistol fire.

"Jack!" Bella screamed. She turned to find him, to be certain he was all right, but she only saw him for a moment before her world went black.

Chapter 27

"Bella! Bella!" Her name slowly leaked into her consciousness. She could hear other sounds, horses pawing the ground nervously, people nearby and at a distance talking quietly among themselves. She heard people wonder if she was okay. Bella slowly realized she was lying in the street. She remembered seeing the gun. Kelly lifted it and aimed. She thought he was going to fire on Jack. She yelled for him to watch out right before she felt the slug slam into her, knocking her off her feet onto the dusty road. She tried to get up, but the pain that had been nagging her for the past hour suddenly took her breath away. She gripped her belly with her good arm and groaned.

Jack was beside her in an instant. He ripped her dress to get a look at her shoulder. He growled curses and threats, but his hands remained gentle. Bella looked up at him and tried to smile. He looked terrified. She tried to take a deep breath to explain she was fine, but she couldn't even manage a shallow one. It was as if the air caught in her throat and gurgled. Bella gripped Jack's arm. She couldn't help but wonder if she was going to die in the road before she ever got to see her baby. She wanted to tell him she was scared, but she couldn't speak.

"It's going to be all right, sweetness. It's just a shoulder wound. Doc Moore is on his way, and he'll fix you right up. You hold on."

She nodded, but the pain grew more intense. Tessie and Noah hovered above her. Tessie cried out, "My baby!" Then Noah grabbed her and held her tight. Bella wanted to tell her Jack said everything was fine, but when she tried to sit up, once again effort was greeted with darkness.

She woke in a strange room. Someone was yelling at her. Shaking her. "Wake up, Bella! You have to wake up. You have to push."

Push? Push what? She tried to think, but the pain in her belly was torture. As if by instinct, she bore down. Someone lifted her shoulders off the bed. Her upper body was sore. She felt hot, so hot she thought she might have died and gone to hell.

"Good girl. Relax a little." She closed her eyes and felt the wave of black relief wash over her. Smelling salts ruined her reprieve. "Stay awake, baby. You have to stay awake."

"Push!" The strange voice barked at her. The sound was harsh on her ears, but she complied as quickly as a shy child. She pushed. She felt her body tremble, doubted she'd survive. No longer cared if she did. She was tired of the pain.

"That's it, child. That's it. He's a blondie like his mommy."

It was Tessie. Bella opened her eyes and searched the room till she found her. When her eyes met hers, Tessie ran to her side and bent down. "Keep going, baby. I can see his head."

"My baby?"

Tessie kissed her cheek. "Of course, your baby. One more good push and you'll be holding your little one."

"Jack?"

"Right here, sweetie." Jack was on the bed. He was the one lifting her off the mattress as she pushed. He leaned forward and kissed her cheek. "Don't you dare leave me, Bell. Don't you dare leave me." His voice was choked off by a sob. Bella stroked his hand and gave it a squeeze. "I won't leave you, Jack. Not ever."

A tear spilled down his cheek. "I'm holding you to that sweetness. Our baby needs his momma."

Bella nodded and was about to smile, but the contraction took her breath away. "PUSH!" the man bellowed. Bella took a deep breath and clenched the damp sheets with both hands, and she pushed with all her might. She felt her body spasm as it demanded rest, but she never relented. She pushed until she felt like she was tearing inside out. Then she felt her child greet the world. Tiny fists and feet glanced off her trembling thighs. She heard his cry. It was a strong, petulant wail. Bella smiled. Her baby was safe. She smiled and relaxed into the velvety darkness.

"Go. Rest a bit, Jack."

Jack shook his head. Dawn approached. Another night was ending and still Bella did not wake. Agnes sighed hard and went to Bella's bed. She touched her forehead and brushed back the sweat-soaked hair. "Did she wake at all?"

Jack looked up at his sister. The shadows of the room hid the tears in his eyes. "Should we call Doc Moore to come back?"

Agnes frowned. She heaved the heavy bucket of scalding water on the side table. She laid fresh towels and rags beside it. "I think we should let Wendy's grandmother come take a look at her. She is bleeding too much, little brother. And she is burning with fever. I think Doc Moore knows more about surgery than he does birthing babies."

"But he's a doctor."

"And his doctoring isn't helping. Wendy can have a midwife here in within hours. If we ask Doc Moore, he'll just say let her rest and ain't nothing else he can do." Agnes dipped a calloused hand into the boiling water without flinching. She wrung out the rag and wiped Bella's sweaty brow. Bella didn't respond. Agnes added, "I don't agree with the laudanum either."

"I don't want her to be in pain."

"She's tough. She needs to be awake. Needs to nurse the babe. Pap and goat's milk won't protect the child from disease."

"Doc Moore said not to let her nurse. It could weaken her." Jack sounded appalled at his sister's suggestion.

"Hogwash. The good Lord wouldn't design a woman to nurse if it was bad for her. Nursing will help stop the bleeding."

"I don't know, Aggie. She's all I have."

"Hogwash again." Agnes lifted Bella's head and pulled her hair to one side and gently washed her neck. "You better take care of her baby. Nothing meant more to her than that. You know as well as I do, she'd nurse that child even if it would weaken her...which it won't."

"What does Tessie think? About the Cherokee midwife?"

"Tessie agrees with me and she is ready to pour the laudanum out in the yard. Being this out of it isn't good for her at all."

Jack squeezed Bella's hand, then brought it to his lips and kissed it. "I only want what's best for her."

"Then you and Daniel take Wendy into the mountains and find this Baka. I once knew an injun midwife, and she knew more about births than any woman...or man I ever knew."

"Daniel and Noah could go. I need to stay here."

"Hmmph." Agnes brushed out Bella's hair with her fingers till it lay smooth across her pillow. "Daniel isn't familiar with the territory, and I'm not sure that Noah has ever ventured much past books and papers. Besides, I need to finish washing her up and change the bandage on her shoulder."

"I'll help you."

Agnes's jaw dropped to her chin. "Why, that's just not fitting."

Jack shrugged. "I don't see why. She's my wife."

"Well, because it just isn't done. And you most certainly won't start a new tradition on my watch. Now get." She waved him toward the door. "And on your way out, tell Tessie you agree about the laudanum. Three days of sleep is enough for anybody."

Jack didn't move.

Agnes dunked the rag in the bucket and wrung it out again. She paused, rag hovering above the bucket. "Did you hear me, Jack? Get on about finding Baka. Before it's too late."

Jack's eyes opened wide. "You think she could…?" He couldn't bring himself to utter the word 'die.'

Agnes frowned and looked down at the fading Bell. "I'd like to say it never happens. That good always prevails and stories all have happy endings, but they don't little brother. I think we need to try the midwife because I don't think we have a thing to lose."

Chapter 28

Jack, Daniel, and Wendy were saddled up and ready to ride into the Smokies where some Cherokees remained hidden away from the government. This was where Manny's family lived and practiced the traditions and medicines of their ancestors. The morning sun crept over the horizon, and the first hearty birds warmed up with a scattering of chirps in the distance. Jack looked back at the house as the horses sauntered away. He loathed leaving, but he knew he had to go. He whispered a silent prayer and nudged the horse to go faster. Wendy and Daniel followed.

Half a mile out the road, Daniel spotted some movement in the trees. He held up a hand and wordlessly cautioned Jack with a gesture and a nod toward the woods. Jack popped the button on his weapon holster. Wendy looked to the woods, her body dipping forward till her cheek grazed the horse's mane. Her horse scampered in response to its rider's nerves. Daniel rode up next to Jack and whispered, "Someone's been following us since shortly after we left."

Jack drew his weapon and rode along the edge of the woods. He heard the leaves rustle and a stick break as someone scurried from hiding. Jack cocked the hammer back. "Show yourself or I'll shoot your lousy hide."

"It's just me, Mr. Jack! It's Manny." The boy came from behind a tree pointing to his little chest.

"What the hell are you doing?" Jack demanded.

"Don't be mad at me, Mr. Jack. I wanted to see where the injuns are."

"They're Cherokee...and who the hell said you could come?" Jack barked.

"Why, nobody. I thought I was trailing you pretty good. I didn't think you'd ever know."

"And why the hell do you want to find the Cherokee?"

Manny didn't have to answer the question. Jack could see it in the boy's face. He wanted to belong. Wanted to know what sort of blood he sprang from. Jack looked over his shoulder a moment. If he sent the child home, he'd try to follow again, possibly even get lost in the mountains. He shook his head. "Get over here, Manteo. I ought to switch you for being so bold, but I haven't the heart. Guess you get your wish. You're about to see Cherokee country."

Manny let out a whoop and held out his hand to Jack, who lifted him off his feet and set him in front of him. Wendy gave him a skeptical look.

Daniel touched her shoulder. "It will be all right. Sooner or later the boy will have to know his heritage. Might as well be now."

Wendy bit her lip. "It's not Manny I worry about." She cleared her throat. "I, uh...I never told the tribe that Manny was born. I never even told them I was pregnant."

"Oh." Daniel frowned. "Should I take the boy back? I'd damn near have to hogtie him and keep him under watch to be sure he stayed home, but I'd gladly do it if him going is gonna cause problems."

Wendy was quiet a moment. "No. You are right. He deserves to know. And they deserve to know him. I have no home. No place I belong. I don't want that for Manny."

Daniel nodded. If he were and eloquent man, he would have let her know that she always had a home with their family. That she had Noah, who loved her enough to follow her through six states to bring her back safe and sound to her son. But he wasn't, so instead he said, "Guess home and family is what you make it."

She nodded and prodded the horse with her feet. "Let's go," she called. "We have miles to cover, and we need to hurry for Miss Bella."

Manny prattled on and on. Jack sighed and shifted in the saddle. Wendy looked back at her child and said, "Shhh, Manteo. Warriors travel so quietly, an enemy doesn't even know they're there until it's too late."

"Really?"

She nodded. Manny didn't say another word. Jack wondered if the child even took a breath until they climbed deep into the mountains and saw the smoke from a fire snaking into the air. Even then he remained silent, wordlessly pointing to the sky. Jack nodded. He could feel the boy's heart quicken against the arm. His own heart hammered as he prayed this medicine woman was as good as Wendy claimed.

A hundred yards from the clearing, a young man emerged. He was dressed in the white man's clothes, but his long hair and brown face were iconic Cherokee. Wendy spoke to him in the Cherokee tongue, pointing back at the men riding with her. They spoke a few minutes, and then the man wandered off.

Wendy turned to them and let out a long breath "He is young. He doesn't remember me, but he is going to get Baka." She looked over the quaint village with its log cabins and muddy streets. She turned to Manny. "So, little one, what do you think?"

"I expected more horses, more warriors. Where are the teepees?"

Wendy smiled. "Cherokee don't live in teepees. The horses are pastured in fenced in fields. And you just saw a warrior."

"Him? He looked like a kid. And why doesn't he wear injun clothes?"

"He's Cherokee. The wise Cherokee adapt. They use what they think is useful of white man's ways. Most here speak English. I spoke the native tongue out of respect. They are at a difficult place. They want to stay here, to get along. But they also want to preserve their culture for their future generations."

Manny looked disappointed as if he expected a full blown pow wow to be going on when he arrived. Wendy was the first to hear footsteps. She turned as a thin woman approached. The woman wore a skirt with a chambray shirt tucked into the waist band. Several strands of beads adorned her neck and her long gray hair was hidden under a bonnet. "Chhaya!" the woman called. Wendy leaped from her horse and ran to the woman. She wrapped herself around her and laughed as tears streamed down her face. "Little Chhaya, you've come home." The woman touched her cheek gently.

Wendy nodded and wiped at her tears.

"I began to doubt, but every spring the Great Spirit spreads the roses," she said and spread her arms wide to the forest, "and I took comfort that my child was well."

Wendy covered her face with her hands. "I am so sorry, Baka. I should have come sooner. I must beg your forgiveness. And, and..." Wendy paused and bit her lip.

"And forgive that even now, I have come because I need help."

Baka nodded. Her wrinkled face pruned up with concern. "Are you in trouble?"

Wendy shook her head. "No. It is a friend of mine. She was shot," Wendy said, pointing to her right shoulder, "here. And she was with child. She delivered the babe. Then fever set in. She has been growing weaker and weaker each day."

"And the young one?"

"A fighter. Just like her momma. But she needs her mother."

"You will take me to her?"

"Yes. Yes, of course I will."

"Come. You can tell me more as we get my bag." Baka gripped Wendy's forearm and dragged her toward a wooden hut with a domed roof. They disappeared inside.

"What did she call my mom?" Manny looked up at Jack, his nose wrinkled.

Jack shrugged and looked at Daniel. Daniel pinched the bridge of his nose. "I think it means shadow. If my Cherokee is any good. And if the Cherokee language is the same here as it is in Oklahoma, then she called her Shadow."

"A windy shadow. How stupid." Manny grunted.

Baka and Wendy reappeared. Baka walked a spotted pony out from behind the house by a bridle. She secured two bags to his thick neck and then hopped on and gave him a nudge to his sides and off they went. Wendy followed her to the edge of the village, and then moved her horse to the front. Baka turned to the men. "Hurry on. If she has been fevered for three days, we must hurry."

"Couldn't agree more," Jack mumbled and gave his horse the command to move it.

Elizabeth Seckman

Chapter 29

Wendy showed Baka to Bella's room with a gentle hand on the woman's elbow. Jack and Agnes followed close behind. Tessie heard the commotion on the steps and met them at the door. When she spotted the withered Cherokee, she burst into tears and grabbed the woman by the hand and nearly dragged her into the room, "God bless ya, bless ya for coming. I pray there's something you can do." Tessie pulled her to Bella's bedside. "This is Bella. She's like my own baby...and she has a baby of her own. I can't lose her, you understand?" Tessie leaned down and stroked Bella's forehead. "She hasn't been awake at all today. Usually I can get her to stir, but not today. I even brought the babe in and let her give a good cry, but nothing." Tessie's words broke off, and she held a hankie to her face and sobbed. "I know it's the blood. I don't know how to stop the blood."

Baka patted her on the back and gestured to Wendy who wrapped an arm around Tessie and escorted her to a seat. "It will be all right," she whispered. Tessie whimpered into her hankie.

Jack turned pale and looked like he might pass out. He dropped to his knees by her bed and held her hand in his. "Please, Bell, please."

Baka went to work, speaking to no one in general and to anyone who wanted to listen. "Yarrow leaves. Crushed in hog fat..." She peeled back the dressing on Bella's shoulder. "...will heal the wound. The bullet is out?"

"Yes. Yes. Doc Moore removed it," Agnes answered.

Baka greased the wound, then applied a clean dressing. "Hot water."

Agnes raced to the dresser and grabbed the pitcher.

"A cup," Baka said.

Agnes nodded and poured the boiling water into a cup. Baka crumpled some of the leaves into the cup. "Drinking yarrow will stop the bleeding inside."

Agnes bit her lip and frowned. "We can't get her to drink a drop."

Baka nodded. "Get the baby." She leaned over Bella as she dug a wad of cotton from her bag. She poured a liquid on it and fanned it under Bella's nose. Bella's nose wrinkled, and her eyes darted under her lids. Baka gave her a smart slap to the cheek. Jack took a suck of breath; his jaw twitched. Bella groaned. Baka slapped her again. Her eyes fluttered open. "Lift her up." Baka barked at Jack. He lifted her limp body pillow and all. Baka ordered her to drink. Bella took a sip and grimaced. "Drink it all." Bella shook her head and seemed to be slipping back to sleep, but then Agnes walked in with the baby who was fussing and struggling against her blankets. "Let her cry," Baka ordered, stretching out her hands for the child. Agnes handed her over. Baka unwrapped the blanket, and the baby let out a lusty scream. Bella's eyes fluttered open again. Baka held the baby in front of her just out of her reach. Tiny pink fists and feet pumped and punched against the air.

Bella shook her head. She needed to get rid of the fog clouding her mind. She could hear her baby. She opened her eyes. Some strange woman was holding him, dangling him above the bed. Bella reached for him, but the woman drew him away and handed him to Agnes. "Please…my baby…" Bella whispered.

"Drink," the withered woman commanded. Bella shook her head. "My baby."

"Drink and you can have her."

Bella's brain worked so slowly. Who was this woman and why was she trying to make her drink. Maybe it was poison? But why would Agnes let her hurt her? Bella thought she heard Tessie. She was sobbing. Maybe the Yankees were back. Maybe they were being tortured. Bella needed to think it through, but she was so tired. Too tired really to think clearly. The baby's wails grew shriller. Bella tried to get up, but her body felt like lead.

"Drink, sweetheart, please." Bella looked to her right. Jack was beside her. He smiled at her. "It will help you." Bella nodded. The woman brought her the cup, and Bella drank. She choked and coughed, but drank long enough to make the woman smile. With great effort, she downed the last drop. She felt as drained as if she had walked a million miles. Jack settled her back against her bed, gently making her comfortable. Bella was about to close her eyes and rest, but suddenly the warmth of her blankets were stripped away and the horrible woman started jabbing her in the belly. She pushed and squeezed, causing Bella's stomach to tighten in pain. She tried to shoo the woman away, shoving at her with weak hands. Baka motioned for Agnes. "Keep massaging her belly. We need to get blood to the womb. I need to make sure they got all the after birth."

Agnes nodded and put her firm, strong hands to the task. Bella let out a yelp and moaned in pain. Jack gathered both of her hands and held them close to his chest as he whispered, "It's going to be all right, Bell, it's going to be all right."

Baka shook her head. "Just as I thought. Give me clean towels." She traded Wendy bloody towels for the clean ones before covering Bella back up.

Tears rolled down Bella's cheeks. Baka pulled the blankets back up to her chin.

Baka leaned closer to Bella. "You're going to be fine. You want to hold your baby?"

Bella nodded. Tessie hurried over, the baby swaddled and snug in her blankets once again. Baka nestled the baby next to Bella and helped the hungry baby find a breast. "Doc Moore says that will weaken her."

"Pah. What does he know? The babe needs the milk, and she needs to nurse. It will stop the bleeding."

Jack nodded. He stroked Bella's hair as she lay with her eyes closed. He kissed her forehead. It was cold and clammy with sweat, but her breathing was steady. He looked to Baka. "Is it all right if she falls asleep?"

Baka smiled. "You could both use sleep." She gathered her bag and motioned for everyone to leave the room.

The door closed. Jack brushed the tendrils of hair from Bella's cheeks and a frown tugged at the corners of her mouth. She was so pale, and her skin was warming again with the damned fever. Her breathing slowed as she drifted deeper into sleep. Her soft breaths and the sounds of the baby suckling comforted him, but he couldn't let go of the fear that she might slip so far into her rest that she would leave him forever. He propped himself up on an arm planning to keep a vigil. He wouldn't sleep. He would watch over her all night, do battle with the grim reaper himself rather than let this woman leave him.

The sun started to set. The shadows in the room grew longer. Jack held his eyes open wide trying to revive them against the heavy feel. The shadows hid the pale skin and dark circles under her eyes. Her beauty was enough to take his breath away. He would never in a million years understand what he did to be so lucky. He stroked her cheek, and she smiled faintly. He whispered, "I love you." And she let out a soft hum. He leaned over carefully and kissed her temple. The baby stirred and kicked a skinny leg, then soothed herself nestling closer to her mother's breast. Jack returned to his watch position. The vanishing light dipped below the horizon casting the room in darkness. Jack's head felt heavy and started to nod, but the drop brought him wide awake. He needed to walk around a bit, maybe take the baby for a diaper change. As he lifted his body from the bed, Bella stirred. He sat motionless for a moment, and then tried to move again. The creaking springs sounded as loud as a train whistle in the quiet room. Bella's head moved against the pillow. Jack held his breath wondering if she was asleep or awake. He sat, one knee on the bed, one foot on the floor trying to decide what to do. Bella whispered, "Don't leave me, Jack. I sleep better when you're here."

A tear rolled down his cheek as he returned to the bed. He put an arm out and stroked her shoulder. "I won't ever leave you, my sweet. You better not leave me."

Bella's voice sounded weak and tired. "I'd never leave you, Jack. You're the silliest."

Jack didn't try to stop the tears. He let them roll one after another onto his pillow. After a while, they started to slow, and his body felt heavy as hell. He heard Tessie slip into the room and pull the baby away from Bella. In his dazed state, he thought he heard Tessie and Bella talking, but he wasn't certain. He did hear the door click closed and felt Bella kiss his lips and tuck herself against his shoulder. He wrapped an arm across her, and felt his body relax. It felt so good, he was certain he had died and gone to heaven.

Chapter 30

Bella woke to the echoing whispers of Manny outside her door. "But it's for Miss Bella. It will make her feel better." Bella couldn't hear who argued against his point, only his voice reverberated off the walls. "Well then if she's asleep, I'll sneak in and leave it." Silence. "I do too know how to be quiet."

Bella's body was stiff and ached every time she moved, but the pain in her stomach was gone. Replaced by a fullness in her breasts. She pulled herself up a little. Jack lay snoring on the pillow beside her. She smiled. She heard the sounds of Manny being dragged from her door, his shoes scraping against the wood floor. "I declare! I don't know what has gotten into you!"

Tessie. From the sound of her huffing and puffing, she was losing the physical battle with the growing boy.

"Now see what you've done." Bella heard Manny's voice crack. "You broke it!"

Bella called out, "Manny. Come here."

Jack stirred and rubbed his face with his hands. Then, as if remembering the last few days, he shot straight up. "Bella, you're awake. Are you all right?"

Bella nodded. "A bit sore and I feel like my whole body is made of lead, but I feel fine." Then her eyes popped open. "The baby! Where's our baby, Jack?"

Jack smiled. "She's fine. Tessie's been watching over her like a hawk."

"Her?"

"Yep. A baby girl. That all right with you?"

"Oh, my, why, yes, of course. I was so sure I was having a boy. I hadn't even thought of any girl names."

The door opened a crack. Two sets of brown eyes, one at three feet, then one above at five, peeked in, "Miss Bella?" Manny whispered.

Bella smiled. "Come in, Manny. I've missed you"

Jack kissed her forehead.

Manny crept into the room. He carried a sack of dirt with a scraggly bush sticking out the top. He held it out so Bella could see it. "I spent a day with the Cherokee, Miss Bella. I even got a Cherokee name and made arrows with a warrior. And I met my uncle! I guess my dad is dead. That kinda makes me sad, but I never knew him, so I guess I'm not so sad. My uncle is a brave fighter. He even fought the Yankees. And he thinks like you, Bella. He reads and writes and wears white people clothes and goes and talks with the people who make laws. I told him you made me go to school, and he said you were a wise woman. He said that, Bella! He said, 'she is a wise woman'!" Manny's dark head dipped. "But then I cried. I didn't mean to, and I couldn't really help it."

Bella's face softened, and she touched his smooth cheek. "Well, that's a lot of changes for a young boy. You were probably overwhelmed."

"Oh no! I was sad 'cause I was afraid you were gonna die."

"Oh?" Bella's eyes opened wider, but then she smiled. "I think I've pulled through."

"It's 'cause I got you this." He held up his bag of dirt. "Have you heard of Nunna dual Tsung?"

Bella shook her head.

Manny shifted the bag to his hip. "It means the trail where they cried. When the white people made most of the Cherokee move west, that's how my dad died...anyhow...the moms prayed for the strength to go on and these grew along the trail. It was a message from the Great Spirit that everything would be all right." Manny set his bag on the floor and came to the side of the bed and handed Bella a flower. "See, four white petals for the pure hearts, a gold center for the gold they were run off for, and seven leaves on the stem for the seven tribes. Uncle Balik, that's my dad's brother, and the warrior I was telling you about...he says this would bring you good luck. Till Tessie broke it." He shot Tessie a scornful look.

Tessie looked embarrassed. She came over and checked Bella's forehead. "Fever's broke. Praise Jesus." She leaned down and gave Bella a kiss on the cheek. "You hungry, child?"

"Starved. And I need a bath. But first, I want to see my baby. Will you fetch her, Tessie?"

Tessie smiled and nodded. A tear slid down her cheek. "She's a spitting image of you, when you were a baby. Just takes my breath away." She wiped her eyes with her apron as she left the room.

Bella turned to Manny. "And you, little man, let me hold that flower. I want to see it up close." He placed it in her hand. Bella took a suck of air. "That is the most beautiful thing I have ever seen! Why, Manny, I want to put this right by my bed so I can see it all the time. I must press it and keep it forever."

"You really like it? Think it's okay broke off?"

"It's perfect. I can't decide where to plant the bush. By the front porch so the whole world can see it, or at the back swing so I can look at it while I relax. That's such a quandary."

"No, it ain't. I'll just get you another."

"Could you?"

"Of course. They grow all over injun, I mean Cherokee land. And Balik, my uncle, he's coming to get me once a week to teach me how to be a Cherokee. Baka, the lady who saved you? She's my great grandma, but not by blood. You see, my mom, she didn't have a clan, and you have to belong to a clan through your mom. So, Baka adopted her. My mom and dad married, but then when my dad decided to go west, he didn't want my mom to go with him because she was having me. He was going to come for her later."

Manny stopped to take a breath. He frowned and continued, "He didn't get attacked by a bear, Bella. He got bit by a rattle snake. That's why he never came for us. Mom says she had to leave the Cherokee to take care of her mother and never went back.

"I'm sorry about your dad, Manny," Bella said taking the boy's hand.

"I really like Balik, my uncle. You'll have to meet him." Manny looked around the room as if to make sure no one was listening who would tell on him. "He's going to help me if they try to lock you up, Miss Bella. He says we can steal you out of prison and take you west where no one will ever find you. He is a brave and knows everything about the forest,"

Bella's heart slowed. How could she have forgotten what she'd done? Forgotten what kind of trouble she was in? She swallowed. "Well, thank you, Manny. I will, ah, keep that in mind."

Jack rubbed his chin and looked at the boy. "You're a good man, Manteo. Watching out for your friends and family is the best measure."

"I won't allow nobody to lock Miss Bella up, Mr. Jack. No sirree. And I done swore to little miss I'd take care of her too. She may be ugly as a bird, but still she'll need someone to look out for her at school and all."

"Ugly?" Bella laughed despite her troubles.

"Yep, she's right ugly. People keep saying how pretty she is, but she ain't. She's scrawny and red and cries a whole lot."

Tessie's footsteps echoed in the hallway. Bella gave Manny's cheek a pat. "Well, I guess I will have to see for myself." She looked to the door and her heart hammered in her chest. That bundle in Tessie's arms was her baby. Jack helped her pull herself up, arranging the pillows behind her. He took the bundle from Tessie and handed her to Bella, who instantly burst into tears.

Manny shook his head. "Geesh, Miss Bell, she ain't quite that ugly."

Bella laughed. She held her daughter close and kissed the soft cheek. "I think she's beautiful, Manny. Simply beautiful. I'm so happy."

Manny scrunched his eyebrows and shrugged.

Jack lifted Bella's chin until she looked up at him. He couldn't think of any words that expressed the feelings that swelled inside him. Instead, he kissed her and buried his face in her shoulder and cried, hoping like hell Manny didn't notice.

"Come on, Manny. Miss Agnes whipped up some cakes for callers. I'm sure she could use an opinion on whether or not they're worthy of company." She took the boy by the shoulder and walked him from the room.

When she heard the door click closed, Bella looked to Jack. The worry on his face made her heart skip a beat. Her mind spun with the possibilities of a life in jail or on the run. Or was the west really that wild they could just disappear?

"What am I going to do, Jack?"

Jack wiped his eyes and kissed the top of his daughter's head. "Do about what, sweetness?"

"I'm wanted for murder. I know what that Pinkerton will find, and I know I'll be headed back to jail. Then when they find me guilty…"

"You're not guilty of anything, Bell. I'm sure the sheriff will clear you. Hell, Kelly's own investigator should be able to clear you."

Bella clutched her daughter. "But, Jack, I am guilty."

Jack shook his head. "You can't blame yourself for Charles. He deserved what he got, and if running away with his tail tween his legs is how he wants to deal with his wrongs, then good riddance."

"I shot him. I shot him in the head and Noah buried him in the field. That's why I was so nervous about you poking around the shed."

Jack smoothed the hair on the baby's head. "You know, she's five days old and has no name."

"Did you hear me? Did you hear anything I said?"

"I've been calling her Punkin', but that isn't nearly pretty enough for my sweet girl." He kissed her gently. "And don't you listen to Manny, little one. You are as stunning as your momma. Manny is just a fool boy."

Bella took him by the chin and lifted his face until he was looking at her. "Listen to me, Jack! I shot Charles. Noah buried him. He's dead."

Jack shrugged and took her hand in his and kissed the open palm. "You shot him, yes. Noah buried him, true. But Bella, he isn't in that grave."

"That's impossible."

"Let's worry about a name. Bella junior? Do you name baby girls like that?"

"Certainly not." Bella shook her head in frustration. She couldn't believe what Jack was saying, or how nonchalant he was acting. Beads of sweat broke out along her brow. How could she solve this problem if the man she counted on most in the world didn't take her seriously? The baby started to fuss.

"See now," Jack whispered. "She knows her momma is upset and it bothers her."

Bella took a guilty suck of air. "You think so?"

"I know so."

"I'm so sorry, baby." Bella cooed as she lifted the baby to her shoulder and patted her back. "Momma's fine. So sweet, so precious."

"And she also needs a name."

"I don't have any girl names. I was certain she was a boy."

"Shame on you. I told you I wanted a baby girl like her momma. You know I always get what I want."

"Hmmph." Bella grinned. "That's pretty arrogant of you."

Jack chuckled. "I'm a happy man. You should kiss me."

Bella grinned and leaned forward and kissed her husband.

"Mmmm, still sweet. Kiss me again."

Bella grinned and readily complied. Jack winked at her. "See, I told you I get what I want."

Bella gave him a playful pinch with a shake to her head. "Well, I assure you, you won't get to name her junior."

"Then just Isabella."

Bella shook her head. "Too confusing. Besides one Isabella per century is plenty."

"Oh, I hardly agree with that. Isabella it is."

"But I don't like it, and I did give birth to her."

"Yes, but I sat up with her for the last five nights while you slept, and I had the stress and worry of what was going to happen to my family. It was a nightmare. I will probably have bad dreams for the rest of my life. I was never so scared. Not even prison compared to the pain I felt thinking I would lose the best thing that ever happened to me."

"Oh, Jack." Bella stroked his hair. "You poor man. I forget. That time felt like a few hours' sleep for me. Were you really a wreck?"

He nodded, his eyes burning with tears. Bella kissed him slowly, then laid her head against his shoulder. "I'll never leave you, Jack. I promise."

"I don't ever want to be that scared again."

"It'll all be all right. And I suppose you can name her Isabella. But I'll not call her Izzie or Bella. You have to come up with a proper middle name she can go by."

Jack thought a minute. "Why, we'll name her Rose. Show little Manteo how grateful we are for his gift."

Bella laid the baby across their laps. "Well now, little Rosie, what do you think of that?"

"Isabella Rose. I think it suits her perfectly."

Bella gave Jack an ornery grin. "And don't you think it passed my notice that once again you got your way."

Jack threw his head back against the headboard and let out a hearty chuckle. It was interrupted by a knock at the door. Jack composed himself enough to yell, "Come in."

Noah poked his head in the door. "Jack, the sheriff needs to speak with you. I told him I'd send you down."

Jack nodded. He looked at Bella, who was suddenly pale as the white pillowcase her head leaned against. Jack's jaw was firm and his words serious, "You'll not worry over this, you hear? Everything is going to be fine."

Bella nodded and chewed the side of her cheek.

Chapter 31

The door closed and she could hear Jack's footsteps fade as he made his way downstairs; once she was certain he was beyond earshot, Bella turned to Noah. "He won't believe me, Noah. I don't think he believes me capable of murder."

"It wasn't murder, Bell. You saved my life. Momma's life."

"Well, the law won't care. There's a dead man buried in my field."

"No, there isn't. I thought maybe Jack was looking in the wrong spot, but I checked. Charles's body is gone."

Bella's face scrunched in thought. She stroked Rose's head absently, cradling the child, and stroking her cheek against hers. "Could Jack be right? Could the bullet have knocked him out but not killed him?"

Noah started to shake his head, but he stopped with a jerk as if his mind just woke with possibility. "I'm not a doctor, but maybe I was mistaken to think he was dead. I've heard plenty of stories of people being buried alive…and I didn't bury him very deep. It was almost dawn and I was in a hurry."

"Oh Noah! If only. I feel as if a huge weight is being lifted. To NOT be a murderer? I mean I never truly blamed myself, but there was always this nagging in my heart, this feeling of coming judgment …does that make sense?"

"Certainly. You don't have a mean bone in your body, Bell. Charles was a horrible man, but you wouldn't have shot at him if there was any other choice."

Bella's smile dropped, and she sighed. "But more likely, Jack has fixed things. When he first came here, he poked around that building a lot. Jack moved the body."

"Still…without a body, the law has no…"

"Maybe…without a body, I get away with murder, but truth is I am still a murderer. I don't know if I can look Kelly in the eye and not tell him the truth about his brother. Charles was a horrible person, but he was still a person. He still had family who loved him."

"Kelly's probably looking for money."

Bella shook her head. "He shot me. He didn't blackmail me."

"Bella." Noah took her hand in his and squeezed it hard. "You have GOT to promise me you won't confess to anything. You have this baby to look out for. And Jack. Jack will die a slow death if he loses you. These past few days have been a nightmare for him. He has walked around this place like a ghost. You can't sacrifice your child and your husband to give piece of mind to a Stanley."

Tears welled in her eyes, but she shook them off. She nodded at Noah, but made no absolute promises.

There was a quiet knock on the door. Noah leaned over and swung the door open. Wendy poked her head in the room. "May I?"

"Of course." Bella smiled and waved her in. Wendy came in and stood by the bed. She wrung her hands nervously.

"You have an official name?" Noah asked touching a tiny pink hand gently.

Bella looked down at Rose. "We named her Rose, after Manny's gift. Isabella Rose.

"That is very pretty." Wendy smiled.

"Jack insisted on the Isabella. I find it a bit much, but it pleased him to get to name her. I suppose I will get even when we have a boy."

Wendy smiled. "Manny is planting the rose and insisting I take him back into the Smokies for another."

Bella folded her lips in and groaned. "I'm sorry. That is my doing. I told him I didn't know if I wanted the rose planted in the front yard or the back. He offered to get me two."

"I am glad he is so thoughtful. You have done much for him. He should want to do all he can." Wendy cleared her throat and added, "Balik, Manny's Uncle, has offered to help us build a house on Cherokee land."

"Is that what you want?" Bella asked.

Wendy looked at Noah and shrugged. "I am waiting for Noah to make his decision. Balik wants Noah to run the school, to teach the tribe the white man's knowledge."

"Why that sounds perfect! You guys will be close by, and Noah, you've always wanted to teach...and they probably have much more clever minds than me! Why, I declare I couldn't have thought of a better solution."

Noah sighed and shook his head.

"What? What's there to decide, Noah?" Bella looked suddenly like the big sister, ready to boss her little brother around.

"It's complicated," was all Noah would offer.

"Not really," Wendy said. "Balik asked you to teach the tribe, you are an excellent teacher, we could live free from scorn, and have a family. And Manny would be happy to be close enough to visit everyone."

Noah cleared his throat. "We'll discuss it later."

"Why not now?" Wendy asked quietly as she cast a quick glance to Bella. Bella caught the look and understood from the depths of womanly sisterhood what Wendy needed from her. Bella bit on the bait and turned on her brother. "When are you going to stop being such a coward, Noah?"

"Excuse me?" Noah looked deeply offended.

"You heard me," Bella said matter of factly. "You love her, right?"

"Of course."

"And you love Manny...and all of us can see how an attachment to his culture has made the boy flourish, right?"

Noah stood and walked to the window and looked outside for a while before turning back to Wendy and Bella and announce, "I prefer to live in the North. I feel comfortable there. There are actually colleges for black men and opportunities there that will never be here."

"Then I will go with you," Wendy announced with a smile.

Noah frowned. "No, Wendy. I think it best that you stay here."

"I don't understand."

"Manny needs to stay here," Noah explained.

Wendy made a heroic effort at staying calm, but she failed, dropping her face into her hands and sobbing. Bella shot Noah a look of death. "Come here, Wendy." Wendy sat on the bed, and Bella wrapped an arm around her, hugging her close and rubbing her back.

Bella cooed the crying woman a moment before turning her anger toward Noah. "What is wrong with you?"

"Excuse me?"

"You heard me. You're a fool, Noah Solomon. Act like you haven't got the sense God gave a goose! You belong up north. Hmmph…bout as much as I belong in polite society. You only think you belong there. You belong with your family. And Wendy and Manny are your family. And Tessie. You really going to leave your momma again? Make her worry over you night and day, wondering if you are alive? How selfish!"

"Selfish?" Noah snapped.

"Selfish." Bella stroked Wendy's hair. "I'm sorry, honey. I don't know how my little brother got to be such a horrible, selfish toad."

"I am NOT selfish," Noah barked. "I AM thinking of Wendy and Manny. Balik would make a much better husband and father than I ever could."

"Balik?" Wendy wiped her eyes and looked to Noah. "Why would I want Balik? I love you."

"Balik is strong and he is smart…he is a better man…"

"Then you marry Balik." Wendy yelled the words and jumped up from the bed. Bella snuggled tiny Rose closer covering her delicate ears and shielding her from the fray.

Wendy poked Noah in the chest. "I love you. You are the better man. You are brave and smart and good. If you want to not love me because I am a bad woman or a sorry mother, then say it."

"Wendy, no. I have never thought that. You are braver than you will ever know, and I know how much you love Manny, how you thought sacrificing yourself would save your boy. No, sweetheart, I want you to have the best this life has to offer. You deserve that and more."

Wendy brushed away tears. "Then marry me. Come with me to the mountains, start a school, and have a family with me. I will make you happy, I swear. I will be a good wife."

Noah grabbed her and held her tight. "Oh darling, please, don't cry. I do love you, and I know you will make a wonderful wife. Bella's right, I am a fool. I love you too and I'll do whatever makes you happy."

"Really?" Wendy sounded as giddy as a small child.

"Really." Noah hugged her close. "I would do anything for you. Anything that would make your life better. Even if it meant walking away."

Wendy shook her head emphatically and held his face in her hands. "Don't you ever think that leaving me is best. I love you, Noah Solomon. And you are braver and stronger than any warrior or chief ever could be."

Bella smiled and couldn't help but cry the happy tears. Her brother looked so happy, and she didn't have to worry about hardly ever seeing him. The mountains were a short ride away. Well, as long as she didn't get imprisoned or have to go on the run...or...the sick feeling washed over her again...if she didn't get her neck stretched by the hangman's noose. She rubbed her throat and wished Jack would come tell her what was going happening.

Chapter 32

Bella scooted to the edge of the bed and put shaky feet on the floor. This simple movement tired her, made her legs shake and sweat break out on her forehead. She gripped Rose tighter, fearing she might pass out and hurt her baby.

Noah was the first to notice. He stepped away from Wendy with a scolding bark, "What are you doing?"

Bella held Rose out toward him on trembling arms. "Take her. I feel…"

Noah barely got his arms under his niece before Bella went limp. Wendy rushed to her side and shoved her body back onto the bed before she slid to the floor. "What was she trying to do?" Wendy asked.

"Hard to tell. Fool girl rarely thinks ahead." Noah leaned down and lifted an eyelid, gently smacking her cheek. Bella moaned. "Go get Momma." Noah looked down across her small body, "I don't see any blood. But someone better check her. If she starts bleeding again. Sweet Jesus, I don't know how much blood one body can lose."

Wendy didn't say another word. She nodded and disappeared. Tessie arrived minutes later with smelling salts and a tray of food. She set the tray on the dresser and did a quick check under Bella's bottom to be certain she wasn't bleeding again. She kissed Bella's forehead, then waved the salts under her nose. Bella flinched, but woke. "What are you doing?" She blinked as if she couldn't focus. "Tessie?"

"Mmm hmm. Fool girl. Where were you trying to go?"

Bella thought a minute. Then she remembered. "Jack. I wanted to get Jack."

"He'll be in shortly. I'm certain young Manny will alert him, even though I told him not to do it yet."

"I passed out?"

"Of course. You got no blood in your body, child! You gotta eat. You gotta rest. Then in about a week you can get up and start walking around." She gave her a narrow-eyed warning. "You can maybe go sit in your swing. If you behave. Get up again? I'll tie you to this bed myself."

Bella nodded and quietly took the cup of soup Tessie ordered Wendy to bring from the tray. Bella took a hesitant sip, but once it hit her stomach, she felt starved. She chugged the whole cup in such an indelicate manner she was certain Tessie would scold her real good. Instead Tessie smiled; a tear shimmered in her eye. Tessie cleared her throat and blinked back the tear. She took a napkin from the tray and gave it a snap, unfolding the linen square in a single movement. "I suppose you remember how to use a napkin? Eating like a field hand, I swear."

Bella took the napkin and grinned. "I'm still hungry."

"Well good thing I brought more." Tessie turned to Wendy. "Bring the tray, child, so miss can eat." Wendy brought it over. Her smile was so broad, Bella wondered if it hurt her a bit. "Baka said when you round the corner, you will be starved and ready to eat."

Bella took a hot roll and devoured it without cutting it open or slathering it with the butter. "She's right. Your Baka. She's a smart, lady," Bella said as she chewed.

"Baka is wise."

"When I can ride? I want to go to the mountains and thank her myself."

"I will gladly take you."

"Good," Bella said, "I will be fit in a week. Unless…" Why did she have to keep thinking about jail? She groaned and her chewing slowed.

"Don't worry over it, Bell. I won't let them lock you up." Noah sat beside her and tugged one of her curls. "You get well. That's all you have to worry about."

Bella considered telling him she knew he planned to fall on the sword for her and that she would have none of it, but instead she smiled and patted his cheek. "You're right, little brother. Things'll work out." *If I have to run away to the hills and hide the rest of my life, so be it*. She thought as she flashed them all a charming smile.

"Jack is coming! And he's bringing the sheriff!" Wendy closed the curtains to the window as if that would shut out reality. She darted around the room like she was looking for a place to hide. Noah gripped Bella's arm. She grabbed hold and took a suck of breath.

The door opened slowly. Jack led the sheriff in. He picked up Rose and held her out for the sheriff's inspection. "Isabella Rose. Prettiest baby in all the South. Hell, all the world." He kissed the top of her head. The sheriff touched a grizzled hand to a tiny fist. "My, she is tiny. I was worried for you, young'in. Not too many gets to be born while the doc digs a bullet out of her momma." He turned to Bella. "Sorry for that, Miss Bell. I never dreamed Kelly was capable of that. Had I known, I'd have offered better protection. I guess those damned Stanley's are all hot-headed beasts. I've still got him locked up, charging him with attempted murder."

"You are?" Bella's voice was barely above a whisper. Her heart hammered. Her body's effort to run it so hard dried out her mouth and made her limbs cold. Noah's grip tightened.

"Most certainly. Though I will say, he calmed down considerably after his Pinkerton brought him the report on Charles. Then once he got to thinking on it, his ire was raised over Charles skedaddling out of town and leaving him to hold all the family's debts. Now seems he wants to hunt his brother down and murder him." Sheriff Clark chuckled. "Craziest bunch I ever saw."

"Charles is alive?"

"Don't sound so surprised." Sheriff Clark laughed. "Your bullet never hit him, Bell. But I daresay, with his temperament, it's probably a matter of time before someone really does put a bullet in his thick skull."

Bella looked dazed. She tried to sort out what Sheriff Clark was saying, but she couldn't make sense of it, especially when the image of Charles with a bullet hole through his forehead haunted her worst dreams.

"Bella." Jack spoke a bit too loudly. "I know you shot at Charles. We found the bullet hole in the barn, so I assume you confronted him there?"

Bella nodded. Noah groaned and whispered. "Sweet Jesus."

"But you didn't hit him."

"But..." Bella began.

"No buts. The Pinkerton investigated. You shot AT Charles, but you missed."

The image of dead glazed eyes shot through her memory. She opened her mouth, but Noah pinched her. She looked at him, and he gave her the look, that look they shared as children when he wanted her to shut up...when her mouth would get them the business end of Tessie's switch. Bella closed her mouth and turned back to Jack and said, "I'm so glad to hear that. I was so worried I harmed him, since, of course, Kelly showed up and said no one had heard from him. Until then I had assumed he knew I wasn't going to tolerate his meanness a day more and ran on home to his momma."

"Seems his momma died during the war," Sheriff Clark explained. "Kelly and Edward are the only family he has left, but he didn't go home to them...probably because he sold off the family estate and didn't share a dime with them. No, it seems your husband wandered north. Got arrested a couple of times for disorderly conduct and had to sleep off the effects of, uh, spirits in jail for a day a few times. Then he seems to have racked up a considerable amount of debt in Ohio to some pretty rough people, so I doubt he'll show his face on the East coast ever again...or he will be pushing up daisies."

Relief. She felt relieved to be free of Charles's murder. She didn't even realize the business weighed on her until she was free of it. "Do you think Kelly would ever try to harm me again?" Bella asked.

"Likely not. And if you wanted to show him some clemency, might save him from being hardened in jail. Most he'll get is a few years anyhow."

"Then release him. Tell him I'm sorry for his pain and I forgive him for shooting me, but I'd rather not have any ties to the Stanleys ever again."

"You've got to be kidding me," Jack said, then turned to the sheriff. "You're seriously asking my wife to look the other way? She damned near died!"

"It'd put this whole business to rest. But it is her decision."

"The hell it is. I'm her husband."

295

"Might be best to let it go, Jack. Time to get on with life. I agree with Bell. Let's put the past behind us." Noah spoke quietly. "As long as Kelly agrees to stay away."

Jack's face reddened, and he didn't look at all convinced.

"Vengeance is mine, sayeth the Lord," Tessie added.

"Please, Jack? I don't want to be burdened knowing I am keeping a man in jail. He was distraught. He thought his kin was murdered. You feel angry that he even wounded me, imagine how Kelly must have felt?"

The muscle in Jack's jaw twitched. He put his hands on his hips and shook his head back and forth slowly. Then with a long sigh, "Fine. Let him walk. But I want to talk to him before he leaves town. Let him know he is only walking away because of my wife's mercy and let him understand exactly what will happen to him if he so much as sends a Christmas greeting."

"Oh, Jack." Bella almost giggled at his comments. He was so protective. Her heart soared, and she wished she had the energy to jump up and hug him.

Jack shook the sheriff's hand. "Well then, seems this business is wrapped up. Now if you all don't mind, my wife needs rest."

The sheriff made his adieus. Tessie offered to show him out as she grabbed the baby insisting she needed a bath and Bella needed rest.

Wendy and Noah excused themselves also. Noah gave her a kiss on the cheek as he left. Bella gave his nose a tweak as she assured him, "I can help plan a wedding from right here, you know?"

"Think I should ask her first?" Noah laughed.

"Oh, I think I know the answer," Bella said. Wendy smiled as they left the room. She held onto Noah's hand as if she feared he would try to escape her. Jack lay down beside

Bella and pulled her in close, nestling her head under his chin. He kissed the top of her hair and breathed a sigh of relief. Bella kissed the hollow of his neck and stroked her cheek against the coarse hairs that poked out from his collar. "I wonder sometimes, Jack Byron, if you're not more my guardian angel than my husband."

"I'm everything and anything you need me to be, Bella Byron. 'Cause you might think I'm your angel, but I know you're my life."

Bella smiled, content in the knowledge that he truly was the best value for any gold she ever spent.

Elizabeth Seckman

Epilogue

Bella scurried around the room, trying to find the lavender bonnet that perfectly matched her lilac print yard gown. As she searched wardrobes and drawers, she was subjected to the petulant pouts of Rose, who sat on the bed, back curved, legs crossed, and her dress billowing about her in a most unladylike manner.

"Momma, you have to stop him!"

Bella bent over and answered with growing agitation as she looked under her bed and dealt with her unhappy daughter. "Manny is an adult. It's not within my control."

"It most certainly is! All you have to do is tell Daddy not to pay his tuition."

Bella let out a long exasperated sigh. She took a minute to remind herself she, too, was once an impatient little girl who thought the entire world should come under her control. She sat next to her daughter and brushed soft blond curls away from her cheek. She answered quietly, patiently, "Ah Punkin', I wouldn't stop him even if I could."

Rose gasped and turned wide eyes to her mother.

Bella put a finger to the child's lips and said, "Now shh, listen to me. Manny is a man with a dream. And he is as spirited as a soaring falcon. If you really care about him?"

Rose looked pitifully at her mother, unshed tears making her blue eyes sparkle. "I know you love him, darling. That's why you have to let him go. You have to let him follow his dream and find his own way in life."

"No! No, he doesn't! He could work here, with Daddy and Uncle Daniel...or with Mr. Joel at his furniture factory. He doesn't have to leave Troy. He's just mean and he WANTS to leave." Rose's stubborn defiance fell apart. She let out a single sob, and then covered her face with her hands.

Bella pulled her hands away and brushed away the tear that slid down her cheek. She hugged her daughter tightly, rocking her back and forth like she was still a baby. Rose was only nine, she couldn't understand Manny's desire to go on to college, to study law and help his tribe move into the next century. She still had a child's heart that simply ached with loss. "He will be back when he finishes school," Bella explained softly.

Rose sniffled and looked up with the small comfort of hope. "You promise?"

Bella squirmed. Who knew what might happen when Manny arrived in Virginia...but his family was here, he may not return permanently, but she could say without any hesitation that he would be back...at least for visits. "I promise."

Rose picked at the pink embroidered bud on her skirt. "But, but...I won't have anyone to play with."

"You have friends at school. And you have your brothers and sisters."

"They're all babies. And the kids at school hate me."

Bella chuckled. She knew better than that. Rose was the butterfly at every gathering, loved and sought after. And her mother knew she knew it.

Rose answered, "Don't laugh. You know they don't *really* like me. They like me because I'm pretty and I have nice dresses and Daddy has money." The little girl sighed. "They don't *truly* like me. Not like Manny does."

"Well, then, you'll just have to spend time with Moxie. She adores you and *she's* not a baby. She'll start primary school in the fall."

"You really should start calling her by her real name, Momma. Kids are going to tease her."

"What? Call the poor child Agnes?" Bella groaned. "I think I prefer Moxie. Besides, she's far too spunky not to be a Moxie."

Rose laughed. "That's true." She fell back on her mother's bed. "How could you ever let Daddy name her Agnes? I mean, I love Aunt Agnes, but really."

"Your daddy always tricks me." She lay back by her daughter and laughed. "That's why I taught you to be so smart, so no man can trick you."

"Daddy tricks you. Ha. Miss Tessie says he spoils you rotten."

"Of course he does." Bella winked at her daughter. "And one day, I'm certain you'll find a wonderful man who spoils you rotten. Until then, you're stuck being a child."

Rose seemed to consider her mother's wisdom as if she was looking into the future and forming a plan to get her way. She must have found satisfaction in her conjectures, because she smiled and said, "I *suppose* I can play with Moxie. She *is* really funny. But I refuse to play with Lily until she quits sucking her thumb. And the twins? Ugh....you should have had two more girls. Boys are such pains."

Bella laughed. "Well, sorry to rain on your parade, but they're here to stay. You better get used to them. They love you and will pester you for the rest of your days."

"Hmmph," she said with crossed arms, but her face revealed a pleased little smirk. "Well...I will put up with them, but...if either one of them brings another frog to dinner? I'm going to let Miss Tess whoop him good. I covered for the brats last time, and they put the awful thing in my bed."

Bella couldn't stifle a laugh. The twins were only three, and they were as smart as they were rotten.

"It's not funny, Momma. That's why they're so bad. You think they're cute!"

"Well, they are cute, but you're right. They're a bit too ornery. You shouldn't cover for them anymore and *should* let them get what they deserve."

Rose frowned and rolled her eyes. "Well, we shall see."

Bella kissed her forehead. She knew neither boy would ever lose the protection of their big sister. "Why don't you run down and see if your father has started the ice cream? We want to make sure Manny's going away party is spectacular."

Rose nodded, pulled her mother's bonnet out from under the coverlet, and handed it to her with a grin.

"I wonder where the boys get it." Bella pulled a curling pig-tail as Rose scampered from the room. Bella went to her dressing mirror and placed the bonnet on her head, smoothing the ribbons and fixing the silk flowers. "Rotten children. It's a wonder my hair isn't gray."

Rose giggled as she ran down the hallway. Tess appeared from seemingly nowhere. "Proper ladies walk. They don't run like a field hand to the supper table. I declare," She grumbled.

"Sorry, Miss Tess. Momma told me to hurry."

Tess clucked her tongue, but said no more. Rose walked till she closed the front door. Then she bolted to the cellar house. Daddy told her all the time how Momma helped him dig it…while wearing trousers! She really couldn't imagine such a thing, but her daddy would never lie. He saw her coming and waved. He and Noah were cranking the handle on the ice cream churn.

"Why if it isn't little Miss Rose! Looking more beautiful every day." Noah smiled.

"Why thank you." She made a quick curtsy and then offered him a look that looked so mature and sincere in her empathy that her father felt a swell of pride and heartbreak at the same time. "Poor Uncle. I know you are going to miss Manny something fierce. Him being your only child and all."

Noah's eyes glistened. "Well, you're right, Rosie. I will." He pinched the tip of her nose like she was still three. "I guess I'll have to come pester you."

Rose laughed. "You must do that!" Then she turned to Jack. "Momma sent me to make sure the ice cream was getting made."

Jack winked at her. "Your momma sent you out to chase your tail so she could finish dressing, eh?"

"Probably getting even with me for hiding her bonnet."

Jack shook his head and grinned.

"Well, Rosie, the ice cream is almost done. Will be before the first guest arrives."

Rose gave him a kiss on the cheek. "I suppose I better find Moxie. See what she's doing."

"She was here a few minutes ago. I think she went to the kitchen to sample sweets."

"Oh, then, I better hurry! The twins are probably close behind!" She hurried on to the house, slowing only a second to yell, "Love you, Daddy!"

"Love you, too, Punkin'," Jack called to the vanishing child.

"Where does the time go, Jack?"

"Slips away while we aren't paying a bit of attention, that's where," Jack said with a sigh. "I can't believe Manny's sixteen already. Seems like yesterday he was a little boy in the back of the wagon staring me daggers after Bell sprung me from jail."

Noah laughed. "True. True. That's a whale of a story. You guys going to tell it to the kids?"

"I do. All the time. And can you believe, of the whole insane tale, the only part they don't believe is that their mother wore trousers?"

Noah laughed. "I'd probably doubt it if I hadn't seen it with my own eyes. You know, there's other parts of the story that are a mystery to me, Jack."

"Like what, Noah? I'd never keep a secret from you."

"Well, good. Maybe someday. Maybe before I die, you'll have to tell me the *whole* story."

"You want to know how I made Charles disappear, then reappear?"

"Exactly. I mean, I'm not a fool. I know the man was dead."

Jack stopped cranking and directed his full attention to Noah. "I buried him in the old privy. He's more than ten feet under in the waste, like he belongs."

"Aha. And how was he arrested in Ohio?"

"Daniel. Haven't you ever recognized the resemblance?"

Noah shook his head. "No, sir. Daniel is so pleasant looking. I guess I overlooked it."

"First time Bella saw him, she damn near had a heart attack. Thought she saw a ghost. That put the idea in my head. So, I sent Daniel off to make a bit of trouble in Charles's name."

"So, you planned it out before you even knew she'd get caught?"

About the Author

Elizabeth divides her time between her beach cottage and her scrupulously clean house in the hills of West Virginia. Ooops. That's fantasy Elizabeth. The real Elizabeth spends her days schlepping after her four boys (five if you count their father) and the assortment of pets they swore they'd take care of. She does live in West Virginia; the house is clean when the mother-in-law visits; and she does have serious dreams of living at the beach. Elizabeth is a Marshall University graduate with a degree in counseling. This has proven very beneficial when dealing with the make-believe friends she hangs out with all day (she calls this 'writing').

Follow her blog at: http://www.eseckman.blogspot.com

www.ingramcontent.com/pod-product-compliance
Lightning Source LLC
Chambersburg PA
CBHW031122210626
46816CB00016B/1759